ANTHiLL

A Political Spoof

United States of America

Publisher, OSAAT Entertainment

First Edition. Fiction

Contact the Author Visit: oebooks.blogspot.com
Email: rycjoebooks@gmail.com

Cover Design by RYCJ

Library of Congress Control Number: 2023912013

ISBN: 978-1-940994-17-8

Printed in the United States of America

For Ronnie

DECLASSIFIED...

Disclaimer: This chronicle has been unredacted and translated in semi-normal English to help readers get the picture.

CHAPTER 1

WeShallOverCome.

Before Roughneck Creek of Providence Hill came to be, Insectivores fought mandible to whisker for the right to exist. Across the Galaxy, from conception and prior to the GreatExodus and Killorbekilled eons, or beyond the DoomsDayHollow epoch, survival of the fittest was in full swing. On grounds so bitter and caustic that most didn't live long, this period was a less gentler, less jovial existence. If bugs didn't meet their demise in battle, then they were consumed by the elements. Staying alive was no joke.

But survivors grew from this dark. The fittest of the fit scrambled and scattered, moving North, and South, and Eastward, and West... and eventually a synovial bunch of Osage Waterbugs braving the Knavish seas swam mighty high tides to settle on a vapid stretch of land later to be called the New Territory.

Stoned, bloated and terribly banged up, the Osage Waterbugs, the first inhabitants, arrived on a barge of unnamed, unmolested terrain relieved they hadn't succumbed to the seas. In swift order they set up camps, duplicated in swarms, and celebrated their good fortune.

And then plagues joined the festivities. And typhoons brought malaise...and soon became apparent the brutally primitive conditions were not designed to be outlived. Actually no bug escaped this reality... ANYWHERE in the Galaxy. But tricked by relief nothing could be worse than surviving the Knavish seas Waterbugs recklessly abandoned their guard.

This all happened as King Gumby dipped into his chess of troubles. Originally from Dnalgne, on the other side of the Knavish seas, Gumby belonged to a Royal band of Silphanyroaches who built the Silpha Castle. These were a wealthy class of bugs that found Gumby an unwelcomed rebel. He took what was not his, and crushed bugs that complained. His kin wanted him expelled. Cast from the Castle. And after enough bidding and bickering found a strategy to push the nuisance out. He was given a sketch...and compass... described as Utopia. All the riches to be had were in this place they expressed to him. "Go! Go at once to see for ro'self!"

This was how Gumby arrived to the unnamed territory, also by chance. He and a bunch of outcasts just like him followed the compass, got incredibly lost, and landed disheveled and in dire need of resuscitation on a barf of land belonging to the Osage bunch. Washing ashore a ribbon thin cluster, as many succumbed during the long voyage, they quickly canonized the strangers. Help us they pleaded. Feed us. Replenish us. Show us your jewels of survival, they begged the Waterbugs reclining on the sea's edge.

The bloated bugs didn't hesitate to befriend and feed the new strangers. But after this generous show of hospitality they were unceremoniously clipped of their Digs, which was promptly claimed and Named. It was not an easy defeat however. A brutal bugfight ensued between the Osage and the Silpha Roaches, lost only by wit, not grit. Lacking a gift to conquer thieves like Gumby, and inept about matters such as celestrial embezzlers magistrating over land, air and water... the Roaches outwitted them.

Really, the Osage didn't comprehend their loss until a huge stone edifice glaring down on them began spilling troves of bugs favoring Beetles. The itsy-bitsy bugs, with these eeny-beeny prickling scissors sliding back and forth across their musks, were absolute pests, nibbling on any and everything directly in its path. This irritation was how and when...along with a BIG SPEECH Gumby gave, it occurred to them that they'd been replaced by massive mixing and mingling.

"I envision a dreg when Roaches will rule the hills and knolls and valleys and rivulet of streams on this great pasture of green," Gumby bellowed, projecting the Utopia he envisioned to his ILK, and illions of beetily bugs he curated; Mosquitos, Gnats, Flies... Fleas...AND MOST NOTORIOUS, BLACK ANTS in bondage. From nothing it's precisely what happened.

The persnickety beetily bugs were ordered to build this Utopia from which Gumby could oversee and rule on ALL BUG MATTERS. Seeds were planted and rocks stacked, soon fashioning his Utopia. Initially all began hohum. The beetily bugs, most illicit spawns of Gumby and his ousted ILK, worked while the euphoric heirs steered and delighted in the sights.

"This land is for US, the upright and morally scripted," swooned Gumby, speaking to a wide berth of air. No bugs paid much attention to the lectures, not even his own ILK. First they'd have to see the LCBs (Lower Class Bugs...the illicit itty-eetles) as Insects to care. For the most part they deduced the speeches down to Piccolos in a grand 'ole bug opera. And as for the LCBs, they barely even understood the Silphanyroach ticks and clicks (language). Gumby could've said anything and had their consensus.

And so, with spectacular ignorance promises were made. "Those seeking wealth and prosperity this is the dreg and the place," Gumby placated his scrupulously exhausted heirs with oaths and laurels upon which to hang their marbles and pearls. "Why...with our pellucid customs, and scintillating strategies plus upright reputations, we are the deserving to inherit this bling forevermore!"

Gumby continued with the BIG ANOMALOUS SPEECHES, subjugating the overthrown and the itsy-bitsy bugs held in bondage, burying them beneath forgotten plagues and long ago gifted generosities. He surpressed the entire lot as he renamed the New Territory, the New Colony.

For a while the New Colony blossomed. Off ill-gained pilferings he and his ILK became richer, like the ignored became less visible. A superimposed prism of boom and illusions nonetheless increased for all. The air turned crystal-cleaner and clearer. The seas swelled, filling gorges and ravines full of fatty rich omega3s. The once desolate landscape bloomed drop dead gorgeous, forests so emerald green that no creature, big or small, wanted for nourishment. Even the nugatory Insectivores... the Worms, Moths, Fleas, Gnats, and of course the Ants benefited as well. All the termitey-type bugs managed to carve out fortresses of their own happily after ever versions.

A lambent future well on the horizon luminaries and visionaries appeared in wide bands. The foreseeable became the conceivable. Trinkets brightened the landscape. And droves and droves of EVEN MORE reckless Bugs populated the New Colony with more reckless abandon. Wasps, Bees, Flies, Grasshoppers, and hoards of yik-yakking Cicadas multiplied, eventually out-numbering the Roaches. And that's when the BIG BOOM dropped on the charade.

The period became known as D-D, the Dark Demise, when King Gumby's successor, Ruthless Malevolent Dastardly Gumby the 200th assumed the throne and denounced every Insectivore not of His ILK. "We are the true strategists, thus inheritors of this great wealth," he announced, reaffirming the Silpha's initial position. "There shall be NO BUG greater than the GREAT ROACH, owning more prosperity!"

"From here on out ALL BUGS are remanded to abide by SEPARATE BUT EQUAL statutes," argued RMDG. Bugs not aboding in Royal Residences suddenly had no rights to access and enjoy justly gained spoils amassed under his predecessor.

Heirs to this enrichment carried on as before, while the NEWLY OUSTED labored on. For the latter, it was futile to argue and protest...given they had no means to craft silken societies... as RMDG cried out.

"ALBEIT," he beleaguered on, "...any NEH possessing a Noble Resume equal to, or exasperating OUR OWN, they shall inherit THE MONARCHY," he openly broadcast with one caveat. "But until such evidences are brought forward, consider YOURSECTS unsantisized and unInsectivized, and forevermore deservant of whatever demise!"

RMDG the 200th swore by this lore for the remainder of his reign. Bugs that looked like Mosquitos resided in thickets. Wasps in Hornet Dives. Grasshoppers in Green Patches...and so forth and so on... right down to ANTS residing in Mounds. Whatever the habitat, NO BUG NOT comprising of 103% Roach glick, in accordance with an unscientific compound RMDG basically made up, were permitted to reside in Castles... or Palace like domiciles. He OPENLY and quite bitterly denounced nonRoachy species. From his preposterous ideologies of species and class, his clarification was RULED SUPREME, MORAL, JUST and A HUNDRED PERCENT RIGHT!!!

NO EXCEPTIONS were made. Off limits were attractive and durable materials to build LC dwellings. And LCBs were ordered to use inferior services and products. If they were deemed less, they must behave and look less. Even abodes fashioned out of mud and clay, the lowest of materials, could be seized if another Roach, ANY ROACH, desired the fixture.

Least to suffice, RMDG's sumptuous new order led to a chaos beyond measure. But he soldiered on, building Palaces like ones he recalled from whence his kilt came, set upon large knolls to rule from. He used lesser... very loyal bugs...to guard these havens, bribing them with praises...and of course extra walnuts.

Eventually feuds and wars broke out. Because NOT EVERY ROACH lived in one of the Royal Palaces, friction arose when Spiders (for instance), moved its Web next to a LC (low class) Roach's pile of debris. Without designated authorities to oversee domicile feuds among the regular LCBs, and the Roach LCBs, THINGS GOT CANNIBALISTIC UGLY!!!

Below the Palace, beneath the Noble Hill in THE VALLEY OF THE SHALLOW OF DEATH, looked like one VERY STABLE & HOSTILE hurricane. The Roach LCBs, who understood the Silpha dialogue, were better equiped to fashion thier Utopias. Meanwhile the regular LCBs, less fortunate, reached out to RMDG for help. Of course help was negligible, if not downright hostile. 'We Shall Overcome' became their mantra.

NOT AT ALL MOVED, RMDG continued the BIG SPEECHES. "We shall soldier on! WE will survive! WE MUST KEEP HOPE ALIVE! But for ANY bug wishing to move on, the SEA IS OPEN. Go! Go! Leave US to our greatness and OUR great land to survive and thrive and keep prosperity alive!"

Of all the BIG SPEECHES, this was the ONE lurid ONE that WOKE UP the regular LCBs. They'd put in a scandalizing load of work building that comfy Palace RMDG and his Royals reclined in, and refused to move on UNREWARDED! Plus, they had nowhere to go. So throughout the D-D era, and well into the WeShallOverCome period they fought like the jevil!

...And it wasn't only the Black Ants fighting. Crickets fought for peace and quiet. And Gnats tried to oust the Crickets for being too vocal. And Grasshoppers fought because they were bigger. Obviously they needed more space.

And the Red Ants (unrelated to the Brown and Black Ants) fought too. They fought by irritating ALL LCBs with their promiscuous work ethics, outshinning the rest by building incredible perdu dynasties from nettle, actually making OVERCOMING look possible!

In one way, or others, the HAVES and HAVE NOTs all began caroling... 'WeShallOverCome.'

Imemine.

The Weshallovercome era was nasty, but didn't last long. The Whooda event put an asteroid dent dead in the moral center of the bickering. It was hard to feud in eternal darkness. Values shifted after a spell of hoping for peace and light. From Palaces to ruts, once the light finally returned, and dark disappeared, the feuding stopped. Bugs were so grateful the worst was over and they could see again that many LCBs no longer cared who had what. Suddenly they were crooning to a few NEW SLOGANS; 'ChangeWeCanBelieveIn', 'StayingWoke' and 'Every Bug for Bo'self'.

At the inaugaration of what officially became the I-me-mine era it appeared the Shalls had OverCome, hopefully forever. Even RMDG had lifted his restrictions. One of the Palaces he in fact opened to all Plebs interested in Magistration (aka Politics).

"From this DREG onward, ALL PLEBS are invited to represent your ilk from the Main Palace," he announced. "My Fortress is now OUR Fortress!"

And so it was in this enviorn, albeit an eon later, that Head Chancellor of the Black Ant Mound visited the Trade Square to do a little flea marketing.

Twice a year... once in fall and once in spring... flea marketing happened. Bugs across the Colony scavenged resources to stockpile. Black Ants howso, picked up the practice in earnest. Rooted in ancient practices dating back to their beginnings, the fashionistas moved in droves to parade its vivid antlers and bounty of accolades affixed to their pelts. They'd been a flashy troop, no matter the era or oppressions, prone to shimmying and flickering and gathering attention. Insects of every Class would stop to inspect the glitzy braggadocious show, especially when the loftiest of them weren't stuffed in Guarded Leafs chauffeuring them around. It was rare to catch one high-stepping in public with their breastplates bowed out, (especially for non-egg-holding Ants). Whenever and wherever they happened to make a splash appearance, with their showy struts, they were bound to draw gawkers.

And so it was on this crespecular crispy clear dreg that Head Chancellor Elder Black, who hadn't been out without his entourage in many eras, dressed clad in the works and traveled on his own tangibles with three Kiddies; Pokey, Giggles and Skimpy.

It was a bodacious outing for certain. Though the Wars in Providence Hill were next to extinct and the territory one of the more flourishing, Insects were still Insects, and thus still confrontational by constitution. Bugs craved excitement, often in the forms of conflicts, and would seek it out at available opportunities.

The youngins' out with their Head Chancellor were sort of showing off too, eager to become grown-up Elders as well. All, or at least the vast majority of Kiddies in the Black Mound hoped to one dreg display the huge sappy antlers and broad breastplates, and of course the stacks and stacks of prestige like their Head Elder Ant. Only the oldest, and most knowledgeable and respected among its Class paraded the Blue Shard Medallion; an accolade the Chancellor wore proudly. He earned the medal in the WeShallOver-Come era, supposedly after surviving a lawnmower assault that demolished one of the largest Ant Colonies that ever existed. He was the only one who made it out of the ordeal, to later describe the lawnmower in such detail that it inspired the innovation of movies, plays, scribes and tunnels across the Colony... and Galaxy. The tunnels, in particular, proved to be a savoir for many Insect Kingdoms. As it turned out, moving underground was safer. And the deeper, the better. Few built permanent shelters above ground in the Imemine Era.

But however notable a figure Elder Black was, and ostentatious and showy his appearance, few associated him with such a major event that had mowed down so many Insects. Out and about in public, without the security forces that helped chauffeur him around in shielded golden Leafs, and the WeShall-OverCome era being such a long-ago era gone bye-bye, he was little more than a moving theatre to gloat at and mock. In short, the Elder was far out of touch with the new social climate.

And yet, the Elder wasn't in need of such knowledge at this point in his journey. He was simply out for a walk with not a care nor concern for who was checking out his wardrobe and medallions, or what might happen if one of the Kiddies got to acting up while in his custody. Those ponderings never crossed his firball. Had he to guess at that moment, he would have resorted to methods used back in the WeShall-OverCome Era when bugs handled derelictions according to the ruling clan's tribal laws. He would have bent an acting up Kid backwards and sideways in fours, and continued his walk, of course totally unaware he would have been in violation of current laws. There were hefty rules for curbing (disciplining) young Ants in public (in the Imemine era). Verbal chastising and physical altercations of any sort were BANNED!

At any rate, there Elder Black was, in public strutting ahead of Kiddies, Pokey, Giggles and Skimpy. At first all was going swell. The dreg was crispy clear and sparkly. The mood mellow. The goods fresh. And visitors of the Square minding their manners and on their best behavior. Without incident Elder Black arrived in the Square and stopped at the Crumb Vendor. His Kiddies were a little playful, but not so much so that warranted anything more than nudging them with gentle reminders; "...come along kids."

Elder Black selected a few grains of salt from cracker crumbs and slats of high-fat bread crust. Next he moved on to the Straw Vendor, followed by the Nut and Berry Vendors. There he bought acorn leaves and bushels of berries. His Queen loved berries, and these were the fattest, sweetest berries he'd seen in a while. It reminded him to inform his Ant Charges to ensure the Worker Ants that normally did the marketing to visit this vendor. Obviously the Workers were either slacking or rushing through this detail. Whichever it was, or whether those Worker bugs were harboring the best for themselves, he planned to lecture the Charges about this frivolous detail upon his return. "...Don't know what this Galaxy is coming to," he muttered out loud to the vendor that passed him a soppy sagging sack of sap. "They've been telling me the markets are drying up, but look at all this bounty," he scoffed.

The Sap Vendor chuckled. Mosquitos didn't speak New Colony language, namely the dialect spoken by a Black Head that didn't get out regularly.

In short order the Elder wrapped up his whimsical marketing spree, packing the Kiddies' back with the goods he picked up. It wasn't a whole lot by common standards for such a trip. After all he hadn't gone out to do any real provision gathering. He only wanted to catch a breeze, and get away from that stifling imperial Gold Leaf that chauffeured him everywhere. Up to this point the trip had been what he expected it to be and he felt dambangle good. He hadn't strutted as far in ages and the attention and treatment he experienced put a smile on his mullet. It was about then when he heard Pokey, aka Slow Poke, whining about the crumbs packed on his back.

"It's too heavy," Pokey cried.

"Kid, it's only a few grains of salt and one crumb," Elder Black scoffed. He intentionally didn't give Pokey much to tote because he was the smallest.

"But it's still too heavy..." Pokey pouted and whined as pelts of salt fell to the ground while he slow poked along.

"Watch out," Elder Black shouted, grabbing the sack that almost toppled off his back too. "You're acting like a little puss-flap," he snarled, readjusting the sack and yanking the kid in the process.

"Oowee," Pokey cried. The Elder wasn't taking it easy on him, tying the sack so tight that his marbles crossed. "Now I can't see," he whimpered.

"Too bad," Elder Black snapped. "You ought to count yourself lucky you can still breathe." Back in WeShallOverCome times this little bug not only would have been put out of his misery, he wouldn't even have ended up as a memory.

"I'm telling," Pokey whined. "Soon as we get back I'm telling Ante Goo—"

—WHACK! Pokey didn't see the tentacle coming at him half speed. One instance he was upright, and an instance later he was down.

"Ooops, Kid are you alright," Elder Black asked marginally concerned. Hitting a kid certainly was against the law, but the Elder hadn't whacked him as hard as he meant. He was irked enough to send that kid into orbit.

Fortunately the kid wasn't hurt because even an accidental whack was illegal, despite Incism being very much alive and well. A full-grown Ant, no matter how celebrated or reknowned, caught touching a bug could spell disaster, not only for himself, but for an entire Ant colony. There were grim consequences for whacking a Kiddie, disobedient or not, or his or not, in public. Only Officials on active duty displaying the proper credentials were permitted to lay whiskers on Insects.

And still, the Elder almost let his tentacles, 'accidentally of course', flop back the other way. He was gunning to execute a well proscribed finishing touch on the kid. It was pairs of marbles that stopped him...and a squeaky squeal.

"Ut oh," he heard Skimpy screech.

Cued up the Elder detected something very, very sinister. This was something else afforded to those hailing from the WeShallOverCome era. They were equipped with solid second senses. "Pull your strut together," he growled, nervously glancing around. That extra whisk would have completely impaled the kid, and then what?

The entire affair was such a one off. First off, in Weshallovercome dregs kids melted to be selected for prestigious trips. Pokey himself all but passed out when another kid, eclipses better, almost squeezed him out for this trip. In a tie-breaking whine fest Pokey edged the other kid out. His pleas were more earnest, and cries absolutely loudest. The noise he made got all the Ants attention, young and old, even though he lost most of the contests by dozen point spreads.

Nevertheless, the one heck of protests he put on proved his desire to be more sincere. So, it was beyond credulity to see the same tike suddenly showing zero interest in this exalted opportunity. What an OBSCENE BRAT!

Realizing the jam he was in the Elder hissed at the pouting kid again. "Straighten up," he snapped. "This is neither the dreg, nor place, to start acting like a puss!"

"Ooouuoolll..." Pokey sang. "You called me a cuss," he chortled painfully loud.

But, like seriously? The Elder was beside himself sizing up this kid and it showed. His antennas were all over the place looking for a suitable landing. Should he wrap them around his lobes and pretend none of what he was hearing had been uttered? Should he whack himself and put his own self out of this misery? Or should he attempt a home run, as in knocking the kid in the background of evolution where noSect would ever know he existed?

The worst part was the fuss Antes put up about taking the chap on this walk. Ante Good, in particular, warned Pokey was too immature to leave the compound with the outdated Head Elder. But she was vetoed by other Elders, to include the Head Elder himself. Once upon a time the Head Chancellor was the smallest among his clan too. He, likewise, eagerly ached to win the affection and approval of Elders. But he was constantly dismissed for being too small, or too young, or too yellow, or too not enough for whatever grown-up activity was taking place. It took eons before he finally was recognized for what he had to contribute, which unfortunately happened when the Lawnmower Disaster wiped out all his competition.

"If you drop that sack one more time, you'll be sorry," the Head Chancellor fumed at the whinny tike anyway. "You'll never become a Soldier and a hero to your kind," he added, hoping the warning might shape up the kid.

But nope. "Sooo," whined Pokey. "I don't care. I don't wanna be a Soldier noway. I wanna be a balletrina."

"Wha—the—Wha—" the Elder could barely breathe, let alone speak. It was next to extraterrestrial for a kid specifically selected for this distinguished outing to behave this way. The Chancellor was well within his crowned right to crush the kid to pollution but considered the repercussions. It wasn't so much as the possible laws he might be breaking, as it was having to explain his actions to the Ante who quarreled over taking the kid in the first place. It was a strange contemplation albeit. In Weshallovercome times Elders wouldn't have given it a second thought. A bug like Pokey would have been gone in one inhale.

From this point forward Elder Black dropped his mullet and looked neither left nor right, letting his gangly antennas and antlers freely sway. If one of the Kiddies got in the way of his sway, so be it. It was the whole reason he had taken the stroll in the first place. To catch a breeze. To sweep debris. To bling. To show off. What in turn made the Kiddies trailing him all the more noticeable. While Pokey moped and whined, dropping crumbs and eventually the entire sack, Giggles and Skimpy played rounds of chase and catch.

"Ha-ha! Gotcha," Giggles celebrated tagging Skimpy. "Now you have to tote my sack," he chortled.

"No!" shrieked Pokey. "That's no fair," he whined. "I wanna play tooooo..."

"But you lost your sack," Giggles noted. "You don't have nothing to barter!"

Elder Black's marbles pulsated like hazard lights but he said nothing as he continued his gangly strut, passing large billboards reminding travelers of the consequences for breaking laws... crimes the Kiddies committed openly as he decidedly ignored them.

"Ante Goo-Goo said I don't have to do stuff I don't wanna do," Pokey sniveled at Skimpy and Giggles teasing him about disobeying their Elder.

"Well, you're gonna get sent to Camp," teased Skimpy. It was a serious offense to disobey an Elder, especially none other than a Head Chancellor. If the Elders didn't offer up the untrainable kid, for sure public Officials would come for him. Skimpy had been picked up twice by Judicials (County Officials) for acting out in public. Both times he was sent to Orphan Camp.

"Yeah," Giggles doused on, in his ultra-thin icky rickety laugh. "They stick simps like you in holes with the yucky bugs...Caterpillars, Lady Bugs and creeps like that!" He, too, had been picked up and likewise almost spent his entire youth stuck in a brutal orphanage.

"Gigs is right, Poke," howled Skimpy. Providence Hill County Officials were rumored to be the meanest bugs all over the Colony. It was the reason 'the Hill' was touted to be the best place to live. The Officials in this turf didn't play. They meted out punishment, particularly against Black and Brown Ants breaking rules, with particular cruel intentions.

"Them POs (Providence Officials) will lop off your doodle too! You'll never get a Dallie," Skimpy squealed obscenely obnoxious.

The irony was what spared both Skimpy and Giggles and allowed them to escape a sentence meant to churn them to dust. Lack of discipline, though Elders argued counter-wise. It was their lack of discipline that warranted their capture, and sheer obtuse luck that allowed their escape. Had their captors not been goofing off, bored with the task of watching a gaggle of incalcitrant kids, they would have seen Skimpy and Giggles, and other incorrigibles sneaking out of confinement. Fortunately, there were so many rabble-rousers that Skimpy and Giggles were hardly missed. NoSect bothered to count.

Slow Poke, however, could care less about any of this jabber. Yes, he wanted to ascend to the pinnacle rank, but hadn't exactly come upon his WHY yet. He had only seen tikes like Skimpy and Giggles appearing tough-like, on their way up the ranks to where the real grown-ups displayed the real influences, and of course wanted to mimic them. But he'd never done all the things they did. He certainly had never been picked up, and like what did he need with a doodle? Other than what the Antes had taught him; 'doodles being used to dribble out what he drank', he didn't know what else a doodle could be used for.

Bare-backed and sulking he batted off the insults and tottered along, kicking discarded crumbs as he moped. And the Head Chancellor clamped down on his bone crushers and strode faster, madder than a swollen Hornet looking for something to sting. He was calling an all whiskers on deck MANDATORY MEETING, ASAP! Something had to be done about these severely untrained and undisciplined Kids! Their future lay in ruins if this willful behavior wasn't curbed. Be damned, Imemine era!

Black Compound.

The Head Chancellor and Kiddies arrived back at the Mound, major calamity miraculously avoided, but not indelibly as obliterated as Elder Black reasoned. As Slow Poke zipped off to frolic with Kiddies playing zing bat, and Skimpy and Giggles jetted off to brag on the spoils and riches collected during their outing (with the Kids hoping like them to become mighty Black Soldiers), the Head Chancellor stormed straight for the Warpit. He wanted answers. The incorrigible behavior he observed was totally unacceptable. The Black Ant Empire wouldn't stand a chance if this was the best of their young brood. Except, the Head Chancellor was intercepted by Ante Good bursting into the Front pit.

"Good heavens," she exclaimed, pearls levitating and rotating as a stream of Antes trailed behind her. "Thank Crisis you are okay!"

Stumped, Elder Black reared back. "Thank Crisis I'm okay..." he muttered. "Why wouldn't I be okay?"

Ante Great cut in, "Haven't you heard!?! Don't you know!?!"

"Know what," replied the Head Chancellor, barely audible.

"Oh Dear Crisis, Our poor Ruler don't know a thing," cooed Ante Woo.

"Well, thank All Crisis he's still in one piece," sighed Ante Love.

"But for how long," muttered Ante Bitter.

"Oh Jenova, come NOW! Don't let wicked and warped divest our spirits," said Ante PrayedUp.

"What in the jevil is going on," asked the alarmed Head Chancellor, placing his scrutiny on Ante Happy pirouetting around the pit doing one of her triumphant dances.

Suddenly his Chief Command Force appeared in the pit. Intelligence Commanders Combat and Coach, and the Head Prayer Master, Pastor Amen leading the pack, followed by his Queen.

"Have mercy O-Loo-Lay!" shrieked the Queen, bursting to the forefront of the Top Command. She was the highest anointed Ante of the entire eggholding berth. She actually was second in command to them all, Chief Command Force included.

"Have you no usable sense!? What have you done," she shrieked, her feelers out and visible.

The Head Chancellor's marbles etched up to meet his mandibles. Visibly he was quite concerned.

Usually whatever his Queen said was supreme. But normally his Jewel maintained her composure, ONLY coming undone in privacy. Her excitement completely threw him off. After all, nothing had happened. The calamity had been avoided. He used the Crisis-given instincts and wisdom that accompanied every Head Elder to avert trouble, and indeed was in fact okay, as likewise were those untrained brats.

"Have I no sense," he hissed at his Queen anyway, marbling her with particular disgust. "That was nothing but a suicide mission," he screeched, swiveling around to address his swelling audience. "Have you all NOT seen that odious Roach posing on those flumox of ghastly billboards, brandishing them gruesome sandblasters," he shrieked as if he had actually been attacked. "His MUG is plastered across each and every billboard," he continued, fuming with ire as he reimagined the hell he experienced. "There are towering alpines of him daring us to train our young! Every billboard spoke of carnage! He's trying to ANNIHILATE US!!! He's calling for ALL OUT WAR!"

This was nothing new. Had the Chancellor gotten out more, or at least involved himself in political affairs, and not been so coddled and wrapped up in his own comfy pillar, served and waited on, whisker to mandible to tentacle, he would have known the signs had been around since the Roach assumed the Nest, some many dinurals ago.

"Another Head could have seen me," the Chancellor continued venting. This was no exaggeration or moot point. His accolades and fixings would mean nothing if he lost the respect of other Ant Kingdoms. They'd all be in trouble, though he winded down his huff as he observed his audience looking on with pity. "In this very instance I could be the laughing block of our stock," he concluded in closing.

Combat, the War Commander, also informally

known as WarLord, stepped in. "Let's get you to the Safe Chamber (the Pedicle)," he calmly replied. "This is not your fight—"

"—Oh, Yes It Is," shouted the Chancellor, regaining some of the vim that seemed to drain from him. "I am a Shepherd and Servant (Sheep)," he protested indignantly, go-to words he regurgitated each and every time a widget was before him, real or simulated. "We shall meet tyranny tall and together," he waged on, ignored by most. The Elders and Antes had moved on, discussing larger matters more central to the impending visit from County Officials, as little Pokey circled him, merrily...and with must zest... playing zing bat with the Kiddies.

"Now, I say we gather the youngins right this instance, in my presence, to lay out OUR code of behavior," continued the incensed Head Chancellor. It was a pitiful plea because while he still saw himself enlarged, enclosed by walls that made his irrelevant colloquy relevant, the leadership beneath him viewed his spiel as lost in the Imemine era way of doing things.

Combat completely disregarded his colloquy. So what the old babbling creature made it through one Lawnmower Event. He, himself, dodged a Foot Bomb. Like the Chancellor, he was the sole survivor too. Coach, Pastor Amen, and almost every other Elder as well circumvented impossible feats. Coach dodged a Picnic Pandemic. In horror he watched fields of Ants drink Kool-Aid that swelled them to the size of Waterbugs before they dropped like poisoned Flies. There hadn't been an event as horrific since a Praying Mantis tried to get rid of ALL bugs by hosting RAID Raves. From coast to coast a suspicious buzz lured acres of young Insects to the Raves where bugs left happy...and sterile, and had it not been for Brothera Almighty, who really should have assumed the throne ahead of the Chancellor, the Insect population would have easily become extinct. But Almighty, who not only survived two consecutive sentences in a D-D encampment, along with outliving the WeShall-OverCome, the Great Exodus, and the KillOrBeKilled epochs, killed the Praying Mantis. This was not normal by any stretch of soothsaying.

Pastor Amen was another heroic. He spared entire Ant Mounds from Sweet Sweeping events that claimed billions of Black and Brown Ants on the regular. In his worship arsenal was a Babylon (Bible) and a Wire (video) he played and replayed to show Ants with propensities to be lured by sap into Sweet Sweeps, how billions went in to the Sweet Sweeps and never came out.

"Listen up bug," Combat said speaking to the Chancellor who he otherwise respected, despite hurriedly grabbing the Elder's gangly tangibles to prepare him for immediate transport... "just because Sir WaWa is in the Nest, doesn't mean he won't let them find you guilty of whatever they want to charge you with, to show All Black Ants who really is large and in charge!"

"Wait a minute," the Chancellor rebutted, snatching his tangibles out of the jumpy Warlord's whiskers. "I shall not be moved," he argued.

At this point it was going to take Pastor Amen's level of persuasion to appease the Head Chancellor because he wasn't yet ready to be folded over and shoved into a Leaf; Gold, cozy, or otherwise.

"Your Highest and Mightiest," began the cooled Pastor, "you've been accused of Kiddie Abuse," he explained. "Our beloved Mound will be crushed to dust if they come to collect you. We MUST get you out of sight."

"Oh, Have Mercy," gasped Ante Hope, bringing her whiskets together in prayer fashion. "Give Him traveling grace," she wished, crossing her breastplate as Antes, one by one, started passing out.

The 'they' or 'them' needn't be explained. EverySect knew unequivocally they and them meant those in charge of Rule, Law and Order; primarily 'the Roaches'.

The Head Chancellor shook his mullet, as his Queen looked on (from inside the Hot Caddy) mad, nervous and every bit ready to get out of dodge. There was no denying the Chancellor made a terrible mistake taking those Kiddies to the Square and she wanted no parts of being held accountable.

"I told you it wasn't a good idea to let Pokey-mon go on that outing," Ante Good angrily spat at Combat. She was one of the most vocal and outspoken of the few Antes that remained upright. "You knew he wasn't ready for his sap just yet."

"You oughta be impaled (impeached)," the Head Chancellor lopped on, snarling at the Warlord too. "Since when have SiTs (Soldiers in Training) desired to be balletrinas," he grunted.

Combat ignored them both as he finished stuffing the Chancellor inside the Gold Leaf with a lot more intent. The nerve of this old coddled humbug. He never should've been put on the throne in the first place. Yet, here he (and his Queen!) were, with his non-involved hadn't seen a real WAR ever, being obliged the opportunity and privilege to ride things out in one of the stateliest mobiles in current times... (a high-rolling Cadillac Castle/3-V Hummer style) ... while the rest were about to deal with the scandal he created!

For this reason Combat took ample pleasure karate-chopping and folding the gangly old creature when and where he could. Sideplate, backplate, mullet connector, his underbelly...he hit all the tight and tender joints while muttering, "...you need to direct that crabroll to your beloved Captains and..." ...and his tone abruptly lessened.

Truth was, Combat could end up throwing Coach and Good under soil. Together and separately, these two... Coach the Chief Trainer and Good the Reigning Mover and Shaker... were a reckoning force. Even above Pastor Amen's moving sermons both corralled large groups by their mere presence alone. Combat therefore needed them, unlike the Chancellor's highly favored Captains he relied on and credited so often.

The Head Chancellor however, hadn't heard much of Combat's mutterings. He was busier dealing with the blows it took to get him in the Leaf. "If this is a set up to impale me, I will find you all," he yelled from the Leaf, cut off by his Queen who had words of her own. "O, hush up you 'ole showoff foo! NoBug set you up!"

And with that, the Hot Caddy shot off, steered by an anxious Soldier almost taking Combat's left foot whisker with him.

"But why didn't he pack the extra crumbs on Skimpy's back if Pokey couldn't tote them," Ante Good asked as the Leaf fled. Being the moral authority for the Kiddies, teaching them their rights, she nonetheless felt guilty seeing the Chancellor whisked off under so much duress. His famous last words really stung. "Those bugs are doomed, ya' hear! They are DOOMED! Mark my word," he shouted as the hot Caddy darted around a corner peeling out of sight.

The premonition wasn't lost on other Senior Elders either. "Look," sighed Pastor Amen, glancing around at Pokey still happily zipping around the pit, not a care in the Passel as he slipped and slid along with his pals yapping, 'zing! zing!' "...We realize the imperativeness of properly disciplining these young bugs if they're to survive the next era, but we also must hold sworn Officials accountable to every letter of Rule as defined in the time-honored Insectivore Constitution."

Combat, Coach, and Ante Good in particular, agreed with the pastor. And so once more, under strenuous circumstances Pastor Amen had done it again. He stitched rhyme into reason... until Brothera Almighty spoke up. "Yeah, but with all due respect," he hummed in a sonorous and strong tone. "I hope we have a rhyme and reason for bugs without rhythm because Roaches don't give a hoot-ninny for song and dance!"

"Aww, pimp...there ain't gonna be no picketing and WeShallOverCome speeches," Coach chuckled. "Survival of the fittest long played out! We rollin' Imemine game!"

"Whatever that is," muttered Almighty, overheard by Combat who belted a string of famous last words.

"Well, we're about to find out!"

The Offies are Coming! The Offies are Coming!

NEWSFLASH!

Recorded on Live Wire; County Officials Headed to the Black Mound! And buttressing the ticker tape was the image of the high stepping Chief County and his bounty of Law Officials; Wardens, Judicials and Peons all strutting in strict military formation towards Providence Hill.

The newsflash stymied complete chaos inside the Black Mound. Although none of the Ants (in Imemine times) had experienced a personal encounter with County Officials on this level of discord, every one of the Ants knew the Chief to be one of the nastiest Officials in current times. He was most famous for indiscriminately terrorizing bugs and carrying out deadly assaults... on Black and Brown Ants primarily. Rumor of his visit alone, invited scores of Insects from near and far, high and low, to the area.

"This could get ugly," muttered one Soldier inside the Mound to another. Neither really understood the unfolding situation, for they were much too young to weigh a hate they'd never met. Studying the Chief's menacing habits during training, and watching blurry old films of him exterminating more bugs than all Leaders (ever recorded) combined, paled in comparison to seeing with their own marbles this next level great horror, all strapped with powerful fuel-fed lethal sandblasters, storming closer and closer towards them.

"Gather the Kiddies and Antes, and secure them in the hold," Combat ordered more worked up than usual. Though he too had never encountered the Chief on a personal level, he was old and enlightened enough to understand the menace coming for them.

"Are you absolutely sure all this is absolutely necessary," asked an amused Captain, tickled by how cool he remained, against the chaotic backdrop.

With the exception of this Captain, noSect laughed. Ants were too busy discussing chores and possible food shortages and looking after the Kiddies and hiding places. Apprehension and tension saturated the mood in the Front pit, leaving no room for wisecracks, no matter how steeped in collywobbles. Combat and Coach started to speak at once, their voices colliding like high volts of opposite static.

"Take a hike," Coach got out first, beating Combat who asked the Captain if he was absolutely sure he wanted to repeat himself. Ants in general, except but for the Head Chancellor now safely hidden, did not care for Captain Ants. Their sharp mental acuity rubbed the general population wrong.

NoSect however, despised Captains more so than Combat.

So the Captain backed off, but not by much. There was so much anxiety and activity prepping for the advancing Officials that his small backwards retreat wasn't noticed until Captain FuFu vaulted from the KIA (Know-it-All) pit.

FuFu was the Senior Captain, assigned to take the rap for ALL Captains, and accordingly, labeled the ultimate of obnoxious curiosity, was most disdained.

"What in Crisis is going on out here," FuFu asked, wildly searching the pit looking for clues. "Is this a joke, a drill or what!?"

"Aah," groused the other Captain, irritated at being blown off by Combat and Coach. "Looks like they got their antlers in a bunch, trying to make a mountain out of a molehill," he snarled, purposely loud.

Combat spun around. "You still here," he barked, darting hard glares back and forth between the twins. "The two of you feel like opening this trap jam when the Offies get here!?!"

No, neither FuFu nor the other Captain wanted no part of the task. Captains did not get their whiskers dirty. They barely even used them. Their battles were fought and won using their wit, why the Chancellor so admired them, and why Combat and Coach so infrequently consulted them, loathing them in particular.

"You ready to pack up your smarts and meet your Crisis," Combat snarled at the Captains. "Do your estimated calculations think this is a good dreg (day) for you?"

The Captains squeezed their lickers tighter and got even quieter. As mean as the County Chief was rumored to be, Combat (to them) was meaner... and he was hot, not an ideal time to challenge his questionable way of thinking.

"Well, what ch'all waitin' on," Coach intervened, wryly humored by their frozen stare. "You heard the WarLord! Take a hike!"

"But take a hike where?"

"Look, go back to your pit and turn on a Wire," Coach sighed. Unlike Combat who returned to shouting orders instead of permanently disfiguring the annoying Captains, he paused to cushion an otherwise grim mood. "How about letting us know if you happen to catch an Offie within firing range," he chuckled humored by their newfound fear.

"Wait a minute," FuFu protested, his pulse pumping so violently that the ground beneath him shook. "The Offies wouldn't fire on us without first giving us the WAFFLE (Whole Affirmation For Fleecing Legitimate Evils). We have—"

"—Fu, Sects don't read that crap," interrupted Coach, again something he didn't have to do. First of all, it was a JOKE! Secondly, he could've QF'd the info famished Captain (using his twin), like he would've done had he overheard the exchange. These foolish overstudied Captains were lucky the WarLord was readying Soldiers for a FA (Final Assault), translating to the severe shortage of time left to be fooling around with their pointless questions. "Have you been watching the Wire, as you should've been doing in the first place," he asked in a not so pleasant tone.

"Huh," FuFu mumbled stupified. Already Captains were mocked and harassed for their intense study habits. So, watching a Wire Elders condemned as FAKE NEWS and openly admitting to digesting its content was like confessing to sabotaging the Mound.

"Look, just go back to the KIA, lay low, and wait for the CW (Classified Whistle)," Coach dismissively replied. "Do ya' think you can handle that much?"

Without further rebuttal the Captains departed the Front pit and crammed in the small KIA with dozens of other Captains arguing about what it meant when the CW whistle sounded.

"It's all over if we hear the CW," said one, marbles turning like Ferris Wheels.

"Not true," objected another. "Right here it says to find the nearest hole and get in it, and remain there, until the Chancellor says the drill is over," he explained reading from a thick scribe of War rules.

"Drill," snarled another. "First show me a hole in this pit, and do you really think those fatards care anything about our survival!?!"

"Yeah, 100%," another chimed in. "They especially hate us! Beside, I already saw the Chancellor and his Queen being carried away...kicking and screaming!"

"Say what!?! You saw them kicking and—"

"—Silence," ordered FuFu, now likewise in a crunch for time. "We must use our wit to figure a way out of this."

"Has Sir WaWa been contacted," asked a young Captain recently added to the ranks. "It says right here in the ROG (Rules of Engagement)—"

"—Put that away," FuFu snapped. "Hench forth, forget the rulebooks," he said at the tip top of his vocals, speaking to the cadre of Captains forming a circle around his sound. "Under no circumstance is WaWa, or any outside counsel to be contacted." This order explicitly went against War preparations, especially in Imemine times, and particularly given the Kingpin was a Black Ant. In their current situation, contacting WaWa should have been the first order of protocol.

"That Bug can't help us noway," muttered another Captain. Ever since WaWa chilly-hilly rolled up in the Colony Nest, the Captains had been debating his rise to power. Most believed he was in collusion with the Roaches, brokered on a jevilish deal.

"Well, then we're doomed," a Captain muttered back. "We might as well light the fuse and impale this Crisis-forsaken place!"

The retort wasn't meant for FuFu to hear but he heard it anyway. He cut off his chat with another Captain, discussing which tunnel was the safest escape route, and spun around to address what he overheard. "How Dare You," he fumed. "How dare you emit that rancor into our sanctuary!" For Captains that prided themselves on diligent research and dutiful reasoning, the very last thing a Senior Captain permitted, was subjecting impressionable Captain's to reckless chatter.

"No matter how desperate a situation we must never sink to the levels of smut-thinkers," he continued. "It is irresponsible and can lead to a holistic annihilation of our CLASS! Now, give me a HooAH!"

"Hooah," echoed the Captains, sounding like an uninspired chorus.

"Perfect," replied FuFu. "And if I ever overhear another Captain speaking so intolerably callous, you will be expelled from the Captain Academy immediately!"

UNINTENTIONABLE.

Tension within the Black Mound continued to climb howso. "What's going on out there," asked a Worker Siss carrying a bushel of clean shells to the Scullary where Senior Antes huddled.

"Hush! And be still," Ante Good snapped, grabbing the bushel. "Go back there and stay out of sight," she ordered. "Help the other Workers keep the Kiddies calm."

That turned out to be a moot order. The Worker Siss got to the back and found the Kiddies happy as larks. Not one had a care or concern. Dressed in their Ante-spun Superhero pjs fashioned out of discarded Swapmeets bug leftovers they zinged and zapped each other, playing like any other dreg.

"Shouldn't we be making them be quiet," the Worker Siss asked another Worker Siss.

"Oh Crisis, no," replied the Siss. "You know how Good and them Antes are. Make one of these brats cry and we'll be a Siss out of Work!"

And Kiddies were everywhere too. Besides the zinger and zappers making up enough noise to drown out a reunion of Cicadas, some napped in corners as others swung from the ceiling, crawled up the walls and basically stressed the Sisses out worrying that just one could cost them their job.

"Look at Pokey over there," one Siss remarked. "He thinks he's some kind of carpenter," she laughed, amused none.

"Yeah, well, a deuce ago he thought he was a pair of wings and liked to broke his main connector (neck)," scoffed a Siss just as unhappy about the impish Kiddies.

"Well, that's one that everySect in here might be better off without!"

"Ooo! Siss," chimed in a Siss who very much agreed. "He the reason we in all this mess now!"

It was no secret. Among all the Kiddies, Pokey was most annoying, especially for the Sisses who had the chore of looking after the brats. "Well, we better keep a pearl on him," one Siss warned. "It's no telling what he's over there digging up!"

On the other side of the wall Brothera Almighty kept hearing a drilling sound. He looked around, trying to figure out where the noise was coming from, but failed to look down. "I'm hearing something," he murmured, glancing around and feeling the wall, and seeing it tremor.

"Hey, come over here and feel this," he even

said to Coach at one point. "Do you think the Offies might've found another way in here?"

Coach strode over and checked the wall. He too failed to look down but felt the bed of stone and watched it move some. "Don't worry about it," he said. "It's probably them kids in there cutting up. Just hang tight. We got the Offies in sight."

"But—"

"—Sssh..." Coach hissed, hushing Brothera. Combat was speaking, instructing the Soldiers on the plan.

"...Now that we know the Offies haven't crossed the Trigger Line, you all can chill some," Combat was in the midst of saying. "But we still need you Soldiers at Attention at ALL TIMES," he emphasized. "I need all lickers tightly sealed and marbles fixed on bik-bloc three! You got that, Ticks!?! BIK-BLOC THREE!!!"

Bik-Blocs were cameras mounted on the wall, mostly internal surveillance to keep track of Workers' comings and goings, and to ensure the Kiddies weren't being abused or noSect was stealing. But Bik-Blok three (on this dreg) was put in use to film the Officials in real time, to document any and all mistreatment or unlawful abuses, to prove any and all retaliation because Combat was committed to not go down without a ferocious fight.

"When the dot turns gold, I want Row 1 to Fire," Combat ordered. "Unload your sandblaster 'til it is empty," he bellowed. "When Row 1 falls, it's Row 2's turn," he continued, completing this sequence in a so forth and so on manner. The show would be over when they all were down.

Rattling something fierce, fuzzy garbled 'yes WarLords' tumbled off a few lickers, serving one overriding goal; the determination to win. No Soldier wanted to see any Soldier go down more than the Soldiers in that First Row.

"Never seen nothing like this," a Comrade in the Middle Row muttered to his left.

"I'll say," the Comrade muttered back. "My feelers say it's about to rain pussola."

"Who's speaking," Combat barked, looking the rows of Soldiers over for clues. He couldn't tolerate a dissenter breaking ranks. If just one bug choked, it could spell lights out instantly, and forever, in the Black Mound.

"I said WHO'S SPEAKING," Combat barked again.

The Soldiers (particularly the first three rows) were terrified, vibrating and shaking uncontrollably. But a Soldier in the next to the last row spoke up. "I think the Offies are gonna get us from behind," he reported, speaking of the chiseling going on behind him, right at that instance.

"Who said that," Combat demanded to know.

"It is I," replied the brave shivering Soldier.

Combat approached the Soldier, chiseling on the other side of the wall still chiseling, with his sniffer flaring. "Did NOT I give the command to keep those lickers zipped!?!"

"Yes WarLord, you did, but—"

"—But why are you still talking!?!"

"Because I hear drilling," replied the Soldier.

"Come again?" Combat said, his voice and energy so blustery that along with the rattling Soldiers, the chiseling sound of the Kiddies digging their way into the pit was washed out. But of course that 'come again' was not meant to be answered.

"Front and Center," shouted Combat, ordering the brave Soldier who spoke up to the Front line, replacing his position with a Soldier that had been holding still in a puddle of his juice. "Now, anyShell got something else to say," he asked, again a question not meant to be answered. "Let me know if one of y'all hear something else because I can play switch-a-roo all—"—and before finishing his sentence a fantastic BLAST burst open the Front trap jam.

County Officials came in hot and heavy and packing much heat. But they had to navigate a tunnel of sorts, before meeting their opposition. This wasn't a War plot. The Mound was designed this way long before this event came to fruition, back in the dregs when Insects crafted stone walls out of rocks to keep distance between its inhabitants and a variety of threats.

"Positions..." Combat whispered, almost giddy with excitement at this once in a lifespan opportunity to test his WarLord skills. One way or another he was confidant they were winning. He even brushed off the suggestion to keep Pastor Amen with them, in the event they needed a negotiator that could also pray. He was so sure of his strategy that he told Coach to let the Prayer Warrior comfort the Chancellor and his Queen, because only their enemies could benefit from prayer.

"Listen up," Combat hissed at the Soldiers. "No heroes. Remember your training. Heroes are first reduced to zeroes!"

With that said, the cavalcade of Officials finally made their official entrance. They looked smaller and sillier than how they appeared on the Wire. The crystal vests, squirrel-hide trousers and mud masks weren't as menacing in real purview. The exaggerated dress partially hidden behind insanely obscene sandblasters proved to be an instant surprise, and relief, to the once trembling Soldiers. In fact, one laughed... brazeningly loud.

"Let's go Blackie," Chief County, bellowed anyway. "Get up off that Throne and stand on your own spineless whims," he snarled at...well, he snarled at absolutely nothing.

A few Soldiers in the rear rows snickered, as did several of the Chief's backup posse. Combat and Coach almost laughed out loud as well. The numbmusk had come for the Head Chancellor but, apparently, didn't know what either a Head Elder, or a Throne looked like. Neither were in the pit.

"What Blackie you lookin' for pimp," Combat asked, visibly humored. The group of Officials looked a clownish malady, about as ridiculous as the shocking appearance of a small cluster of Kiddies dressed in superhero costumes suddenly seeping into the pit.

Coach didn't see the Kiddies because he stood guard on the other side of the pit. And the Soldiers didn't see the Kids because although they were less fearful, none dared to look down. Only Combat knew the Kids were in the pit, but kept focused on the out of character Chief and his Wardens.

"Stallin' ain't gonna git ch'all nowhere," replied the Chief, still speaking into a vapid marginal space. It was the oddest inspection because although his marbles were clearly visible, they looked like empty inanimate objects, sightless and detached from reality. Every Insect alive knew Black Elders apart from other Ants. Their tangibles were humongous and rarely mistaken, even from heavily sapped and decorated WarLords like Combat and Coach. The battalion of Wardens lined up behind him seemed to even know the Head Chancellor was not in the pit. Like, who was the Chief addressing?

"Well, if you see him, you can have him," Combat replied, calling the Chief's bluff. The answer he got back would tell whether the next era was about to begin, or if the Imemine era would continue uninterrupted.

"Oh, come on will ya'! We got things to do," the Chief lazily growled, waving his sandblaster, oddly turned the wrong way. The muzzle pointed towards his sole line of defense, the zaniest part of the spectacle. Either the bug had been hitting cocktails along the way, or this was NOT the 'rumored,' meanest Insect in the Colony.

Combat almost burst out laughing for the second or third time, but coughed instead. "Umm..." he stammered, puttering around for a neutral reply. "If you came here for our Head Chancellor, he's not—" —and he didn't finish. His careful reply was tartly interrupted by Pokey, flying between him and the Chief, or more like tripping, wearing Dragon Fly wings and a huge super-soaker capable of squirting jet streams of sand in rapid long-distance blasts, strapped across his tiny backplate.

"Over our Black dust," Pokey belted in an ultra squeaky buttery voice, catching the Chief in a lower whisker with a by-the-book well proscribed kick.

Now, that was funny. The bugs all laughed, to include Combat, Coach, the Soldiers, and especially the Wardens, and Chief County too. Pokey, albeit, wasn't laughing. He unhooked the super-soaker and pointed it directly at the Chief. "When YOU go high, we go low," he squeaked, kicking the Chief again.

This time the Chief was not amused. 'Fool him once, shame on the Kid, but fool him twice, the Kid wasn't going to shame him again!'

Although the by-the-book well proscribed kick didn't hurt, the Chief seemed to come off whatever had him acting HIGH as a flook. "Junior," he shouted, foam oozing from the crevices of his lickers, "you best get your black carcasses out of this ragged sand mound before we—"

—Clunk! Cla-boomp... the sound of the Chief hitting the ground.

SHOCKED, none of the Sects moved. Combat and Coach stared. The Soldiers all stared, and so did the Chief's back up posse. All of them marveled at

Ante Good chewing out the pummeled Chief. "Don't you dare talk to our Kiddies that way," she snarled, shaking a hammer-nail pulled from her apron at the downed Chief. "We practice good manners in here!"

The Judicials and Wardens woke up and closed in, circling Ante Good. "Did you see what she did," one asked still startled.

"He's unconscious," another remarked.

"Yeah, don't expect he'll be rising in the foreseeable future," said another.

"Is that a 6-1-2," asked a fourth; apparently a high-ranking Warden, for he wore snake skin wings and plenty moth medallions. Holding an open law scribe he read from the page. "It says here we must tag the City before taking her out!"

Combat and Coach continued watching in amazement, looking from one Warden to the next Judicial, waiting for the cue to press the pin-dot.

"Well, fix her up in the rings, will ya!" snapped the snake-skinned Warden. "What we waitin' on!?! We still got to get the Head!"

And so it happened again. Intsy-wintzy Pokey raised the huge super-soaker and squirted a razor straight jet stream of sand directly at the speaking Warden, knocking him clear off all eight of his whiskers. "Don't you dare touch our Ante!" he shrieked at the cartwheeling Warden.

All crisis broke loose at that point, captured on the Bic-Blok live-streaming the ordeal. The Wardens raised their sandblusters, but were cut down by the first row of Soldiers that pulled their triggers first, despite the gold pin dot never turning on. In sync the other rows of Soldiers followed suit, as the row preceding dove to the ground, though no Soldier had been hit. Warden parts hurricane'd around the pit and the area filled full of smoke and debris, perhaps why the Warden's failed to return fire. The confusion was overwhelming. When the dust settled, the Bic-Blok had been disabled and bug parts, accolade paraphernalia and shards of law scribes were everywhere.

"Pimp, you see that," Coach sighed at Combat, coming from beneath a rock that had rolled on top of him.

"Yeah, that was wild," Combat smiled amazed. "Looks like we got 'em all..."

CHAPTER 2

WIRE FLASH!

At precisely 22:10 Insect dungs (hours), .00273 dings (minutes) after all hell broke loose, and 6602 dueces (seconds) since the Cavalcade's fracturing and dismemberment, the first Audio Wire was received on one of the Official's communicators. A Kid in the Black Mound heard the crackling static and picked up the com-com to play with it.

It was a young Peon left in charge (outside the Mound) calling. He wasn't supposed to, but left in charge, and of course not knowing what else to do after waiting extra dungs to hear the Chief give an 'All Clear' command that never came, panicked after hearing the BLASTER FIRE. "Chief! Chief! This is ID 415239. Is this you Chief!? SPEAK TO ME!"

"At Ease 415. The situation IS under control. I REPEAT, THE SITUATION IS UNDER CONTROL! FALL BACK!" shouted a razor thin voice that sounded frighteningly nothing like the Chief.

The Peon didn't challenge the order. Prior to this visit he caught the Chief tossing back Spirits during the transport to the Mound. The cocktails might've messed with his soundtrack. That happened a lot. Every Sect in the County Nest knew this, which the very last thing he needed was to rile up a sauced up Chief who had the propensity for demoting Peons for breaking rules as minor as polishing their shell a tad too shiny. Hearsay about the Chief's temper was very much true, sadly witnessed most often among his own Peons. Already the Peon in charge had broken TWO MAJOR protocols. A third could cost him more than rank. He could be spun around until his mullet twisted off.

"Alrighty! Yes Sir... hear ya' Loud and Clear! 415239.out," the Peon replied; which proper response from the Chief was to provide his own ID. That didn't happen, so the Peon timidly asked for it.

"I said, GET LOST you crum-bum," screamed the voice.

Get Lost?...And Crumb-bum? So obviously this SCREAM DID NOT belong to the Chief. But the Peon didn't know how to address, so he paced around the barriers outside the Black jam, bossing Comrades (also called Peons), and examining the unfolding (exterior) scene.

"Straighten up," he ordered one Peon looking irritably tired, bored beyond measure and criminally hungry. "...And keep your marbles on that trap jam!"

"I don't know why," retorted the parched Peon.

"Because our shift ends in .50 dings," the in-Charge Peon shot back, doing his best to appear big and in control, despite shameless crowds of Insects, of all classes; Wasps, Spiders, Gnats, Bees, Fleas, Flies, Crickets, Cicadas and etcetera breaking countless laws. In an open field, within clear view, both Peons watched a worm juice a handicapped Bumble Bee. It was disgusting, inspecting in excruciating detail a worm blow up a crippled Bee. Even the lowest, the gray Fleabag, avoided milking Bees, or watching them get milked. And other Insects, breaking other laws, wondered why the Peons weren't doing anything about it. The bugs were clearly crossing a Class Line!

"What are you smutruckets out here for," a large Horsefly passing through smirchingly asked the gloating Peons. "One for the show, two for the golo... hahahaha," and he (or she) flew off.

Shameful. For gender-neutral Horseflys that spent a majority of their existence looking exactly alike, without functioning optical portals among them, made it blasphemous that even they could mock the Peons. What a disgrace!

"They laughin' at us Charge," replied the lower ranking Peon. "Deez bugs out here making spools out of us and we ain't doing nuttin' about it!"

"He's right," noted another low-level Peon. Out in the clear discernable open field bugs were spinning webs, thievering, and selling highly iffy Official do-dads; also confirmed as doing everything but observing the law.

"Well, I isn't a spool," piped in another Peon. "I'M out here waitin' to see that big black bug drug out by them sappy antlers he been paradin' around Trade Square like a caboose!"

"Yeah," huffed yet another Peon. "'Cept we haven't seen nuttin' yet, 'cept deez goo-gobs of specs waitin' on the same thing!"

The in-Charge Peon understood the gripes, and like them anticipated having a swipe at curbing and dusting such a prized Black Elder too. He even brought along buggie-baggies planning to pilfer a windfall of valuables off the big-time Chancellor. Except now here he was, pacing out a disturbingly long wait, waiting for Chief County and the Wardens to exit the Mound, WITH THE BIG BLACK ANT IN TOW! Waiting ALWAYS was hard. There was only so much of the lawlessness he could take.

And ALL BE if just as he was about to answer the Peons, telling the bugs to keep the gossip down, when a smelly Lady Bug climbed out of the bushes, followed by a Weevil. He was smelly too. "Have we missed anything," asked the stinky bugs.

"Yeah, let us know if you want some ink," the Weevil laughed. "We've got bowls of it, in all shades too! We even got fuchsia and bright green for y'all tippers! Hahaha!"

Tippers was another word for sissies. All bugs knew low-ranking Peons in training used colored Ink in their Blasters. It was the biggest whoo-ha. Even if the bug was a sharpshooter they couldn't hurt a Flea using colored Ink. Whoo-Hoo! Not even these smelly bugs feared them.

But to the contrary, while trainees used bogus Ink for training purposes, the Peons' Blasters (on this MISSION) were positively loaded with 100% bonafide pure Grade-A AMMO. They could unload on the stinkbugs and rid the AO of this smelly gas instantly. GO AHEAD! MAKE THEIR DREG, except all that stopped them was they couldn't get the go-ahead. Chief County was out of communication!

Trying to appear in charge (as such his rank and assignment), TCP (Top Charge Peon) attempted to dismiss a Beetle accosting him with what sounded like unassailable info. "Did you know some bugs around the corner from here are selling some of y'alls buke?"

TCP struggled to hide his surprise. Buke was slang for medallions, and this was a Roach speaking, albeit a LCB Roach that looked, dressed, and smelled sane. He called himself Mr. Protege.

All the same TCP ordered the Roach bug to move along. "You're not crossing this barrier either," he weakly added. "It's off limits."

"I'm not thinking about crossing your little funky barrier," Mr. Protege shot back. "But you might wanna watch out because you're wearing some pretty fancy doo-dads too," he laughed, dragging behind a lot of tin, gratefully none belonging to the County.

Still, following Official rules this news needed to be verified and communicated to upper Ranks ASAP, except TCP kept getting sidetracked, this time by another Roach, again one well-dressed, but definitely no Royal. She called herself Crema and claimed to work for Blitz Media...why he knew she was no Royal. They never did public work.

"So, what are you Peons up to," Crema superciliously purred before turning on a recording widget and turning him off instantly. Minus the widget she was a hottie, but wielding an onion protocol absolutely dictated that he, UNDER NO CERTAINTY, either covort, convene or conversate with this Medium. ONLY Top Officials answered slick, shrewd audio sound bytes, because only they could sue the MEDIA for defamation, and later imprison and enbalm them, AFTER wiping out their coffers.

"We're on an Official Assignment," TCP crisply told the Media flirt, in an authoratative BIG voice, but an otherwise wimpy tone.

"And exactly what assignment is that," Crema coyly asked.

"It's classified," replied TCP.

"Hmp," she huffed amused. "Does this mean your assignment is so classified that you Peons are running around dressing in disguises?"

"Huh?" TCP looked around. Wasn't one Peon out of uniform, much less out of line. Not even faintly. Their shells were straight and shiny, and as polished as his. Fixed to their left side plates were brand new blasters... never used; all upright, safety ON and displayed correctly. And hungry as many Peons were, not one showed signs of bending from wear and tear. Not a one. Even the REALLY tired hungry one behaved in an unblemished fashion. Sharp, good posture and stiff as sticks, there was not a thing amiss about any of them. He would promote them himself if he could.

"Section 68934AntsyAlpha0 says we're acting in accordance with the proscribed law," TCP replied like a robotic recording.

"Well, isn't it against the law to be knocking off and hocking County insignias?"

"What are you talking about," TCP asked more than alarmed, again looking left and right for signs of transgressions. It was true however. He had heard unsolicited rumors about bugs parading around illegal regalia, BUT he hadn't personally witnessed this with uncut trust. As far as he could tell (from his angle), while other laws were IN FACT being broken, consistently and without hesitation... the aping Officials was as offensive and illegal as Crema's questions.

"Do you realize you, yourself, are breaking the law," he shot back. "I have repeatedly reminded you, We are ON OFFICIAL DUTY! You NEED TO BACK OFF!" Like, what words did she NOT COMPREHEND? 'Don't cross the barrier' or 'Keep moving?'

"Are you blind," Crema both shrieked and laughed. "Look," she pointed, showing off a set of gorgeous whiskeys. "Look at that Wasp over there making off with an Official County Sandblaster!"

TCP looked, and his marbles nearly bounced back in its sockets when he spotted the Wasp. There was no mistaking the blaster belonged to the County. Not only was the Seal on the Artillery official, but the Official whisker attached to it was clearly visible. It was the Chief's left front whisker!

"Why aren't you doing anything? Aren't you supposed to do something," Crema egged on.

TCP's shell crunched down some. He had no ready explanation. And when a noisy Cricket inserted herself between them wearing a small iron star, making no attempt to hide the jewel belonging to the Chief as well, he shriveled more. Every Insect that resided in the COLONY knew that star. Chief County went nowhere without it, because it was his time-beater (alas pacemaker)! "Where'd you get that," he asked the Cricket, sufficiently shocked. The Chief needed that thing. He couldn't function without it!

"I'll give you fiddy weeds for it," the Cricket offered, extending another trinket the Chief went nowhere without; the copper cord that connected the STAR! To onlookers it looked like a fancy jewel, or perhaps a high-ranking GEM, but those fancy jewels helped that bug breathe!

Meanwhile, Crema had whipped out her bic-blok and started filming. She swung the blok around (from the Cricket to TCP) to get his reaction. The footage captured him backing up, and trying to run. He didn't want to be identified, hiding behind his blaster he used to shield his mullet. It was a comical, if not the bizzarest interview because he was already in dereliction of his assignment. Running in circles squawking 'Leave Me Alone,' trying to escape Crema's glacial strides AND hapless questions wasn't going to spare him from ridicule, even if he wasn't charged.

Finally he stopped running and screamed, "YOU are hereby ordered to leave me alone," he cried. "I feel harassed. You are trespassing and offending me," he squealed before his own awed Peons...and viewers on the other side of this footage.

With his mullet turned, desperately trying to fend off the filming blok, he carried on crying, "if you do not bug off, you and your counterfeit contraband will be seized!"

Of course he, and the Peons, had no way of effecting this threat, despite how clearly he enunciated each word in flourishing iridescent syllables. It was too late anyway. Crema got what she wanted. The footage was permanent. She and the raunchy Cricket disappeared without further incident, both fusing in with the law-breakers.

"Look, I need for you to take charge," TCP said to the closest Peon. "I'm going around back to see if I can put an end to this!"

The Peons laughed. "Aww bug, you don't hafta' do that," replied one. "Can't you see 'dem concession stands over there? The real racket is going on right here before us."

TCP saw this. Any bug with functioning marbles saw the cocoons (bleachers) and trading coffers swarming with maggots. The thing was, he wasn't going around back to stop a thing. He pulled off his Peon bells and whistles and joined the mayhem, sinking to a next level low that once echoed throughout the WeShallOverCome era. 'If you can't beat 'em, join 'em'!'

The new Peon in charge pulled out his personal node and called the Main Nest. The Chief's personal secretary Miss Cootie answered his call. "ID," she snapped into the node. She was irritated. For too many dongs she waited for an update from TCP and was worried beyond measure.

The new Peon in charge gave his ID, which obviously didn't belong to TCP. "Well, go ahead," Miss Cootie snapped again. "Headquarters needs an update!" She didn't bother to interrogate the new Peon because the need for information on the Chief's where and whatabouts had reached the critical phase.

"Well, where are you," asked the new Peon. "Is everything ok?"

Miss Cootie just about lost her lid. "Where AM I!?! What in the puss oasis do you mean where AM I!?," she shouted. "Where in the cramfrackle are you!? AND where is TCP!?! We've been waiting to be connected with Chief!"

The lawlessness had ratcheted up to such a riotest degree that the entire fleet of Peons had taken cover wherever they could find refuge. Crushed stone, bushes, tree bark, mole holes... the Peons took cover anywhere they could pilfer safety...everywhere except the Official vehicles they traveled in because wasn't a speck left of those vessels. They'd all been ransacked or ravished. The new Peon himself hid in a pile of Horsefly droppings.

"Well," he stammered, his voice muffled by the muck that surrounded him, and the clamoring of rioting bugs above him. "Chief told TCP to instruct us to get lost," he said.

Miss Cootie only heard half of his reply, and the half she heard had her yelling back. "Chief would NEVER, EVER give that command! Now if you don't patch me through to the Chief right this instance, I'm calling City," she threatened.

The new Peon muttered more incomprehensible utterances. Actually, he talked over Miss Cootie, leaving her no choice but to carry through with her threat. As long as she had served with the Chief, far longer than the new Peon, almost as long as the Chief presided over the County, she had never dealt with this level of insubordination. Promptly she severed the call and indeed called the Mayor of Anthill Providence, Constantinople City.

Rank & File.

If Chief County was purported to be the meanest bug in Providence, then Constantinople City was known to be the biggest, baddest and brightest Grasshopper alive. City outplayed the Chief by magnificent yards and bounds. He ran the city ERROR FREE... and almost all ABSENTEE. No bug bucked City. EVER. Not one even tried. To look at him was frightening enough. But if he had to announce what he was thinking... WOO WEE... the scramble got real. He wasn't the leader to put up with double-talk, back-talk and by no means a CODE TALKER. He did to backstabbers what flames did to moths. Under his auspices bugs had to come correct, contrasting sharply to the Chief's arbitrary dispensary of meanness.

Unlike most Grasshoppers, City wasn't green. He was orange. Flaming, brilliant bright, Kilimanjaro orange. He survived prior epochs on instinct alone, what made him a frightening standalone COLOR.

He had only caught a clip of unfolding events at the Black Mound when he got the call from Miss Cootie. Understandably she, like him...and many Law Subscribers existing on instinct, at first, were confused, though not to be lumped with shaken.

"What do you mean a Peon called you for an update," he barked.

"That's what I said too," Miss Cootie replied. "He's lucky I couldn't reach him!"

"Patch me through to that SOB right now," barked the Constantinople.

So Miss Cootie, with her well-manicured whiskets, only trembling because she was so angry, switched to the node the Peon called on. A buzz later a Peon answered, but not the Peon she initially spoke to. "Chief is checkin' things," said the next Peon left in charge. "He said stop buggin' him. He'll—"

"—You pusscrum, I NOW HAVE CITY on the node," Miss Cootie snarled, using so many of her features that her mullet was barely recognizable. "Hold on," and she switched the node so vehemently she'd be lucky to place a call from that wire... EVER AGAIN!

The Peon holding on the node was Lower Case Icky, one of Chief County's long trail of Kin who sifted through the Academy the old-fashioned way. No skill. No wit. No care or concern whatsoever about law or order or class or City and his big, bad reputation. He joined the ranks for the Walnuts (money), and because the Chief asked...why the other Peon left him next in charge and joined the rank of rioters.

Icky told City the Chief told TCP he didn't want to be bothered, essentially the same thing the other Peon told Miss Cootie.

"What's your ID Kid," City coolly asked.

"What's yours," Icky shuffled back.

Oh no, this level of disrespect superseded all levels of insolence City would tolerate. Talk like this definitely wasn't going to fly with the Grasshopper. But like many old bugs coming out of other eras, seeing most young Insects as intolerably flippant and cheeky, City decided arguing with this acreage of horrendous logic was pointless in the given brewing situation.

"Get his ID," City told Miss Cootie upon severing the call with Icky. "I'll—"

"—Oh, I can tell you who that one is right now," Miss Cootie replied. "He's one of Chief's poo-poos."

"Should've known," City muttered. "Well, keep trying to get the Chief on the node," he grumbled. He didn't bother to inform her of his intention to pay Roughneck Creek an immediate visit. Wasn't no need. He lumped Miss Cootie in the same Creek as Icky and the rest of County Roaches working under the aegis Chief crawled out of. Bottoms Up! He planned to drain the gully!

Headed for his Lyft, the vehicle that transported him to and fro, he shouted directives. He ordered nearby Recruits to suit up. And he made sure the Lyfts were mounted with Cherryblasters. And he rattled off one more directive. "...And get Maz on MY NODE ASAP!"

Despite surrounding himself and his city with the best of the best, his ONE Ace-in-a-Hole was Maz BLACK... and this majorly BLACK ANT was no studied scholar or looker...or GAME PLAYER. Part Black, part Brown Ant, and somewhat part Weevil she came to the Municipal Mound (by Insect timetable) ages ago, via a City Worker that found her crumbled on top of a heap of scraps. She was a mess. Bent whiskers, no fur, inside or out, and real smelly. But when the Worker introduced her to City he liked her pizazz right away. It was her brutal honesty. Despite the hardships she brushed off, the cauliflower bulbs stuck to her shell exemplified her real heroism. Maz was a fighter. She was a self-starter, a do-gooder, and go-getter! Maz became his everything, but a mate.

It wasn't hard to get Maz on his node because she called him first.

"CB, have you heard about that ruckus going on over there on the Hill!?"

"Just heard," City replied. By-the-Way, CB was an affectionate term Maz gave him. Stood for City Bug. "I'm headed for the Creek now," he said. "I suspect them shrunks are sauced up...as usual... because they're not answering their communicators."

Maz was on it. She detested those rice slurpers and had the County Waterworks digest open and plugged into the County Roster before he asked.

Most of the calls went straight to vacay voicemail. A few rang and rang. Wasn't a fantastic surprise. It was pretty much the norm for activities going on in the Lush's Nest. Abject truth be, Maz rarely had a need to contact the County's Nest. It was the other way around. County needed City's help, often to be bailed out of one of their many binge imbibing torts.

Finally a sole Worker answered, and without introduction or invite Constantinople City jumped on him. "What in a Timbuktu is going on over there," he snapped.

The Worker stammered, sounding more loaded than frightened. He muttered something about a 'Mound Pound' initiative...and AOC (Acting Out of Control) Black Ants, plus some other garbled nonsense.

City allowed him the leisure of rambling for a Sushi amount of time before cutting him off.

"GET THE CHIEF on this NODE ASAP or BE GONE WHEN I ARRIVE!!"

The Worker wasn't frayed or dismayed. "Well who in a tootin' is YOU!?"

Maz cut the call. There was no need for City's response. She already had the Worker's ID splayed across her node. It was LS (Lead Scriber #2), a dead weight that constantly called about a County Walnut issue. "We need to clean OUT that Nest soon as we finish restoring order," she suggested after morbidly severing the call.

"Way ahead of you," City grumbled.

Though intel was sketchy, and shakey at best, WORD on WIRES was some real brew was stewing on the Hill. And the reports were stacking up claiming the County, thus the City, was falling apart. Not only had nothing to this magnitude ever happened during his command, NOTHING of this PITH had occurred since the Crawler period when Rankazorouses stalked the Galaxy.

City summoned his BBB Unit—a Squadron of Soldiers regarded as his best. They were created to deal with serious UNREST, an occasion never manifested, though Darth Vader attire and Blazing Black Blasters (i.e., BBB), real scary stuff was the brand City kept as a part of their readiness. In uniform they looked like ROACHES... their ACE strategy!

Cocked and loaded the Constantinople and his BBBs hopped in Lyfts and started the boots (engines).

"Wait..." he suddenly said. "I'm splitting us up. We don't need this much artillery for those snacks!"

Maz, monitoring both the LIVE WIRE and City's transmitter from her Nest got her concerned. "Ceboo," she cooed using his other pet name. "Is everything okay? What's going on down there?"

"We're scaling back," he told Maz. "I only need Casper, NuGro and Piriah."

Casper was an albino Spider with exceptional tactical skills. He could disappear like a whisper; extremely helpful for quelling RIOTS. And NuGro, the only Black Ante in the BBB, was NOT a he, but a she. Like Maz she enshrined a temper. Those two were forces not to be played. They'd fall a bug with a look, which NuGro could accomplish on sight. She wasn't a looker, not that Maz was either, but it was rare to encounter a Tarantula that wasn't a Tarantula.

As for Piriah, he was a chilling martial artist. He could unarm and dismember a bug in a tick. So City wanted these three Shibings with him on this trip to the Creek. Though he didn't know what to expect, he hardly considered the County lushes a threat.

"I wish I could go with you," Maz worried as she simultaneously monitored the RIOTS airing in streams on the Tube.

"Oh, it won't be necessary," City replied with an irritated sigh. "We'll have those lushers barbed and be back here before you know it..."

A lot was happening as Maz was worrying. The Live Stream was rolling...and there was no shortage of activity occurring on the Tube. Looked like more than a simple RIOT by her take...not that City and his Top Shibings couldn't take care of whatever the cut up on the Hill, while draining the Creek of the Lushes, but between the tusseling transmitting from the Lyft and her node ringing, the worrying ratcheted up.

And then she heard a shrill scream! She looked over at the Tube to discover a Ziprazone Reporter, an egg-holding Lady Bug, wailing about being chased by a Prayin' Mantis. Just then the Lens switched views and sure enough a Mantis wearing the Chief's chiffon wings was INDEED crushing hard on the bug, and in a not so complimentary way!

"Listen," Maz said, interrupting City's tussel. "I have the Governor on node 62. He must be seeing some of this Hakari going on, on these Feeds!"

"What?" huffed City. His attention split too, he was busy reassigning his BBB Squad and plugging coordinates into the Lyft as he and his chosen Shibings suited up in the Darth Vader attire.

So Maz repeated herself, adding... "Sounds like this nugget is mad as a yellow flu," she chuckled.

"Go on and patch the flu through," City huffed again. "Might as well pile on the ju-ju. I'm good and prepared for some jit-jitsu!"

It was no secret. The hostility between the County, City and State was palpable, best objectified by Governor State's annoyance at City taking so long to answer his call. By the time City picked up he had passed the call to one of his OLO (State) Guards.

"Whatcha' got," City bleated prematurely, not knowing he was speaking to an OLOGuard.

"Well, why don't you tell us," sneered the bug. "We hear y'all done flubbed up!"

The outright disrespect, as usual, stung City. He had to restructure himself, since he couldn't reach out and reconstruct his BOSS. He had hardly messed up, YET!

"Glad you find this funny," City replied, still not realizing it wasn't State speaking. "Wonder how laughable this all will be when the Kingpin calls.

This was a silly retort given the Colony Kingpin happened to be a Black Ant so few respected. Most in Official positions didn't dig the BIG switch from the historical Roachy-like Kingpins occupying the Palace. They spoke through clinched chippers (teeth) when WaWa was mentioned.

"Ah, yeah," replied the OLOGuard. "Ya' got me All Shook Up on that one," he laughed. "Maybe State will feel different," he added laughing harder.

The OLOGuard's response aptly confirmed it wasn't State peeling off the stodgy remarks. City suspected it on the first cut but wasn't convinced given how infrequently they spoke...and... (save for over indulging in the spirits), how closely State mirrored the missing Lush.

After a terse reminder to the jokestar OLOGuard, refreshing his recollection of how he over delivered on promises, he was promptly transferred to the next OLOGuard.

"These muggle-fuggle salabasters..." City muttered to himself. He'd never allow this dereliction of discipline under his authority. The only reason he hung on the node was because they (he, Casper, NuGro and Piriah) were within sight of the Hill.

So he ignored the trove of 'Yellos' and 'Hold ons' from an entourage of NO MOXY PUTZless OLOGuards transferring State's calls around the State Graveyard. "Yeyyo," one OLOGuard greeted him for what became the FINAL transfer. "How can WE help you?" he asked anyway.

"Tell YOUR BOSS, a FIRE BALL is HEADED YOUR WAY!"

It wasn't true, but EOT (end of times) did look menacingly close according to the Creek City and his Shibings failed to see because the Hill was so swathed by bugs; and all kinds too... A FIRST!

Besides Brown and Black Ants, there were Slugs and Leeches, and a variety of Ticks, plus those vulgar peddling Red Ants slinging slimy meals and sides they clearly did not own. The crisis appeared 198.98% dire because not only was there NO CREEK in sight, but there was NOT ONE County Official on site, not even a PEON!

And YET, what did the OLOGuard clap back? "ID?"

"Listen here you pussmark," growled City, "If your Pally is too busy to communicate with me, then you can tell him to ENJOY HELL—"

"—Oh no, heeb on," cried a suddenly terrified OLOGuard. "Deeba jeeba jall 'dem bews walla halla," added the licker-twisted, obviously LCB.

City didn't reply. He said nothing because not a lick of what the bug rambled could he identify. But he didn't sever the call either, due to being so busy inspecting the sights.

Besides the Red Ants operating unlawful concession stands, and Brown Ants merenguing in the middle of travel Lanes, along with Black Ants providing lit lyrics, there were Leeches, Flies and a hedge fund of Fleas swinging from cobs spun by Spiders caught in their own webs. This was SHOCKING, but not as shocking as what they witnessed next.

A huge Grasshopper, huger than City, chopped on what appeared to have once in a lifespan been a healthy Roach, as a Horsefly hovered over a grill barbecuing its nether bits. A pair of marbles belonging to an Earwig looked right at him, as flames framed the bug's mullet while his lower bits wriggled around on the grill... independent of its upper half mourning its lower half cooking. Deplorable, more disturbing than a nearby belly up Sardine spitting up eggs.

"You wanna take 'em ALL," NuGro asked, seeing exactly what City was observing.

"Naw...looks like this clean up is going to be easier than—"

"—What are you doing disrespecting my Rank & File," spewed State, his command suddenly coming up from the Lyft's floorboard.

Given the limitless crimes just peeps in front of them, City and his Shibings only caught bleeps and bits of State's YELLING. In short he wanted to know, 'As their "Governor and Chief", why was he just hearing about the blasphemous ruckus taking place "ON HIS HILL!!!"

"I got bugs FROM THE HILL TO THE PALACE TELLING ME the whole derogatory territory done flipped to ALL CRISIS," he continued ranting.

City and his Shibings ignored the rant. They were on the ground and already had a remedy. The sweeper and vacuum attached to the Lyft was enough to rid the AO of the lawlessness without ever deploying the Blasters. One click and the RIOT would be swept up, sucked up, and spit out in the Creek, likely on top of bathing County Lushes.

"I'M WAITING..." fumed State.

"Me too," City replied.

"Wha—wha—what..." State stammered. "What do you mean YOU TOO!?!"

"I'm mean, give me the CUE GOV'NER," he amused himself...and his Shibings.

Though the scene looked 110% horrific, like nothing seen since the Crawler period, ONLY viewed in historical tomes, but ALSO nothing he and his Shibings couldn't extinguish with but a touch of a nodule. They literally were ONE CLICK away from ridding State of his anguish.

But the Governor was having a moment. "Look, I just want to know why in a Seclusky HAM am I just finding out about this mayhem..." and he muttered some other words to avoid calling the Chief out of his name. Instead he accused an unnamed source for 'negotiating with them uppity Blacks.'

"Well Sir, and with ultra due respect, YOUR NEWS is ALSO NEWS to me," replied City.

State's feelers somersaulted backwards before flipping forward. "What in an Eifel Tower do you mean YOUR NEWS!?!"

City, far ahead of State, knew the County, ALL 100% HIRED and PAID out of the Governor's fat budget, meant this MAYHEM was ALL on his Walnuts. Like it OR NOT, accept responsibility OR NOT, these RIOTERS were really HIS MONSTERS!!!

Just roll back the tapes to clips where he rallied hardest for every one of the Sects he cheered into the County Nest, ALL AGAINST city objections. Whisker held high, squinting and sweaty, he swore to do everything in HIS POWER to ensure Chief County ...and HIS Peons, Wardens, Judicials and every other imbileSect employed under HIS reign, had HIS unwavering support and backing. And that was exactly what happened. Every single one of (HIS) KIN who wanted a job, HAD A JOB! And NOW LOOK!

It didn't stop the screaming Governor from lifting OFF however. He was HOT. FUMING HOT! And he was on a Roll. "It's ALL OVER LIVE WIRES," he continued, for crying out LOUD.

"...And making matters worse," he wailed on. "YOU AND I just met on this a few sprinkles back," he raved, referring to a bundle of strategy meetings that, among other unsavory elements, covered curbing Black Ants and other LCBs.

"How DARE YOU go above my mullet to order such a curbing!"

WAIT...WHAT? Was the Governor trying to kickball him under a TANK?

"There is not one IPMC request (Issued Public Misdemeanor Citation) anywhere on my board," so spewed on the lit up Governor.

So, YES HE WAS trying to kickball him/City under a TANK, just as lo and behold he looked up at a GIANT billboard where both the Chief AND STATE were posed side by side, shaking whiskers, and grinning beneath a BOLD headline that read: 'Break One of ***OUR*** Laws and We're Coming to Get Ya!'

"Well, guess Chief went over my mullet based on Y'ALLS whisker-shake deal," City wryly replied.

"Wha—What," State whispered, before levitating his vocals to its greatest volume. "Who in the Crevil do you think you're talkin' to Bug!?!" He paused to catch his breath. "First of all, I DON'T ANSWER YOUR QUESTIONS! You got that!?!"

"I DO," City replied, the snark in his tone unmistakable.

"There WAS NEVER NO DEAL between the Chief and me," State carried on. "Got that Pally!?!"

"I do," City again insurly replied, albeit more curd in his tone. "It's just that these billboards lined up on this road are speaking to the contrary." And again he gleamed, though only observable to his Shibings quietly enjoying the wrestling match.

"What are you talking about!?! What billboards!?!" State wondered aloud, just not as vocal.

"Oh, the ones spaced about every few paces," City replied. "The ads where you and Chief are posed together promising to get tough on—"—City didn't finish because State knew exactly what billboards were being described.

"Where are you!?!" he cried.

"I toldja'... on our way to—"

"—Stop! STOP!" shrieked-screamed the Governor. "I want you to STOP RIGHT NOW and take 'em down! That's an ORDER! I WANT YOU TO TAKE ALL THEM BILLBOARDS DOWN RIGHT NOW!!!"

Official RIOT Report.

Once the haze and fog cleared only a few bugs stayed. For the most part Insects came, looked, looted and left the Hill in shambles. Only a very few emerged from the dust cluster; an old weathered Red Ant folding up her concession stand, Crema, and a Worker Ant who had a whisket poked out, trying to catch a ride to her Scrubadub job. Her name was Teasa Tweaza.

"Hey," Teasa called out to Crema, the Leechy but cute bug anchoring for Blitz Media. "Where you headed," she asked.

Crema was beat. Dead tired beat. Since the arrival of the Officials she'd been on her game scooping blok bits for Blitz. Pilfering, hawking, dating and mating and rough rousing playing... she'd editorialized it all for those unable to be there. In the thick of the mayhem she got the goods. Now she just wanted to kick up her whiskets and suck down a tube of gook.

"Hey!" Teasa called out again, "you ain't talked to me yet," she teased. "Come on over here and ask me some questions!"

Crema stopped and looked back at the shifty Teasa dressed in Scrubadub attire with a whisket poked out. Reluctantly she gave in, given how badly she desired to get back to normal and kick up her whiskets. "Where are you headed," she asked.

"To Work," replied Teasa.

"By chance is this Work in the city?"

"Of course," replied Teasa. "Right down the road from where you Work."

Tired as Crema was, her mullet jerked some. How did this Worker bug know where she worked? During the RIOT, along with her energy, she lost her Blok equipment, and as well much of her identity. Her mullet was almost completely covered by sand and shell bits, rendering her unrecognizable. Minus the Scrubadub attire she kind of looked like Teasa. The query didn't last long however. She couldn't help but own up to her desperation for transportation.

"Well, I accept," Crema dryly replied. "Traveling together has to be safer than hitching alone!"

"Oh honty bunty, whachew talkin'!? I ain't eva been scurt traveling these parts by my Sexty Sect! I been hatched here and gonna turn to dust here," Teasa waged.

"Hmmp," Crema wasn't impressed. "Guess you are one of the lucky ones," she muttered in a snarl.

"No, I just don't be currying around widgets to record other bugs business," Teasa snapped.

But Crema could get snappy too. "Maybe you oughta' be a little more concerned about more bugs than just you," she clapped back. "Sects like you are out here destroying—"

"—Oh No, hole' up honty bunty," Teasa interjected wagging a bunch of digits at Crema. "First of all you need to take that 'tude down a notch 'cause I ain't 'da one!"

"Well, thank goodness," Crema faked, rolling her pearls out of view of the Scrubadub bug. "Last thing I need is to be associated with a riotous rioter!"

"Rioter!?!" Teasa gasped. "Awwwlll, jevel-to-the-naw! Where you seent a riot!?! And a RIOT wid me in it!?!" And she waited, with a whisket on her sideplate. "You can't," she snapped after waiting on a clap back that never came. "You'da the riot, running around wid your smear campaigns!"

Crema kept quiet because in addition to being tired, she really, really wanted to get back to Blitz, and preferably unscathed. So she let Teasa blame her for being in cahoots with a juiced up Brigade (the County Offies) making a mountain out of a molehill blitzin' up her (once peaceful) Hill. "Y'all 'da ones that blew eva'thang up—"

"—We didn't blow up anything," Crema objected when she had had enough. Blitz was a respectable Media. Fact to the matter, she had witnessed masquerading Officials behaving well outside accepted norms. But the other fact to the matter was she knew none of them. "When we got here the RIOT was already—"

"—PULeezze," huffed Teasa. "I ain't seent no riot and neither have you!"

"Well EXPLAIN what's going on up there," Crema spat, gesturing up at the Constantinople, along with his BBB Squad, ripping down billboards.

Teasa turned around but instead of glancing up, she (first) noticed a gang of Fleas huddled around the Constantinople's Lyft. "Oh Snap!" she cheered. "Looks like we got us a ride into the city! Come on," she squealed, scurrying over to the Fleas.

Meanwhile, elevated a good distance above the fracas, the Constantinople pulled out his Scoptacallas (binoculars), to observe the activity below. "Looks like some bugs are making off with our transpo," he announced to Casper, NuGro and Piriah.

The BBBs looked down but couldn't see much without Scoptacallas. "I'm going down," NuGro said, first to offer to right the wrong.

"Hold on," interrupted Piriah. "I'll GO," the jit-jutsu master said. "It'll be much less noise," he added.

"No," City intervened, calling back all three. They were almost halfway down the pole. "Let's focus on tearing down these billboards. I'll call Maz."

And that's what happened. The BBBs went back to removing billboards while City called Maz. "Look," he sighed aggravated, but not defeated. "State got us out here covering his backflap, pulling down billboards while some rogue Fleas have taken off with the city Lyft."

"Oh really," replied Maz, clicking on keys like automatic blaster fire. "I see 'em on the scanner now," she said clicking even faster. "Looks like they're headed to Blitz."

"That's interesting," City replied. "Think they want to report a Tank they stole," he lamely joked.

Maz became naturally concerned because this wasn't her Ceboo. He wasn't a jokey type, especially in situations as this. And he rarely obeyed orders he disagreed with, even from his BOSS.

But Maz didn't disobey her BOSS either. "Well I got something for them Fleabags," she replied. "I'll dispatch a few of the BBBs to take 'em out," she said. "We'll give 'em a little shower."

A shower was different than a blast. A blast would've gutted the Hill. A shower only would have shriveled the immediate threat, reducing a bunch of Fleabags to carbon potpourri.

City didn't object. He could care a high cliff less what happened to the Fleas...and any other bug that decided to catch a lift in his vessel. He had bigger plans and a larger agenda on his radar. This billboard issue wasn't over by a far cry!

Fortunate for Crema however, she lucked out. She arrived at her destination before the shower, while Teasa continued on up the road to her Scrubadub job. It was a great relief for Crema, until she heard the unmistakable hiss of shattering cartilage. That's the material Tanks were made from.

"OhMyGawd," Crema cried after peeking behind her and seeing the teflon Tank disappear.

A Reporter in the Media Mausoleum rushed to Crema's aide. "Oh my WORD," gasped the Reporter having abandoned her podcasting post. "Crisis, are you okay!?!"

Crema got theatrical, going into hystronics. "NO! I'm not," she cried long, LOUD and hard. "They peppered me with sand and grit... stole my Blok pack... I even saw an egg-holder besmirched and a Wasp almost got me! Now I just saw the Tank that save me blown to smithers! We're doomed! We must go! LEAVE!! Crisis is Right! EOT is REAL! I think JUDGEMENT is HERE!!!"

The Reporter gaped horrified, not only at the reflection of what stared back, a clearly ravished bug, but ALSO at what she was hearing. Though it sounded like Crema was making it all about her, AGAIN, the podcaster had seen Crema's onsite ground reporting and feared for the safety of the entire Colony.

"Even the Officials bounced," Crema carried on. "Not ONE ever appeared. But I knew it was all over when I spotted them flying Black Blattos up on poles ripping down our precious billboards!"

"Oh sweetums," gasped the podcaster, moving aside as other Mausoleum bugs rushed to Crema's cries. Baroness Bigdata and #1 Anchor ...Colony-wide Cokenasmile came running over to scrape scoops off the 'grounds Reporter'.

A few ticks later, as Mausoleum Anchors and podcasters were super hyper experts, Bigdata hopped on a LIVE WIRE and blew it up. "It's OFFICIAL," she began in a voice so grim the crypt got dim. "Earlier we brought live pics and interviews of Riots taking place on the Hill, but we've just discovered some disturbing news. One of our beloved Reporters has just been found besmirched, fleeched and stung over 100% of her shell. Currently she is enroute to the dispensary, so WE ASK ALL TO PRAY for her speedy recovery."

Cokensmile cleared his trake and reported a similar tale, adding one frighteningly alarming detail. "What was initially perceived to be a simple RIOT stirred by bugs angered over the Black Mound visit, now appears to be a coup on the Colony. The troubling removal of billboards leads us to believe a new governance has already conquered Providence Hill."

Inside the O-ring.

The air inside the O-ring smelled of heavy sweet hot sticky BeesWax when the RIOT news finally reached WaWa's lobe. The Fan-fab Four...him and his advisers Tiramisu, Starbucks and KFC were discussing the rising cost of collard greens and its impact on the Colony when Maz's call came through.

WaWa and his Advisers kept silent as Maz's promenade voice came over the node. By policy no call was patched through to the O-ring without being verified, corroborated and introduced. But Maz's sound ...a mix of dare, scare and conflicting flair... was how she navigated protocol and got through. Even WaWa and his Advisers failed to discern if she (or he) was Silpha Roach, Just a Roach, or Ant or what.

"One of you bugs at the O-ring level need to get up off your O-rings and get the O-ring out to Providence," was how Maz greeted the Colony's Sir Kingpin. Truthfully, few bugs respected WaWa. Past Kingpins had ALL been Roaches. Not one Black Ant had led the Colony from INSIDE the O-ring. So few bothered to figure out how to respect his title with him in it.

"Come again," WaWa replied, straightening his posture to project strength and loyalty, and his sincere OATH TO SERVE. Regardless of HOW he got the position, dissing was dissing, which Black Ants didn't take kind to any dismissing.

"I said..." and Maz repeated herself verbatim, cluing her listeners that she definitely wasn't a Roach. This kind of mattered, BIG TIME, why WaWa let her finish the call, which she did... adding how a certain Governor had her Constantinople (and City Officials) UP on a scaffold pulling down HIS flockup!

The call led to a ballsy exchange with a Field Palace Scribe assigned the task to surveil a quadrant of territory covering the Colony. In all there were 64 quadrants, and this Scribe had the 5th quadrant, a 5000 acreage of land which covered the Hill and surrounding territories such as Roughneck Creek. In comparison to other quadrants it wasn't a large area, and thus a mundane task, particularly given how sleepy the area normally was. Many bugs handling the task had to create controversies just to stay on the bursa; that being to remain on payroll. But now WaWa wanted to know why he hadn't been informed about what was going on in Providence, along with how in a muddy untailored Crisis had Maz gotten through to the O-ring with this info, instead of he who should have been enlightening him on the matter!

These conflict of interest issue entanglements ended up getting addressed in a heated exchange, in the order asked. 'Was not the Kingpin monitoring his Feed,' voiced the Field Scribe, to which WaWa voiced in defense, 'there was NO FEED in the O-ring!'

That was a germane lie! Though it wasn't the Field Scribe that swung back. The First Wingbourne occupying the jump position with Scribe jumped on the node and filled WaWa's lobe expeditiously. "LOOK at YOUR ALERT NODULE," shouted Wingbourne, a blistering red-colored Roach. "LOOK at it! YOUR ALERT NODULE IS FLAMING RED YOU PUSS PUTT," he screamed. "Them nodules are in every Chamber in the Palace. Don't YOU KNOW THIS!?!"

Of course WaWa perched over his histrionic plank slurping up sweet sticky BeesWax and discussing the cost of collard greens with his three Lord Advisers had known this...and seen this...BUT INDEED IGNORED THIS!

However, WaWa didn't come undone. During the course of his jerry-rigged Kingmanship almost every bug in the Palace had yelled at him and called him all kinds of unsavory epithets. He got this flack a lot. He was used to it. In his defense, had he activated those nodules every time it blinked he'd never gotten a thing done, or word in edgewise, let alone have a chance to enjoy a hot saucer of Beeswax with his Top Advisers. He loved this stuff; the sticky red brine was culled from Bee juice and curated rubber. It took thousands of Worker Ants to create the dish, and he oh so loved vibing with his favorite Top Advisers while slobbing down the delicacy. So yeah, he had ignored the flickering nodule...like the yelling and screaming and calling him lascivious names. And even still he had a job to perform. "Well, are we getting crushed or what," he asked.

"What!?!" cried Scribe. And he wasn't only upset because of the noise and feedback in the Eagle preventing a clear line of communication. He detected some churlosity, prompting Wingbourne who was at the controls trying to avoid flying into a squall of Dragonflies to correct the transgression.

"Deuce, you got something for us," Wingbourne howled back.

WOO! Now that moniker came off really cussy. But WaWa didn't curl. He wasn't the one weaving and dodging, trying to out-maneuver cooky drunk shelly creatures coming from a lake brouhaha. So he sort of repeated himself. "A gassy sounding Sect told me we're gettin' crushed! So, ARE WE!?!"

The Bald Eagle Wingbourne and Scribe were flying flipped upside down. That REALLY pissed them off. They almost got dumped but managed to right side up the Eagle...churning up the squall party in the process... before delivering WaWa a sting.

"Listen up you PISS ANT," Wingbourne yarked into the node, "It ain't no WE up here, you hear! Your name ain't on any of our bursas! YOU'RE NUTHIN' BUT JUKEHICK SCHMUCK paid to take orders, NOT ASK DUMWIT QUESTIONS!"

WaWa's turn. "Sounds like you know what to do then," he spat back in a wry chuckle. "Good luck!"

WaWa got no rebuttal. He disconnected the call and pushed the node aside so that Palace Servers could use the space to spread out a tray of fried Gnat tendrals. "Sounds like them red bugs know what they're doing," he laughed, returning to his delicious helpings of haute bites... and company.

"Aah yeah, no need putting that on the radar," Lord Tiramisu agreed. "They'll figure it out. It's their job, what they're paid for," he laughed mightily.

"I think you're right," WaWa nodded. "All of 'em need to eat the dust far as I'm concerned!"

"Hahahaha," laughed all four Insects; WaWa (a Black Ant), Tiramisu (an Albino Spider), and KFC and Starbucks (both Cicadas). All had zero tastes for Roaches or Colony plebs like Scribe and Wingbourne ...unless served on platters.

"If they survive to tell the story, we'll blame the connection. And if not," and WaWa shrucked, "WE ALL will exist happily ever after!"

The laughter inside the O-ring was riotous. WaWa, Tiramisu, KFC and Starbucks flipped forward, backwards and sideways laughing. They were about to call out for more brine when suddenly Deputy Adviser Falaffal burst into the chamber.

"The MA (Moral Authority) in Providence has been wiped out... decimated," he explained panicked. "Governor State wants to borrow our Artillery."

"And if we don't get it back," WaWa coolly asked, still amused, supported by three smirking and smacking Advisers.

Falaffal started to part his lickers and then froze, realizing he had interrupted a sort of private celebration. "Ummm...just wanted to inform you, we are on RED ALERT," he nicely offered, easing backwards out of the O-ring.

"Tell Gubnor to hunker down," Tiramisu tossed after him. "...And tell 'em to watch out for a gurgling Bald Eagle," he lopped on, falling backwards laughing. Falaffal, of course, didn't find the humor funny.

"Yeah, it might get kind of breezy out there," WaWa chimed in. "The Bursas got some creodonts doing real fast donuts in the air," he joked merrily, to the utmost amusement of his company.

Falaffal left the O-ring outraged and plainly insulted. He was another one who believed the kingpin had been jerry-rigged into the position, but this display of bamboozlement was intolerably outlandish. He bowed to a stone guardian symbolically protecting the O-ring and said a quick prayer. He hoped WaWa would catch his karma...SOON!

Inside the O-ring WaWa watched a dull bulb blinking beneath his plank. This had been going on for a while, before an alarm sounded. "Bet it's that Hill Governor," he chuckled at the trio still smacking and slurping. "Let's listen to this," he chuckled.

Kicking up his whiskers on the plank and reclining back with a half dozen tentacles clasped behind his mullet he greeted his caller. "Go ahead," WaWa spat real cocky-like.

"Who's this," came back a stern staid far away voice laced with anxiety.

"You're speaking to the Honorable Sir Kingpin Yahinus Blackspan," he replied... his full legal title and name.

"Ugh, yeah," Governor State began. He hated WaWa infallibly. Always had, and forswore he always would. Ever since learning Kingdoms paid a hefty sum of Walnuts to ensure the flaky fluky fake presided over the Colony his assumption never wavered.

"We need some heavy Artillery down here," State asked anyway, as if scraping molasses off his lickers. He hated every bit of this conjugal session. "I'm getting reports that high levels of ceratopsian vapors are downing my plebs," he reported.

The ceratopsian vapors resulted from the Showers Maz ordered. But it shouldn't have affected his plebs, unless they were part of the motley crew that had commandeered City's Lyft.

Starbucks, KFC and Tiramisu burst out laughing. What a plumongous flapjack! Who did State think he was dousing soup over? Like they didn't know he was among believers doubting the Kingpin's legitimate Right to Rule. Now suddenly he was calling for help.

WaWa how so didn't laugh, or at least not out loud. "Who's we," he mildly snorted. He knew the deal too. After the epochs of horrific misery State's kind inflicted on Black bugs speçifically, and Galaxy-wide plebs in general, Roaches deserved to be shooed into the Rapids...if that's where they were in fact being shooed. Still, he needed to be careful. Despite how the power hungry greedy tards succeeded in growing a carnivorous hate, and not by only WaWa's stance, but indeed was an Atlas purview, he couldn't lose this thing. His rule on the throne had to count, be worth his while!

An amorphous silence followed before State spoke. "My Guards, that's who," he finally shot back.

"Hey...hey! Watch the pitch," WaWa chuckled, winking at his amused audience before curling forward to grab a scribe. "Tell me whatcha need, and if it's available we'll try to get it out to ya'."

"Great," puffed the Governor, picking up the inertia in WaWa's tone.

There was no way in a SamGleason smirk that the jokesters in the Palace hadn't been warned about the swarms of bugs... Flies, Fleas, Wasps and whatnot over taking the Hill. They had to know. At that very instance a video feed was playing a band of Yellow Jacks parading Official mohawks (helmets) in public. And on his personal audio feed a tinsel-sounding bug was trying to offload, purportedly authentic County insignias. By all means the Palace had to know of the gelatinous Riot!

Gruffly the Governor belted out the Artillery he needed, summing up the request by asking for a dozen tanks.

"Whoa... where WE going with tanks," WaWa interrupted. "Who's going to be operating them? You got Soldiers trained to navigate this type artillery?"

And that did it. "That's your duty, YOU PUSS BUG..." and the Governor raveled up his ugly finishing sentiments quickly, severing the line before things got really raspy.

"You think I should send them some tanks," WaWa asked his company after his lobe met the click.

"Ojeckles No!," huffed KFC. "I met the Chief on the Hill before. He's as fickle and dysfunctional as the Swine Sea. I wouldn't trust 'em with my curio Platoon set. Let them sort it out... while we recline back watching this unpartisan regime come to a fantastic fabulous karmatic end!"

"But what about the Governor? And Falaffal?" WaWa asked. "And Crisis help us if those Bald Eagle fliers return with another version to this story. Last thing we need is a long redundant investigation tying up more important work."

"Look, let's not get distracted," Starbucks chimed in. "So long as we keep the Media on our side, we're ALL GOOD. We continue to roll the dice until we hear from them flim-flam-fake-flakers!"

CHAPTER 3

Clean Up.

Rolling back to the unveiling sequence of events was where Combat, Coach and the Captains were, in the Warpit pre-semi-celebrating. Not one County Official got off a single blast, and no other Offies burst in to rescue them. Amazing, though not too surprising.

"But are you sure them Bloks were working," Coach asked Combat.

"...Before that samfluggin' kid blasted it off the wall they were..."

"But how can we be sure? We don't want no—"

"—It's not the point," Captain FuFu cut in. "We don't need to be fooling around with doctoring footage. We need to ROLL OUT!"

Combat and Coach exchanged a quick vigilant glance. FuFu might've been right, like he stepped in and took over the Official's com-com, forestalling a certain calamity, but none of it was the point. They despised his input, especially if he had a point!

"How about you and your Captains return to the Front pit and collect any Bloks or gadgets, and examine them for possible transmission," Combat retorted. "Let us know what you find...WHILE WE deal with impending escapes," he snarled.

FuFu didn't protest. He never did when Combat got like this. There was a very good reason he and the other Captains stayed in a Mound where their expertise was not welcomed, otherwise they'd been long gone. They abhorred the WarLord and his amaurotic shuffleboards about as much as they detested him. Luckily a higher morale favored them more.

"That Cappin' irks the lactose out of me," Combat fussed once FuFu and his Lackys were gone. "Think they know every blasted thing!"

"Yeah, I'd be fine pulling them apart and tossing 'em on a pile of those broken up Offies," said one Elder.

"Just say the word. I'm with you Bug," jostled another Elder.

"Well, before we start breaking up and tossing pests, how 'bout we get some numbers straight...and find out what's what," Combat said.

"What's what," muttered a dumbfounded Elder that couldn't piece together a puzzle if it was already assembled, minus one corner piece. "I'll let you in on a secret of what's not," he ribbed anyway, laughing way too hard at humor not only incomplete, but at a joke that failed to land.

"Well, when you get those numbers, give 'em to me," replied yet another Elder a thread less swifter than the dumbfounded Elder. "I only need a seven or elebben!"

"Hot dang!" cheered the dumbfounded Elder, excitedly bouncing around. "'Dats MY number!—"

"—Hey. Hey. How 'bout we pipe down," Combat interjected. They still had lots of loose ends in need of cleaning up. "We need to—"

"—to get out Front," Coach reminded Combat. "...And make sure those Cappins' are doing what we told them to do!"

Sure enough they strutted out Front to find one of the Antes... Ante Good... arguing with Captain FuFu over Combat's instructions. "Look, it was just an accident," she fussed. "He was only trying to help me," she lamented, referring to a kiddie that had gotten in the way of the clean up. "Besides, why do we want to save all this junk anyways!"

Quickly Combat slid between huffed up Good and FuFu trying to hold onto a busted-up gadget the brat kid wanted back. "It's not even working," he tried to explain to Good. "I'm the one that ordered the Captains to collect these scraps."

"I KNOW!" Good shouted. "That's what I'm talking about! Why are we saving this stuff!?! None of it was here before...so why we need it now!?! It ain't going to hurt the kiddies to play with that junk!"

"It's not junk Good—"

"—but it's mine," Pokey butted in, trying to pull the gadget away from Combat. "Nooo, give me...give me... I want it," he whined. "I found it first!"

Combat looked down and grinded his scissors. "Go to your pit before I sock you out you little—"

"—Stop it," Good sort of like hissed back. "I won't permit nothing of the sort," she said, bending over and coddling wailing Pokey. "Don't worry Pokey-mon," she continued, patting his mullet and wiping his tears. "Your Good isn't going to let anySect hurt you," and she glared back at Combat still grinding his scissors. "Not even some big bad mean WarLord," she promised.

"I just wanted 'der 'dem wings," Pokey went back to sniveling. "My dugonflys are old and ugly. I want new ones..."

"Good, this is NOT GOOD," Combat argued. "You can't keep spoiling these kids! We almost got roasted!"

"But we didn't," snapped Good. "Plus, I told y'all not to take Pokey out in the first place!"

"And I said there were to be NO heroes," Combat shot back, glaring HARD at pouting Pokey.

"I'm soddy," Pokey sniveled, laying his best doe look on Ante Good. "Now can I keep my soubenir?"

"Of course you can honey," Good said taking the gadget from Combat and giving it to Pokey.

"I SAID NO!" Combat howled so savagely both Good and Pokey fell back. "IT'S NOT a toy!" he fumed. "Now give it here," he snapped snatching the gadget and passing it to FuFu. "Don't make me chop you! This just might be our barter out of here!"

The gadget fit a recording device, likely a part of the Offies' shell-cam that filmed the entire fiasco. But Good didn't care what it was, or how it might be used to exonerate them. After brushing herself off she got up in Combat's mug.

"How dare you," she hissed. "These Cuts have been beaten up enough over this! They're just beanies, something you seem to have forgotten!"

"And that's the problem Good," Combat rowed back. "These buds will never bloom into Warriors if they're raised to be spoiled, sniveling, rotten non-producing Tikes! They'll be no good for anything!"

"Yeah, well, just tell me one thing," Ante Good smarted back. "Where would we be if Pokey hadn't done what he did!?!"

Good had a point. Combat called FuFu back. "Give the kid the dang gadget," he said.

"But—"

"—But nothing Fu," seethed Combat. "Give the danggonit thing BACK!"

FuFu relinquished the gadget, definitely a part belonging to one of the cams. He saw the ribbon, and the spindles Pokey pulled on as if it was a trigger.

But there was no arguing with Combat, especially if his pursuer was a Captain. Perhaps he could later try to reason with Good... as he most certainly wasn't winning a squabble with one of the Brats, Pokey in particular.

FuFu moved on, muttering about the busted up gadget he probably was going to find in another blink laying discarded somewhere after Pokey got bored.

This was the problem about working in this Ant Mound. No discipline...at all layers. Rumor claimed Combat fought in Battle of MANTS, (the Macho Ants Nukem Tactical Strike). Supposedly when his enemies went high, he went low, how he ended up a sole surviving coward among an entire fleet of Cadets. That was his decorated strategy...before the Foot Bomb Strike he also cowardly lived through. The WarLord was no scholar of either strategy or strength. He was a LOOSE HOPE... and cannon!

"Just clean up this pit," Combat ordered. "I want every trace of these sumbats swept up ...and Captain," he broke, specifically addressing FuFu. "I want you to collect ALL the gadgets and inspect them ...if you can!"

FuFu kept his lickers compressed and followed the order, encouraging others under his helm to 'look and learn.' They sifted through the debris looking for critical parts, a near futile task due to kids hindering the effort.

"Give me that," one Captain snorted, tugging a battery away from a kid.

"Noooooo..." cried the kiddie holding on to the Lithium with all its might.

FuFu bumped into the kid, not purposely (wink, wink), hitting the snit with the sharp edge of a shield. Instantly the kid stopped whining and fell to the ground, HURT! Seeing the mishap work so perfectly, motivated all the Captains to try this again and again...until Antes seeing the misfortunes happening over and over, began shooing kids from the pit.

"Scram! Scram," they shooed, but they couldn't catch Pokey. He remained... ripping around with his prized new toy shrieking, "Bang! Bang!"

"My blaster is better!" Pokey bragged. "Bang! Bang!" he teased and taunted, showing ZERO fear or empathy for Captains he irked, slipping between them, trying to prevent them from nabbing his Bang!Bang!.

"Oool, let me see," one Captain coyly asked.

"Nooo," sniveled the pesky brat. "Ante Good said it's MINES!"

"Well, I'ma find a bigger and better one," the Captain played along, trying to lower the brat's guard, using a gaggle of time they didn't have to lose.

Eventually FuFu saddled up beside the brat and bumped him HARD. Pokey fell instantly, like a stone he hit the ground, losing the gadget. Quietly another Captain scooped it up and pitched it to FuFu doing a LeBron pass while the brat screamed. He wasn't hurt but bawled anyway. "Ouwee! Waaa! Waaa!" he blared at a siren's pitch, drawing attention from none other than his favorite doting Ante, Good front and center.

Swiftly FuFu left the Front pit, distancing himself from Pokey's lingering cries and his most beloved Ante coming to collect the mulish mullet of whoever or whatever made her brat cry... and of course to find the infamous Bang! Bang!

AI'd Footage.

By the time the Antes finished searching Pokey over for damage, the real evil was being dismantled and in process of being forever edited. FuFu commissioned the science scholars of the Captains to dissect the bang-bangs.

"This is URGENT. Work quickly," he warned the experts ahead of a MAJOR INVESTIGATION ramping up at the bequest of Combat...via the Antes, namely Good crying about finding Pokey's bang-bang.

"Look, the brat said you took his bang-bang," Coach yawned at FuFu. "He seems sure of it in fact," and he yawned again. "We just want the thing back, so the Antes can get on with their chores. They haven't been able to get a thing done."

FuFu watched Coach's lickers sliding around, not offering anything more than 'he didn't know what Pokey was talking about.'

"Un huh," Coach continued yawning. "Well... do you think wit all your smarts, you and your magicians can whip up some magic and fashion something the kid can play with?"

FuFu looked at the Warbug like a drifter and said nothing.

"Well, just so you know, whenever Good ain't happy, ain't NOSECT 'bout to be happy. So my advice to you is to come up with somethin'," Coach yawned his hardest yet. "No tellin' what's 'bout to come out of this investigation," he added shaking his mullet as he strolled off.

Totally Fatuous! Of all the garanimals to be wrecked about and this was the animus the Security Council chose to grapple.

Captain Fessy, a second LT along the Captain base, looked at FuFu. "Maybe we should just give them the thing back," he suggested.

"And maybe you don't get the dynamics of the situation here," FuFu contested. "If they are willing to delimb us over a dang bang-bang with everything riding their backflaps, no matter what we do hardly matters."

"But all we have to do is give them—"

"—No Fess," FuFu interrupted. "Dysfunction is coming full speed at us and we don't have time to be trying to appease fragility."

Indeed the investigation soared to grotesque azures. A cluster fuster of Warriors, dispatched by the WarLord, descended upon the KIA convinced of the Captain's complicity in the missing gadgets.

By then the bang-bang was long gone. No more. Wasn't ever resurfacing, no matter how hard they looked. Useful data had been scraped off the device and what remained was no longer recognizable.

"Yeah, kind of see what you mean," Fessy said after seeing what remained of the gadget. "That brat wouldn't want this thing. If their toys don't have the most bells and whistles, they don't want it."

"Yeah, it's kind of a Y2K bang-bang type thing," FuFu replied, though it was none of his argument.

"Well, how are we going to explain this," Fessy wanted to know. A mandatory meeting had been set up about the missing toy and they were required to attend.

"Just let me do the talking," FuFu said on the sly as the last Warrior left the KIA with a sac of Official parts that included gut innards and loads of doodles. Combat was going to have a conniption to see those very mature doodles! Ha.Ha.

"Ummp. So sad," Fessy said shaking his mullet as he too watched the Warrior triumphantly traispe out with the sac full of doodles. "Poor saps doing the best they can with them flattened firballs."

Flattened firballs was basically batter-butter for brains. Many Insects suffered from this issue. The condition spanned across bugs. According to a study done by Galaxy Scholars, less than 1% of the Insecta society harbored reasoning skills. Captains were among that minority.

"Just remember," FuFu warned. "We're their best ally...their greatest hope. Without us, they are DOOMED!"

"Ummp," Fessy hummed again. "Not sure how to cipher that one for bugs making simple decisions on minusa."

"Well, we've been managing the minusa all this time. Let's not shake now," FuFu banked on.

FuFu and Fessy convened in the Conference pit following normal protocol. They moved to the rear of the pit so that the Senior Security and their rah-rah Warriors could position themselves and their point of views front and center.

"Oh no, you two, WE want you up FRONT," Combat loudly announced, speaking of course to the surprised Captains...and not surprised by the callous invite, but caught off guard about the possibility that a ceremonial lynching might be taking place in their sublime Conference pit...an amorphous first!

Instantly Fessy started sputtering and shuffling, taking careful steps as he looked left and right, possibly for an escape?

"Easy...easy..." FuFu muttered in Fessy's lobe, taking careful steps himself . "FBF... FBF..." he quietly and VERY sneakily chanted, reminding Fessy to chill.

FBF stood for Flint Before Fire. It was a code taught Captain Cadets on initiation into the academy. A FIRE couldn't start without the FLINT.

Lowkey as it was kept, the leading reason they were in the Mound and remained in the Mound was due to the Head Chancellor's unyielding respect of the inviolable training built around this code.

"All'ight, WE made a decision," Combat belted ahead of usual formalities; roll taking, grand gestures and noble nonsense. "We've concluded y'all both stole said missing bang-bang and must be charged and punished accordingly!"

"Let His WILL Be Done," shouted Almighty. And he banged on the plank.

"So be it," Combat added, having settled the matter after seeing those doodles, one or all of the Captains sent with his Warriors. "Do you two have any last admissions before sentencing," he smirked.

"Yes," replied FuFu, about to speak on the unfairness of the trial when Good raced in, abundantly late, followed by her posse; Antes Great, Bitter, Hope and PrayedUp. "Wait," she shrieked. "We didn't get to speak! We got something to say!"

"Oh no, Good," Combat objected right off the cuff. "We don't need NO extra—"

"—Unt un, NO Comby! We got RIGHTS! We got something to say about all this too!"

The Conference pit quieted and they waited.

"We got a witness. We got someone you need to hear," she said, turning to the dantiest among her egg-holders. "Go on Hope, tell 'em what you saw..." she prompted the shy Ante.

"Well I seen a Captain deliberately jab Pokey in the marble," she replied.

FuFu almost laughed out loud. And Fessy did laugh out loud. All mullets whipped around to look in their direction.

"You find something funny," Combat snapped.

Fessy didn't respond so Combat asked Hope to single out 'the Captain' among the only two Captains in the pit held accused of shafting the kid.

Meekly Hope peeked up and astronomically indicated it was FuFu that hurt Pokey.

"CASE CLOSED," Combat ruled. "Now get 'em out of here and take 'em to the brick—"

"—Oh NO!" Good protested again. "Before you shake them, we want to make them turn over Pokey's bang-bang!"

"Good, forget the bang-bang," Combat huffed. "It don't matter. It's gone," he said eager to move on but unable to do so because Good DISAGREED, and VEHEMENTLY SO.

"I WILL NOT BE MOVED UNTIL—"

"—I can get the kid's bang-bang—"

"Oh NO YOU CAN NOT," Combat snorted at FuFu before turning on Good. "The only thing these Cappins' are gettin' is a GOOD SHAKIN' & BRICKIN'!"

Ante Good reared back and arched her visors. "I know good and well you aren't addressing me with that tone," she hissed back. "Now, if that Captain has confessed he has that bang-bang, THEN I WANT IT BACK!!! NO IFs, ANDs or BUTs!!!"

Combat grunted. No matter how tough he tried to be with Good, it was pointless trying to win a debate against her. The only way he got to her was by making moves without her knowledge or consent... the strategy he used to make it out of the MANTS excursion. "Just listen to me," he pleaded. "We don't have the luxury to argue about silly—"

"—Ugh! SILLY!?!," cried Good. "I can't believe you have the unmitigated GALL to call me SILLY!?! Are you ALL out of your noncompeting firballs!?!" she huffed at Combat... before panning a glare across his mesmerized audience.

"Now I don't give a hoot hot dang HOW SILLY YOU THINK I AM, but I want Pokey's toy and I want it this instance!!!"

Combat looked over at Almighty, looking back at him, while Pastor Amen, Coach and a filled galley of Elders and Warriors lowered their mullets.

"Now where is that bang-bang," Good said, moving into FuFu's space. "I can get it myself!"

"Look Good," Pastor Amen calmly intervened. "Let's not make things worse than—"

"—Ut," Good said, waging a widget in the air. "Pastor..." and she paused a tick to change her tone so as not to insult the gods. "You know how I revere All Say and Crisis, but I must ask you to kindly step back and shut up," she said shaking her mullet in an 'about to explode manner'.

The Pastor obliged, although his move looked more reflexive than intentional. "My apologies," he said. No Ante had ever told him 'to SHUT UP', even if some of the backlash he'd gotten over the course of dealing with many Antes meant about the same. "I'm only trying to coffer a little—"

—And good was off once more. "What!?!" she shrieked. "Your job is to PRAY for US! Not be in here defending some no good whatchamacallit treasoners!"

And when no bug interceded, she carried on, accusing the Captains of everything but protecting their interests, the only reason they were there. "I know y'all poked out Pokeymon's marbles and stole his toy," she wailed. "...Like I know y'all planning to take off with our Dallies!"

"Whoa...Whoa...enough," Combat said putting a halt to the verbal rampage. He let her vent so long that he actually ended up growing a soft spot for the Captains.

"Look Fu," he began, keeping his marbles off the pair. "I want you and Fess to take Good back to the KIA and find the kid's toy and give it to her."

Then he turned to his Senior Security. "And I want ALL OF US to focus on WHO STOLE THAT DANG BANG, WHY, AND WHERE IT IS!"

"—But why?"

"—Because IT'S AN ORDER," Combat shouted. "It had classified intel on it," he argued, trying to come off knowing when he had no knowledge about what fascinated Pokey about that bleating bang-bang and why the Captains didn' want to return it!

No Good Deed.

Up to this event the Captains hadn't dealt with Good much. She hung out in the Scullery and they in the KIA. So it was a surprise learning she wasn't that boiler bug they encountered in the Conference pit.

"Yeah, I have to keep the WarLord straight," she said. "Sometimes he forgets there are more bugs in here than just him and his Warriors!"

Particularly Fessy considered the revelation a giant leap in confidence as she accepted the doctored gadget cheerfully, and went on chatting about vacays and getting away as if it was the first time they met. "I expected her to be a stiffy," he said. He'd gotten used to bugs jaded by scholars, which was odd given his history.

Prior to arriving at the Mound a scholar-hater betted intellect could never incapacitate ignorance. Action would beat academia every time the hater foreswore. But Fessy proved the hater wrong. He won. The brawl was over in the amount of time it took a garlic-filled bug to figure out it was paralyzed. For the longest few understood what happened, to include those that filled an arena waiting to watch Fessy's demise. Spectators couldn't figure out why a healthy full-grown Bullet bug wasn't moving. How could a bug many times Fessy's heft get whipped like that? While many got it, the haters were plain wrong, few could prove it like Fessy.

"Yeah, I kind of dig her too," FuFu admitted. "She gets us," he chuckled.

"You mean YOU," Fessy teased.

FuFu hadn't fooled Fessy. He more than KIND OF digged Good, proven in how he responded when he heard her screaming.

The disturbance got the attention of many in the Mound shortly after the trinket exchange. When FuFu and Fessy heard the screams they knew better than to rush into the storm. The pitch sounded like the trinket was going to require explaining.

To the contrary, Pokey beatified the haphazardly soddered trinket. He was so enrapt, he stuck it inside an immobile County Offie and somehow brought the stiff back to life!

"What the jell is going on," Combat muttered, confused about what he was seeing.

"Look," Good squealed as if the bugs circling the dazed Offie couldn't see. "Pokeymon fixed him!"

FuFu and Fessy hurried to the Front pit on that pronouncement. This may have sounded profound and phrenic and phenomenal, but they heard CRISIS!

By the time they joined the huddle questions and curiosity engulfed a dopey bug trying to get a grip on his bearings.

"Which one is that one?"

"What they do to him?"

"I don't know about this," said one observant and skeptical Ante. "What if he ousts us?"

Combat couldn't decide whether he was seeing devilment or real ingenuity. "Who did this? How—"

"—Doc needs to speak with you," Almighty slid in his lobe as he teetered over which priority to take on first. Should he squash the cheering or recrush the dope trying to lift his mug? To FuFu and Fessy's chagrin he chose Doc.

They traded glances and made their way back to the KIA to do some eavesdropping. Doc spent his effervescence in the box, a tiny lab where he proved and disproved theories...mostly experimenting on live varmin like Leeches, Lice, and lesser spores.

"What's up Doc," Combat asked.

"I think we have something," Doc replied very casual like, as if the WarLord didn't hate him even more than FuFu, if that was even possible.

Foreboding confirmed the very next question Combat asked was if FuFu had something to do with what was happening in the Front pit.

"Absolutely Not," Doc quickly answered. "Fu knows nothing about this. I've been in here working on reassembling the Officials alone," he giddily replied.

He was telling the truth...somewhat. FuFu and Fessy did know Doc was in the box doing some very depraved work. He was a collage of sin from creation.

Captains even avoided him. No bug that really knew Doc, and was familiar with his work, cared to end up on one of his slabs. But FuFu and Fessy absolutely DID NOT KNOW what Doc had done when they asked him to add a few bells and whistles to the bang-bang toy. Perhaps it was a mistake telling him the toy was for the sniveling kid, BUT THEY WERE DESPERATE.

"Perhaps if we get enough Offies assembled we can release them and not have to bother with exit strategies," Doc shared with Combat.

Rarely did Combat miss a chance to disagree with a Captain, and especially Doc, but on this one the WarLord was rendered speechless.

"Come in here," Doc continued, going as far as to extend an INVITE touring HIS BOX! "I've almost assembled a half dozen of them Offs."

"What the WELL," FuFu muttered listening in from the other side of the Box. Was the Spore Sicko showing the WarLord THE GUTS OF HIS HELL!?!

"Gee, this could be it," Fessy whispered too.

A swish later Elder Elon came ambling into the KIA. He was the WarLord's preferred scientist, paged to provide oversight over Doc's nefarious work.

"What do you think," Combat asked his Top Trusted Make-Believe Source. "Do you think these stiffs will be harmless if unfrozen?"

FuFu couldn't see Elon but distinctly heard a shrug. "Looks like good work to me," he replied.

"Well, I want you to hang around here to make sure no subterfuge is going on," Combat instructed. "Last thing WE need is Good finding out about these depraved operations!"

"In that case you might want to collect those bang-bangs the tikes are running around out there playing with," Doc suggested.

FuFu and Fessy held their breath until they heard Combat speaking again. "Why? What's wrong with them," he asked, just as a youngin' known as lil Dap, heading towards the box, bumped into him. "Hey, hey...where are you going with that!?!"

"He needs he whicca fixed," replied chummy lil' Dap holding what appeared to be an Official whisker. "FruitLoop assadently crushed it," he explained.

"Gimme that," Combat snarled, snatching the whisker away.

"Oool," whined lil Dap. "Give it BACK," he said suddenly turning combative. "...Else I'm telling on you!"

CLABLOOMP! Combat knocked lil Dap on his lil bulb while muttering... "gotta do something 'bout these smar—" —and he didn't finish the mutter.

Suddenly Good appeared, in midst of him also lifting the tike off the ground by the backflap. "What in the name of Crisis are you doing," she gasped, looking from Combat to lil Dap being held by his end flap.

"We need to round up these toys because—"

"—Comby, I'm tired of this! I'm not letting y'all keep getting away with hurting these kids trying to zap away their fun!"

"Aww, come on, it was an accident," Combat grumbled. "Besides, he's not hurt. But we have to get these dangerous toys out of their whiskers."

"Dangerous?" Good asked alarmed.

"Yes, dangerous," Combat replied. "Just got—"

"—No Comby, I'm not hearing it. Do you know what will happen if we keep confiscating their toys!?!"

"No! Do you realize what will happen to ALL OF US if we don't," Combat argued back.

Lil Dap wasn't interested in hearing what Combat had to say either. "I want it! I want it," he wailed reaching for the prop toy the WarLord had taken from him. The whisker belonged to an Official, and as it turned out, had tendons that still worked.

"No, you can't play with this," Combat told the kid. "Now move along before I—"

"—Before you what," hissed Good narrowing her pearls. "How can you be so cruel," she snarled before looking down at lil Dap and gently kissing the top of his mullet. "Don't worry honey, Ante G will get you another doll-whisker to play with."

"—Good," Combat snapped, pleading for what accounted as his final appeal. "This is NOT a play toy," he repeated. "Do you know what grown Offies like to do in the dark with things like this?"

Ante Good's pearls pulsated and twirled, and her lickers popped open as she mused on the choices. She didn't dare reply.

"That's right," Combat iterated, doubling down on his point. "They like to poke things," he clarified. "Do you want one of these kiddies getting poked while trying to sleep?"

On that note, without further protest, Good spun around and took off. She inserted herself among playing kiddies, grabbing as many of the Official (so-called toy parts) and tossed them aside. "Time for bubbles," she sang, ignoring those that whined. And when Pokey tottered by, of course leading his new toy by a whisker, she stopped him too. "Let Ante Good take this sweetie," she said firmly holding onto a big reassembled digital bug.

"Waaaaa waaa waa," Pokey broke out wailing. "I can wash him myself," he cried.

"No honey," Good gently coaxed. "He needs to take a bath with your Elders," she replied, hurling the crazy looking creature resembling the actual Chief with all her might in the WarLord's direction.

Switchin' It Up.

Neither Combat, nor the Elders saw a clear path forward. Too much going on. Too many distractions. Too many choices. So they rallied around indecisiveness.

"This is next level technology," Elon excitedly told Senior Security; Combat, Coach, Almighty and a nexus of others. "I don't see us having to go anywhere if the Offies are patched up and freed," he hubrisly cheered.

Elders apathetic about the prep work it would take to leave their wonderful Mound, yet numb about the consequences they might foment if they stayed leaned in to hear more. "See, when we take this piece here and stick it in this thing here it responds," Elon explained.

On a rational algorithm, mending bugs wasn't an altogether radical discovery. Insect scourges and breakage happened all the time and was typically repaired in this manner. Also, numerous Insects lived long existences missing vital parts, many carrying on eating, mating and enjoying well-rounded pleasures without its mullet.

Elders watched Elon work, having been shown by Doc how to take the front grill from a pile of grills and stick it to a bane (vein) from a tub of banes to expo how the procedure not only brought Offies to life, but also created their personalities.

"Aww, that's no big deal," huffed a particularly cranky graying Elder that thought, lived and breathed the WeShallOverCome past. "All the Cap is doing is patching them swinewhips up."

And again, TRUE. None of this presentation was evidentiary. Depending on the Insect, many could function with missing, and especially switched parts. But what the graying Elder failed to see was these weren't just ANY BUGS!

"No, but check this out," Elon goes. "See, his granolas (firballs/brains) are totally fabricated—"

"—Awwwl jawll to the BIG Lowball No," Elder Insane scoffed.

"Yeah, wonder what Amen gonna say about all this," inserted Elder Surmise.

"He ain't got a digwiggin thing to say about it," Combat lamented in return. "That bill (slang for Bible) he totes around don't mean nothing when he's in here chowing down on earwigs, locusts, termites and any other rebel crawler coming out that Scullery just like the rest of us!"

That simmered the groaning down some. No bug was eager to duke it out with the WarLord. And it wasn't like what he said wasn't true. They all were hypocrites. In that very instance they were munching on a platter of Saffron; one of their staple delicatessences culled from Lightening Bugs that suffered greatly to allow them to enjoy the taste of their guts.

"But come on Comby," Elder Wise sighed anyway. "We're not talking about what we eat. We'll be destroying parts of our ilk for nefarious gains."

"It's not nefarious," Combat snapped. "I'm sure our ilk would rather we survive this thing than have no ilk left to judge!"

Save for Elder Ddawg's muttering, he was the only one struggling with the operation. "This is EVIL," he upchucked, causing Combat to spin around. He couldn't tolerate dissension. One sour vote could enable disaster.

"Who's choking," Combat snarled. "Who feels like surrendering their firball without the benefit of pain juice? Elon can put out your misery right now!"

No bug volunteered, unless Pastor Amen rushing into the War pit counted. "What's going on? I hear there's some depravity in our midst," he said with one whisker raised and looking alarmed.

"Oh, you got the concoction," slurred Combat ignoring Amen holding THE Holy Ant Missive (Bible); Version 991 like elixir.

"No, but before we move forward with any

major decisions we should pray for the offended," he said.

Combat grumbled and rolled his marbles. Any other bug and he would have let them have it. Amen was the only bug he refrained from coming down on in the real. "...Should've prayed before they got here," he groused nonetheless.

"It's never a bad time to pray," Amen insisted. "We all need prayer, even the condemned."

"Well, too late. They should've prayed long ago too," Combat chuckled, joined by Coach and Almighty.

Amen went on and read from THE MISSIVE, though few followed along. The chatter was too clad. Feelers too high. Sensibilities too extended. They were entering a point of NO RETURN.

And then came Good. She burst into the War pit when she heard nefarious rumors floating around too. "Is it true what I'm hearing," she shrieked, held by a gang of Antes struggling to contain her. "My bugs will NOT BE DEGREGATED," she screamed. "How dare you Comby! How dare YOU! I will have us ALL of FRIED before I go along with this blasphemy!"

"Sssh," Combat hushed the indisposed Ante. "Your trust has not been misplaced," he said before laying down a lie he not only misquoted, but he MADE UP! "We're only tinkering with those in the brick," he said out of an amorphous chimera.

Good BELIEVED HIM. "Well, just so you know we've got quite a few youngins missing their bits...and Pokey is now having a fit about his bang-bang. Can you find him something to play with?"

"I'll take care of it," Combat replied. "Matter of fact, I want you and the Antes to scribe down all the things missing, and we'll take care of it. Trust me, everything will be fine."

Satisfied Good and the Antes filed out of the War pit and got back to their duties, while Combat proceeded to double down on the lie. "—Alright..." he gnarled once the pit cleared of Antes. "Listen up," he shouted over mullets sauntering in trying to confirm the rumors. "Doc is going to need help. Therefore I'm asking you to look around for spare parts...or anything not serving a purpose...even if it is something of your own you have to spare...and bring it to the KIA."

His audience, a swelling group of Elders, as well as Warriors, Workers and even young Cadets, looked askance. What parts was he speaking of?

"Just sweep up all the mess out FRONT," he ordered, rather than spell out what he meant and have to REALLY put out a riot. Good, for one, would explode if she heard bugs were asked to donate their vital ensembles just to reassemble the Officials.

"But what if one of them pimp us out," asked a Worker Ant in the rear.

"Don't worry about pimps," Combat shouted to the back. "Just grab a mullet and do like this," and he demonstrated, yanking a near completely assembled Official shell propped up in a corner and slammed its mullet on the ground. The Official yelped when its mullet cracked open but the WarLord ignored him. "Oh, hush," he said, yanking out the stuffing inside and filling it with a clump of dust he found nearby.

"See, it don't matter what gets stuffed inside," he continued explaining, replete with this demo that elicited waves of gasps.

"See, you'll know if something isn't plugged in the right port because it'll yell, or won't work," he went on. "And don't worry," he added. "None of this has to be beautification perfect work... SO LONG as what gets swept up OR DONATED is COMPLETELY EXPENDABLE or unusable to us."

The ad hoc assembly dispersed; bugs leaving the pit with only ONE unifying understanding. The Officials were being released to save their Mound.

Woke Officials.

Combat left the 'stuffing' affairs solely to Doc ...and Elon in charge of minor fixes and monitoring the overall operations. Problem was... noSect but Doc really understood the science behind the work.

Once the job was complete and Combat left to approve the final work, it didn't take much to see the Official tags didn't match up with the reassembled bugs. Clearly Aufguten didn't match the short Moth, like Sangria didn't match the big, gargantuan Beetle.

"Let's not worry about it," Coach shrugged. "So long as they kind of look like the tag."

"But do you think the WarLord will get behind this," Almighty asked. "These DUDS look NOTHING like the tags," he said looking at Bokchoy, a ranking Offie wearing entry-level insigna. "And listen at him. He sounds like a Mosquito!"

"Agh! Try to ignore it," Coach tossed over at Almighty, looking at Warden Kundarhauffen (aka a Butterfly) smiling inappropriately and seeming pleased about his frothy wings.

So they tried to look sideways as Combat got on with the inspection, commencing and ending in nano micro ticks.

"What the what!?!" How could he be okay seeing Warden Kundarhauffen flapping wings no Warden would be seen wearing in ALL the light of power. It was SHOCKING! And when Kundarhauffen asked for a 'kit of Prissy'...basically a fruity liquid no WARDEN would ever request, full leap the WarLord FLIPPED.

"WHERE'S ELON...and DOC," he YELLED.

"Whoa...hold up," Coach intervened. Time was moving and not on their side. "What if we just respin the narrative," he giddily rapped. "Plus, you did say it didn't have to be perfect work. Maybe we can sell their release as a 'Coming to Crisis Movement.'"

Combat twisted around to get a good look at his second in command. "Yeah, I did say that, huh?" He turned back around and gazed over the swatch of reassembled Officials. "I still think we can do better than this. No bug, specifically AN OFFICIAL, is going to buy this trope of—"—and he failed to find a proper phrase for functioning imbeciles.

"But what does it matter," Coach gently pushed back. "By the time they figure it out, we'll have time to be long gone."

"But this isn't about being long gone, or else I'd been long gone," Combat argued.

Coach didn't reply. They were broaching a delicate topic. Not good. Particularly given Almighty was headed towards them...escorting the jacked up Chief.

"So what you think," Almighty asked, looking relatively pleased about the shabbily repaired Chief. He looked nothing like the inebriated Chief that had stormed in demanding the Head Chancellor's mullet.

"Maybe sauce him up a bit," Combat replied, trying hard not to look at the plagiarized coot.

Almighty didn't move. The touch up would've been easy enough, even if he simply doused the coot in licorice on the way out of the Mound.

Combat didn't press the issue either. It was a joke. "Now, we treated you well, haven't we," he asked the dried-out Chief.

The coot stumbled backwards, though he had yet to be doused in licorice. "Comby," he began, more like asking than saying, "I still want my bang-bang. You let that toffy bug take my toy!"

Combat's mullet swung wildly around as he looked over at Coach, just as Elon who overheard the coot's quip, flew over to join the inspection. "Don't panic," he blurted, profusely leaking pulp as he threw up his whiskers. "The kid is just fine!"

Except, WHO SAID POKEY WASN'T FINE!?!

Under the exigency Combat kept cool. "What the NEVEL are you telling me!?!," he shouted at Elon. "Did you do something to that kid!?!"

"Wait...NO...but let's think about this..." Elon rattled. "The kid kept getting in the way..."

"I trusted you," Combat blindly fumed, never really hearing what Elon said. "I put you in charge of this operation," he waged on. "I put my trust in you!!!"

Elon tried to explain but couldn't. Blaming Doc wouldn't work because he was in charge, NOT ELON. So he waffled, emitting sounds that made no sense.

"NoSect is gonna go for this," Combat spewed at waffling Elon. "This entire dang experiment is ONE NOTORIETY EPIC FAIL!"

"But I love you Comby. You's my fabeborite," slobbered the Chief. "And I forgive you," he added, leaping forward to embrace the WarLord.

Combat leaped back but it was too late. The Chief planted a sloppy kiss on his side crushers, and drooled over his aft connector. Now Combat was extra hot...and extra embarrassed too. He let a lot slide, but one thing an Alpha non egg-holder didn't let go was his virile NGH status. He almost dealt the caoky coot a serious blow but instead shouted to no bug in particular, "FIX this shrimp NOW!"

Hurriedly, and relieved, Elon hustled the Chief off, pricking the coot as hurried him away.

"No way we can let them out of here acting like that," Combat scolded Coach. "You trying to get us smoked!?! Or rather, what are you smoking!?!"

"Look, at least he's drooling. It's not like we can get them 100%—"

"—Well I WANT 100%," Combat fumed. "We can't afford nothing less!"

A few dings (minutes) later Elon returned with the remodified Chief. "This one might be better," he said exhausted.

Combat snarled, grating his scissors. "Better better be better than a wild hope!"

"There's no need for intolerance. It's unbecoming of a gentlebug," replied the upgraded Chief, speaking in a cant that sounded like he'd been hanging out in one too many licorice tubs filled with Captains.

Though the corrected Official didn't mirror the original mean talking Chief, Combat let the new version slide. "Yeah...yeah," he muttered before turning to Coach. "Let's get this shrimp on the node with his bugs before I turn this Mound upside down!"

Coach placed calls, first checking in with a bug he knew from back in the WeShallOverCome times who hosted hot topics on Audio dial WBBA-ZAM.

"We's Be Black Always (WBBA), you're on LiveWire, whatcha' got," squealed LadyBug Squeeta.

"Hey there Exy, it's your big bug who know how to do you," Coach greeted back. "Say, I got some TNT for ya'," he lathered on.

"Whatcha' got Cocka," she smiled wide.

And Coach poked her, telling her in chopped up WBBA lingo about the County Officials that came, saw, ATE, DRANK...and now were on their way OUT. Squeeta didn't miss a ding hopping off the call to spread this news, meanwhile a large tumbler filled with licorice was passed to the Chief.

"Make sure he drinks it all," Coach instructed before placing the next call to Miss M.A.A.R.S.I.HFS Cootie, the flummoxed Chief's no-nonsense haughty-taughty secretary.

"Hello? UGH Hello," the Chief slobbered and slurred into the stone.

"Ugh...Yes, go ahead," Miss Cootie uneasily but sweetly eased out.

"Is this MY Cootie?"

Miss Cootie froze. Only ONE Offie spoke to her as such and so far he hadn't returned to the Nest.

"Chief, is this you?" she gasped.

"It's me Sootie," he slurred. "How arst you," he asked like the trustworthy drunk he'd always been.

"How am I!?! How are you? How are you holding up in this hostage crisis?"

"Hostage crisis?!" the Chief shrieked insulted. "Where's the hostage crisis?"

Combat, Coach, Almighty, Elon and even Doc clamored closer to witness this important exchange. The next utterance out of the Chief's lickers would ascertain their next move.

"Nombasense," Chief County giggled.

The Leadership quickly conferred. "We did it," Elon rashly celebrated, confirmed by Doc and Coach singing "...WE!?!"

"Hey...Hey...keep it down," Coach said, overhearing the Chief suddenly bragging.

"We're coming back lil pea," the Chief gurgled. "Yes blossom, WE have come, made new copines, ate, DRANK and now will bid our farewells to our dovey hospitable hosts," he said in a big toasty voice.

"Oh, okay," stammered a montrously alarmed Miss Cootie.

"See ya' in a snippet," cheesed the Chief. "I can't wait to squeeze my—"

—The Chief didn't have a chance to end the call on account of Miss Cootie doing it for him. She severed the call in a gigantic hurry, positive it was NOT the Chief she'd just spoken to. He called the right ID, and parroted unacceptable but his regular gibbous lingo, YET it would take seeing to believe.

DIDN'T MATTER inside the BLACK MOUND.

"Dayhem!" laughed Coach. "I think WE got something here! These Offies are some kind of WOKE NOW! We just might pull this thing OFF!"

CHAPTER 4

Operation Cover Up.

Hornets with its hair-trigger tempers vying to buzz loudest about the new developments arrived in the vicinity of Providence Hill just as a small cluster of Fleas were leaving the Black Mound via the spit ducts of Mosquitos.

"Hey, what's up Fleezs," asked a psychedelic Hornet Reporter for Honeycomb. "Y'all hear anything about Chief County and a bunch of his Under Chiefs leaving the Black Mound!?!"

"Did we!" shrieked one Flea. "Wiggers WE saw it ALL!" she exclaimed. "Them tiggas rolled out drunk as gunk!"

Stinger Ray1 looked at Stinger Ray2. They had to get back to the Comb, and quick! Fleas weren't the greatest communicators, speaking languages few got... or rather respected... and known for their generous attention deficits. BUT it was no telling if they were the only bugs that witnessed such a sighting.

Ecstatic still, Stingers S-Ray1 and 2 jetted off with what they hoped was LATE-BREAKING NEWS! All they had to do was get to the Honeycomb and spin the story first. This looked doable, given their incredible speed...and their natural temperments. No matter who saw what, they kept focused on *their* NEWS BREAKING FIRST!

So S-Ray1 and 2 revved up their jets, traveling in speeds excess of nano ticks, watching traffic and scanning for more gossip while scripting how they intended to spin the story.

"Yo, Ray-Ray, look up ahead," S-Ray1 buzzed slowing up a bit. "Looks like a band of Bigbutts buzzing about something.

S-Ray2 agreed, and both were correct, reaching the mob in time to hear a similar buzz as they heard from the Flea.

"Where y'all Bigbutts bouncing off to with all that humming?" asked S-Ray1.

"Who you callin' a Bigbutt," smarted back the Bigbutt Bee.

S-Ray1 didn't even bother with a reply. He, like S-Ray2, knew what was up...and just what to do. They pulled out their long pointy needles, and in a shot a piece, very impolitely pollinated the Bigbutts over a field of hemp seeds. Looked like beds of floral fertilizer below. Hornets didn't play.

"We better hurry," S-Ray2 said. "No telling if them other Fleabags trying to tell others."

And that's exactly what the Hornets did, along the way knocking off bugs they suspected of carrying *their* gossip. CANCELING bugs slowed them down a bit, but they arrived in the Comb in record time... only to see *their* gossip scrolling across Wires.

"Yeah, we're waiting on State to come on THE WIRE," TopRay casually explained as if their breaking news was old boring news. "Apparently he got some 'splaining to do," he chuckled.

S-Ray1 and S-Ray2 were p.o.'d. They wasted perfect stingers, and not without mention TIME, eliminating competition that never existed.

"Puss for crust!" grumbled S-Ray2. "And we flew right by the State Domain!"

"Well, we can always go back," said S-Ray1.

"Why?" replied TopRay. He was THE BOSS, and HE wasn't asking.

"Well...so we could've gotten more goods first," replied S-Ray1.

"I fail to see your logic," THE BOSS, TopRay replied.

S-Ray1 & 2 couldn't explain, and didn't even try. The culture in their Honeycomb, like every other News Outlet, had always been 'TO BE FIRST!' No bug wanted to hear OLD NEWS!

"Look, I don't want ANY OLD NEWS," TopRay explained. "I WANT SOLID ACCURATE NEWS!"

The Rays exchanged confused looks. This was a first, though too, the event they were collecting stories on was a first as well.

"Now, I want y'all to fly back out there and get the goods," TopRay ordered. "Bring back something every other Reporter is looking RIGHT AT, but ain't SEEING!"

This was going to be a tough ask because they hadn't trained for this. Speed they had, and accuracy somewhat too, and as well it could be argued few bugs ever saw them coming, BUT it was going to involve real antalytics to see something more than that!

"So what you thinking," asked S-Ray1.

"I'm not," replied the other S-Ray.

"Well, don't State scribe our Walnuts?"

He sure did. And he did one more thing that put them at a disadvantage. Roaches, as State was, liked to rule, and analyze and tinker around with what bugs saw.

"You think we should take him out and like... just get this whole thing over with?"

"But what about TOP," S-Ray1 asked doing his greatest thinking EVER!

"Maybe we should take him out TOO."

"DAYYAMN..." chuckled S-Ray1.

But they didn't take out their BOSS. Instead they flew into State's Domain unannounced and not invited and asked for him right away.

"Governooor-alooooo," sung Governor State's beautiful golden secretary, floating into her boss's Nest uninvited as well.

The Governor didn't immediately reply. He was busy, really busy, deep in a fruitless search looking for expendable Artillery to deal with whatever crisis was shaping up on the Hill, on top of reading flurries of scribes shaking his core down to its foundation. He just didn't have it within him to answer right away, especially when he read allegations about him being IN CAHOOTS WITH BLACK ANTS!!!

"Aloohoo," his golden QueenB Roach floated in his Nest on her gorgeous chiffon chassis singing.

"What is it," he snapped.

"You have two Hornets out here asking to speak to you," she replied.

"Well, what do they want!?!"

"Why you boobaloo. They want you..."

"For what," he snapped again.

"Ooo!" cooed the golden QueenB. "Could you be cross with me?"

The Governor settled some and lowered his tone. "No," he replied. "You know I could never tire of you. But what is it these Hornets want...besides me?"

The golden beauty could achieve one task at a time, so she returned to the Hornets and asked why they needed to see her boobaloo right away.

"Tell him firing squads are coming for him!"

"Ooo!" pooted the class act beauty, bolting for her Boobaloo right away. Out of breath she panted, "dear boobaloo, they're coming for you!"

"For what!?! WHO!?! WHY!?!" snapped State, really agitated now. He just read there were scillions upon scillions of accusations alleged against him.

"Oh my precious sweet boobaloo, let's not tarry," cried his Golden Nugget. "Let's concord to the Palisades. We can uncoil and sumerset in the Magnolias of—"

—State pushed his sweet Nectar aside. He wasn't that addicted to her fructose. He had a real Queen...and oodles of small noodles in his pad. They needed him. His QueenB didn't. Scores of hallow bugs just like him wanted what she floated.

So he pushed her aside and went to get the info he wanted, bursting into the receiving Alcove and stopping immediately. The Hornets had their Rays out and aimed right at him.

"Pick up the node," S-Ray1 ordered.

State didn't bother to ask why. He picked up the node and waited further instructions.

"Now call our Honeycomb. Our BOSS has some questions he wants answered," ordered S-Ray1.

State looked around, confused. He wasn't in his Nest and didn't know how to operate the elaborate switchboard he'd purchased for his sweetums from across the Galaxy, for a significant sum of Walnuts. But even if he could work the sophisticated equipment, he didn't have the digits to the Hornets Honeycomb... and of course (staring into two spears pointed directly at him) he was afraid to ask.

Shaken and shakey he tapped on the node, hoping on a miracle which showed up in the form of his sweet tater tot. She'd been pouring coconut juice... the spiked kind... the kind that made her boobaloo relax and chill.

"Oh Boobaloo..." she purred, twitching into the Alcove about to serve him when she saw him doing something she'd never seen him do before.

She dropped the platter on sight. "OH Lynx Crisis forbid, what in the swells are you doing!?!" she shrieked.

Broken shards and spiked juice scattered over the ground, and her a nervous nicky she rushed to her Boss. "Oh my sweet pooch, who do you want to talk to? Let me call for you..."

"...Get Honeycomb on the node," State uttered not only fearful, but ill throughout his shell.

The golden beauty didn't notice the stingers pointed right at them. She was more pressed by her Boobaloo attempting to do something she had never seen him attempt.

Frantic about her boss acting so out of zinc, she placed the call fidgety. "Hellooo," she sang into the node when TopRay answered. "I have the State Governor calling for..." and it was the first time she noticed the stingers pointed at her and her Boss.

"Ooo..." she cooed, before dropping in a clump to the ground and promptly passing out.

Quickly State took over, picking up the node and stammering a greeting. "Ugh, hello?"

"Whatz'sup!" laughed TopRay. "All be dayyam, what I do to get a call from the Governor!?!"

"Ummm...well..." stammered State running into a blank. He didn't know why he was calling, but wasn't going to say this, NOT with two stingers still pointed his way.

"Well, whatz'sup," TopRay yelped again, clueless about the situation on the other end. "I hear you're around there trying to cover your backflap removing billboards and whatnot!"

"What..." State gasped. "That's not True," he heedlessly blurted. Of all the accusations, this one ruffled him most.

"Aww, come on Gov, 'da bugs ALL KNOW you're CROOKED," laughed TopRay. "But hey," he lopped on, about to cut a deal. "When my bugs get there, if you give them an interview to put your side OUT FIRST, you just might avoid an Impeachment. Hahaha!"

Operation Nitty Gritty, Gettin' Down to Business.

City was outraged hearing State on a Hornet Broadcast blatantly rolling him under SMUT. And he wasn't the only bug outraged. Maz, his devoted secretary, WAS TICKED TOO!

Though it wasn't Galaxy knowledge, much less many bugs in the Colony knowing about Maz, but she was a FIGHTER, and not just with her knock out hit and licker service. She MOVED MOUNTAINS and MADE STUFF HAPPEN!

"Oh, we'll see about this billboard business," Maz muttered hearing State relaying the BIG LIE aired on a MAJOR WIRE!

At the time she happened to be in her private dive chilling but wasted no time calling the Palace. How dare State! City ran the best Nest of all the regiments...that being County, the State Government, and especially the Colony (or Palace). His Workers showed up, punctual, energized and loyal. They kept the grounds clean, the communities crime free, and there hadn't been a scandal...until now. The fact that State consistently overlooked them for accolades and Colonial recognition, preferring to reward a drunk Chief and his mean Roaches for their unnecessary acts of pure hatred, didn't deter them from doing what was right to serve their bugs. Of course Maz was incensed, and she did something about it.

One of Kingpin WaWa's Advisers answered her call. She said she was Garam Masala and wanted to know HOW Maz got her digits.

"Let me tell you like this," Maz began. "Don't worry about HOW I got a hold of you. Be scared to dust if WaWa ain't in the Palace dealing with this crook over here doing my Hopper dirty!"

Masala was smart. Normally she'd sever a call like this, but she knew this call was different. "How about we do this," she offered. "How about I let the Kingpin know you called and ask him to call you back?"

Maz wasn't satisfied. "No, how about WE do this? How about you find WaWa and let him know I want to speak to him NOW!"

Garam Masala didn't bother asking Maz to hold. She contacted Speaker of the Palace who grilled her for a few ticks before apprising WaWa of the call.

'Take a message' WaWa told the Speaker.

The Speaker relayed said message verbatim, politely asking Maz for her contact data.

"What is so dayyam important he can't take my call right this instance," Maz wanted to know.

"Listen, the Kingpin keeps a busy schedule," Speaker kicked back. "He can't—"

"—No. You Listen," Maz interrupted. "I don't care if the Kingpin is D-E-A-D, WAKE that DEAD KINGPIN UP, if you don't want to meet my WRATH in NANO TICKS!"

Truth was, Speaker wasn't scared of Maz's narrow watery threats. The Palace received no less than a scillion threats a ding (minute). It was the nature of ruling over the Colony. If she, WaWa, or anybug in the Palace jumped every time they got a threat, there'd be no roof!

Again Maz waited.

"Ugh hello," came a flat unconcerned voice belonging to the Kingpin.

"Well hello," smiled Maz, really impressed by her patience, resilience and insistence...and the fact she didn't have to pull out her HIT LIST. Had WaWa elected not to answer her call, he was getting a visit... and his CHOPS busted. He probably didn't know it, but she was in possession of his greatest secrets. And unlike other bugs, she had the proof.

But he answered, so Maz cut him some slack. Instead of making a trip to advertise his secrets, she stayed put debunking State's nefarious dealings, regurgitating chunks of grit she overheard about the Billboard Affair. "I just want you to know," she claimed before adding... "...since I know you're a BIG GROUPIE AGAINST LIES, SCANDALS & RUMORS!"

"...But why would I be concerned about rumors happening in Providence?"

It took a lick for Maz to regain her patience and readjust her composure. A part of the secret was WaWa kind of being FAST-TRACKED for the Kingpin position. Before he slipped in the Palace most didn't know where he came from and how, or more important ...WHAT he was doing for the Colony.

"You should be concerned because some know exactly how you got in the Palace," she coolly replied.

WaWa *tuffed.* That's the noise that sounds like 'yeah right... and WHAT ARMY could prove it?' He was protected by the Works.

Aside from Speakers, who he would deal with later, he had Expert MegaBlasters, Jackpot Sharp-Shooter Fighters, a Trillion Voters and a Colony Constitution scribed ages ago. And if all that wasn't enough, barbed fences surrounded the Palace. There was enough voltage in those spokes that only Crisis could penetrate. 'So Yeah, sho' ya' right,' he chuckled. 'Go ahead. Make his dreg.'

"...And like OUR histronic kin used to opine... since you seem to be an oblivious nonbeliever..." Maz breached on, "A Hard Mullet Will One Dreg Require Soft Scissors."

But WaWa was good and arrogant. He betted on the side of bureaucratic polemics. He had traded rationale and practicality with a jevil he guarded more sophic than a Black bug that for Crisis sake couldn't even pronounce words right.

"Yeah," laughed the aporetic Kingpin. "'Dem Antas sure were some quotas..."

OKAY, SO WAWA WAS DISSING HER. So be it. Like FAMOUS LAST WORDS, 'Watch This.'

She didn't allow WaWa the added satisfaction of cutting her off. She severed the call herself and returned to the City Nest where the contested Billboards were temporarily stored. She didn't have the strength to tote them but was able to operate a city forklift capable of scooping them up and making a trip over to State's personal pad he shared with his real oodle and their many small noodles.

"Hey Siss," she said in a quick call to Mercedes Benz, another Reporter for WBBA. "I got a scoop for ya' Widget. I just pulled up on the Governor's plot of green. If you want a front row view for what's about to show, you better get your spotlight and bring some ricocheters!"

Siss knew what that meant, and the party, INDEED, was on. Didn't take but a midget for her to corral a sea of bugs to camp out on State's green. Black, Brown, Green, Golden... EVEN ALBINO bugs showed up, and of ALL Classes too. In an instance the Clickers were OUT... and poised for CLICKING!

State heard the commotion from one of his upper sleeping alcoves. He looked outside, saw the clickers... and Billboards, and wasted not a midget calling, NOT WaWa, but the Governor a state away. "These elfin napalms have gone a Creek too far," he roared into the widget. "I've tried to be patient and let them bugraggles slide. I've tried to negotiate, and accommodate, and ameliorate and for jukes sake compensate those undeserving ingrates! I've tried everything up and including consecrating them mudruckles, BUT I TELL YOU they have plucked my last firball!"

Governor Vodka, better known as simply G-VD, stayed quiet during State's opening address. Even he knew this was a ramshackle calumny. State HATED, with extraneous emphasis on HATED, BLACK ANTS!

But rather than point out the getatable he simply asked the insufferable comical. "So what do you need from me?"

"WE NEED TANKS! WE need artillery," State bleated. "I've had enough! I'm rolling over all these mumsumtuckets!"

"Ummph, interesting," replied G-VD, cool as white lice. "And so now you're trying to roll me under a leaf?"

"Huh? What..." gulped a suddenly calmer State.

"It's all over the Wire," replied G-VD. "...Your attempt to frame your City Con and possibly wipe us ALL out."

"What the—" —and he grabbed the gizmo that sifted through channels. As images flashed by he muttered. "This is pure..." and then he stopped...and his tone changed. He went from muttering to gasping out loud. "...What in a Judeeni!!!"

"You gotta help me," State 360-pivoted in the tone of his plea.

"Look, I'ma help you out," G-VD began, "...but only because I sense some real unnatural stuff going on over there."

"Wait, what?" State asked confused. What was his cohort inferring? He knew about recovering the signs, on account of County Officials getting over zealous in observing laws and keeping the peace, but what was so unnatural and seedy about that? A few dangs back G-VD had gotten tripped up in a Spider-web trying to snooker a Fleahooker. State wasted no time letting him beg for help. He sent a Guard to the area and dehydrated the hazard ASAP. Didn't even expect a thank you. It simply was how they rolled.

"Look, I've personally met Chief County and that's NOT the Chief coming out of that compound," G-VD flatly explained. The bedraggled line of County Officials filing out of the Black Mound were NOT any bugs he ever saw coming out of the Official Academy. He knew a farce when he saw one.

Again State breezed through channels, but failed to find what G-VD alluded to. From his end, the broadcast he watched, and rewinded to rewatch, the Offies filing out of the g-forsaken BLACK compound looked like the sack of ribald Roaches he unwantingly encountered on many kinky and inconvenient junkets in the County Nest. The Chief especially, who due to his habitual indulgence in tabu libations and his frequent flubs as a result thereof, looked EXACTLY like the fried drunkard he dealt with on more occasions than he cared to count. "I know one thing," seethed State, "whoever that is, once I get these Tanks rolling, neither that samgussie nor the blackened bamboozled gussies I ROLL OVER, WILL EVER DARKEN ANOTHER WIRE!"

"Hahahahahaha," laughed G-VD. "That's what I want to hear! Dust the whole sha'bang," he agreed. "Just make sure I get my Tanks back in the shape I'm lending them to you," he warned.

Operation Providence Hill.

The Tanks rolled in, a cavalcade of huge Humdees... washed, polished, shined, modern, neither a dent nor blemish anywhere...and not A ONE ever used. Brand spanking new. State came out of his pad, the first time since the protesters' arrival, and approached the lead Humdee, and driver operating it.

"What is this," he asked the G-VD Guard planted behind the wheel.

"What do you mean," the Guard asked back. "You are P(Providence)-State, right?"

"Why Yes," replied State. "But I didn't expect a fleet, and definitely not any personnel with it."

"Hey, I'm just following orders, not enforcing them," the Guard replied, raising the Humdee visor to make it clear the chat was over.

So State returned to his dive and called VD. From an upper visor, while waiting for his call to be answered, he surveyed the scene outside. It looked like a major press conference about to convene. Aside from bugs of all sorts... Bees, Flies, Gnats and Ants comingling like it was perfectly normal to mix with Roaches, Crickets, Wasps and the likes... there also were long cables and humongous cords dragged over his lavish green lawn.

Right away he detected a protest. He didn't know what personal beef these bugs had with him, but Reporters only attended gatherings to blast big Show & Tells across Tubes and Live Wires. Definitely something major was in the works, YET when he looked past the film crew setting up tents, and caught Red Ants selling cuisine from concession stands they were explicitly told, not once, but many times was strictly forbidden and against the law, he just about lost his cool. He couldn't wait to order every single last one of them shiny splendid looking Tanks to crush and mash any, and everything, deep beneath HIS GREEN!

Finally his call was answered, VD greeting him mightily. "How you relish them big tubs," he laughed over the razor thin wire. "Enough heat for ya'," he brashly boasted.

"Ugh...well..." stammered State. "Umm...yeah... well I only needed a few Tanks 'ya know. I certainly didn't expect personnel to come with it," he replied.

"Well wha'ja' expect? Boogaloo spirits," VD laughed abnoxiously loud.

"Well..."...well he didn't say it out loud, but...

"—But what!?!" Now VD was insulted. "All you got to do is USE what you need HOWEVER YOU SEE FIT and send them ALL back!"

A shaken State scrambled around his pad and found a horn. VD just wasn't catching his drift, but he went on and tied the horn around a whisker while wrapping himself in a thick sheet of armor. 'Better be SAFE than SORRY,' he muttered before returning to his green where he raised the horn and shouted directly into it. "IF YOU DON'T HAVE AN OFFICIAL BADGE I WANT YOU OFF MY GREEN!"

Only Guards wore badges, but none were on his green. Regular dressed bugs occupied the green, though none moved. Insects of every class and color, old and young, flush and flat broke, chilled on blankets of woven grass blades eating dessert crumbs and scraps purchased from concession stands. The flush, typically Crickets, Cicadas and (of course) Roaches, ate with fancy hollowware whereas the flat broke used crudely scribbled signs as placemats, and its whiskets for utensils. Just Unsavory!

Those not chilling on spreads meshed in crowds, most waiting in long lines to buy food and souvenirs... or joke with Reporters acting as if they were at a kinship reunion. Even Guards, both Providence and VD Guards, partook in the festivities. Not one Sect paid State an iota of attention. They acted as if he wasn't there.

So State crossed his green with his horn and approached the lead Humdee to have a word with the driver. There he met VD's Senior Guard, chatting up one of HIS Senior Guards.

NOW HE WAS DOUBLY PO'D. He got straight to the point. "What's happening out here," he argued. "Did you bugs NOT GET MY ORDER!?!"

The Guards looked at him, as if he'd fallen off a fig tree. "But no peace is being disturbed," replied HIS Guard.

State almost lost his mullet. His whole mullet. "These bugs are on MY GRRREEN," he frothed at the lickers. "And they are operating concession stands out here! You know it's illegal and AGAINST THE LAW to sell without MY permission, ANYWHERE!!!"

"Well, not all of them," sassed VD's Guard.

State whipped his mullet around and directed his wrath at him. "What do you mean not all of them!?! EVERY LAST ONE OF THEM ARE BREAKING THE LAW! THEY ARE ON MY GREEN!!!"

"Okay...okay," replied HIS Guard. "I'll ask them to get off YOUR GREEN—"

"—Whoa! Whoa," State said, stopping the Guard from moving towards the mob. "I don't want you ASKING A FLIM FLAM THING! I want you to get in that Tank and roll them ALL OVER!"

"WHAT!?" HIS Guard asked shocked. "I'm NOT ROLLING THEM OVER!" There also were itty bitty bugs out there. And old egg-holders too! One, a crippled old Lady Bug pushing an acorn of tiny Bedbugs strode right up to them and asked if they would be kind enough to give the tikes a tour inside the Tank. And that was the other thing. HIS GUARD couldn't even operate the Tanks, even if he wanted to. VD's Guard had to tell him, running down Proper Procedures and Protocols (PPP) he had to follow.

"You sumgussie, when YOU CROSSED THOSE STATE LINES, YOU CROSSED ON MY TURF," State objected, shouting at the top of his vocals.

"But you don't boss me," VD's Top Guard back-talked.

"Careful..." interjected HIS Guard, speaking to HIS Governor. "The Courts can slap an Article 69 on you and hem you up for Offending an Intrastate Guard."

State swung wildly but didn't connect. Damya! HIS Guard stumbled backwards, assuming the swing was a clumsy mishap. "Are you alright?" he asked, reaching over to help HIS BOSS up.

"Get off me! Don't touch me," State yapped, refusing assistance. His whisker had snapped, though it wasn't the reason he stayed grounded. He needed a tick to collect his bearings and come up (quickly) with a strategy to fulfill his elected obligations.

Governoring rules had acutely changed. Back in WeShallOverCome ecades this exchange would've never gone down like this. A smartinoff backtalker would've been impaled on the spot, WHICH would have been after clearing HIS GREEN the RIGHTEOUS WAY! It was gonna take much stamina and tolerance to deal with Imemine bred Vores that hadn't seen bugs split in halves for so much as a huff. In his dreg he had buried quite a few colicky bugs and led the greatest club of Soldiers of all Outfits in doing so. This was effective leadership, how he rose up the ranks to Governor.

But he needed a tick to shake off this bitter dizziness and, once and forevermore, work up a plan to rid the blasphemous circus juking up his spatial patterns ...AND infecting his GREEN!

"Let's get you inside," His Guard insisted, seeing his boss so wonky off his spinners. "I'll have a Medic put your whisker back on right," he said hooking the vexed whisker beneath one of his auxillary whiskers as he led his discombobulated State inside.

There was little State could do but oblige, until HIS Guard got him inside. "Look!" he pounced the instance he was propped upright, snatching HIS Guard by his main connector and bringing him quite close. "Take them Tanks over to that grassy Black Mound and roll over them blackbussie's compound," he hissed. "...I don't want a one of them Black Bugs standing when this is ALL OVER...

...And MAKE SURE YOU take all them bugs out there on my green with you when you go!" Using ONE stone to achieve TWO objectives was a BIG WIN!

EPIC FAIL.

The cavalcade extended far as the sight could see. G-VD hadn't slacked on accommodating State with the Tanks requested. He didn't have to, but he gave State all he had, even tossing in his Guards, which was more of a necessity than a bonus. Although these Tanks were second to none, they didn't operate on its own...and most certainly were not equipped to clean up evidence afterwards.

On State's green rumors swirled. The protest was headed to the Hill. Supposedly State was going to officially apologize to the Black Ants in the Black Mound for the trouble caused by overzealous County Officials unduly harassing them. Luis Obispo, State's Ranking Guard, transported this concocted Big Lie over to VD Guards... who passed along this jello to a Reporter holding a giant megaphone.

Maz heard the BIG Concocted Lie and was satisfied. Fact was, ALL SIZE LIES mattered. So long as the billboard rumor was REDACTED she could move on and get back to her regular job. Despite how smooth the city ran, it didn't run on its own.

So she returned to the city while Guards on both sides, Obispo (State Guard) and Alfa Romeo (a high-ranking VD Lieutenant) fed coordinates to get over to the Black Mound into the Humdees.

It was a clumsy effort howso. Algorithms fed into the Tanks' NexGen fancy navigator were wrong. Unintentionally Wrong.

"See, even if you had authority to drive, PPP only authorizes me to plug in it's coordinates," bragged Romeo, clueless about the Black Mound's location, and more clueless he had plugged in the WRONG GPS. Other than making them go, incorrect coordinates aside, these Tanks were complete mysteries to even those that assembled them.

But Romeo did look the part, as did all the high-ranking Guards, proved by protestors that left State's Green to flock to these staples of probity.

Protestors, Instigators, Rebels and Reporters ...young and old, nice and not so nice, from Cicadas to Gnats popped off the spreads and closed down the concessions to make their way over to the Guards... many marveling their gallant gander and asking about the BIG LIE, but some... like the Dallies and young egg-holders stirred by alterior motives.

"So, what's this bell do," asked one particulary hot Dallie. Dallie was the term given for attractive hydrophic egg-holders, distinguishing them from general egg-holders.

"We wanna lift," one Dallie flirted.

"No," Romeo belted, big, bold and brassy.

"But why not," cooed another Dallie, pouting pretentiously. This one was a real sweetie too. Long lean whips (legs), and large dancing pearls (eyes), and the prettiest red suckers (lips).

But Romeo didn't capitulate, provoking Obispo to needle him. "Oh come on..." he wheedled.

Romeo gave in. "Alright, why not," he replied. "There's enough room to mollycoddle a few zoom-boom-shakers."

"A few," shrieked the Dallie, a flirty Butterfly. "You can take US ALL!"

She WAS NOT ONLY speaking of the Super-Duper hot Dallie flirting alongside her, BUT ALL THE BUGS that had left the green. "Hop on bugs," she projected through a horn of her own. "We're about to roll to the Hill in style!"

In a flash bugs flew aboard the state-of-art Tanks. None of the Guards were prepared, especially not Romeo and Obispo. It was said, done and too late to disrupt a building TREASURY of grave bloops and unorthodox blunders.

Romeo and Obispo were in the lead Tank, with the gorgeous Dallies; the Wasp with the whips and her equitably dazzling Butterfly crony. They had lots of questions about the Tank; another BIG NO-NO.

The operation of the Tank was TOP SECRET. But then Romeo didn't know what many of the gadgets did anyway... and neither did Obispo, so what would it hurt breaking one more PPP by giving them a tour?

Infractions aside, State's green was cleared. The party-like atmosphere that began on his lawn, morphed and continued in the Tanks on the ride over to the Black Mound. Tubs filled with unvetted and unauthorized bugs naturally created a severe lack of oversight. Neither VD Guards, and especially not State Guards, bothered to monitor the navigation equipment. Instead they played with gadgets, showing off for their unauthorized passengers, along with gossiping about a myriad of topics.

At one point Romeo noticed Tank2, operated by VD Guard Mercedes, a petite Bumble Bee who liked everything her way or the highway, riding too close. "That whonanny is busting my back-flapper hard," he complained.

Obispo and the two beauties ignored the complaint though. They were busy snuggling and snickering. But the navigator didn't. The navigator thought the voice was talking to it, and went bonkers attempting to lose the tailgater, which (accordingly) the Tank was off track to start with.

Co-jointly, inside Tank2, Mercedes missed seeing Tank 1 veer. She was busy explaining to her passengers how she abhorred processed influenced air (Air Conditioner). So, instead of using the Tank's cutting-edge technology air, which regulated inside temps to suit singular preferences, she opened the visors, despite the drastically fluctuating weather outside. One of her ride or die companions that rode with her because she was upbeat, friendly and down with the egg-holder power, tried to convince her to reconsider her view on the temp situation.

But Mercedes wouldn't budge, and so it got miserable inside the Tank quick. That's how she, and her ride or die allies, shivering and fanning themselves simultaneously, didn't realize until much too late the Tank was headed for the treacherous Snake River, a direction totally opposite of either Tank 1 or the Black Mound.

These two small oversights threw the entire gangling Cavalcade into a bizarre twist of events with disastrous results. While Romeo desperately tried to regain control of his Tank, Mercedes got busy punching in coordinates trying to get back in sequence with the caravan. The rider who tried to hip her to the Tank's cutting-edge air situation, was the same rider that tried to warn her to JUST STOP! "You're headed for Snake River," screamed a bright Yellow Wasp.

Meanwhile, bugs riding in trailing Tanks, approximately a killion paces behind (about 2000 or so kegs), were steeped in heavy debates about everything and nothing. For instance, in Tank#15 the hot topic was on the Kingpin. Some liked WaWa, others didn't...and then there were some that ONLY liked the work WaWa was doing, and others that plainly had NO clue what WaWa was doing in the Palace... or moreso...HOW HE GOT IN...in the first place!

In Tank#267 (for another instance) the VD Guard piloting that tub was in the midst of showing off the incredibleness of the Tank's system and how it worked. As it would be, he, unlike Mercedes, marveled over the sophisticated navigation system. "See, you really don't need to insert this long code to get to the Black Mound," he explained, as the Tank bounced along following Tank #266, operated by a VD Guard who'd turned off its electrical equipment altogether.

The constant robotic hum emanating from the system was bothering another kind of socialism taking place inside that Tank.

But one of the bugs inside Tank#267, listening to his personal portable wire instead of the Guard's solictious babble, suddenly wanted OUT!

"I can't go along with this! There's a Report on WBBA (WesBeBlackAlways) that this convoy is about to level the Black Mound! Let me out NOW," he screamed terrified.

But the Convoy couldn't cold stop in the middle of a transport. Besides the necessary leaflets that needed to be filed, read, approved and disseminated, a sudden stop could cause a wreck, just what ended up happening when the Tank ahead, Tank#265 slammed to an abrupt halt after witnessing Tank#264 disappear like a whisper.

"Did you see that," asked flummoxed VD Guard Chevy.

"No! See what!?! I ONLY saw YOU," retorted VD Guard Pontiac.

"Two-Sixty-Four dropped out," gasped Chevy.

All tallied, the Rollover Black Mound Mission was a bust. A super big bust!

"Gee, how long is it to Providence Hill," asked an exhausted Prayin' Mantis swelled with eggs. "I might hatch before we get there," she kind of joked.

That's when ALL in this portion of the caravan looked around and realized something was very wrong. They were on a path ALL to their own.

"Oh My Cranapple Crisis! Krispy was RIGHT! We've been set up," shrieked a Ladybug.

"I knew something was wrong," fretted a large Black Waterbug. "There was absolutely no reason for us to leave that dirtbug's GREEN!"

"I think we're just lost," yawned a Gnat.

"No, we hit something," noted another Gnat.

"Well, I'm not trying to be out here for dregs and dregs," cackled a Flea. "I got things to do and mo' Fleas to see."

"Yeah, let's pile everyBug in the able Tanks and get moving," suggested a State Guard.

"But get moving where," huffed an annoyed VD Guard. "In case you haven't noticed, WE ARE IN A DESERT!"

"But we can't be that far away from our starting point," inserted a young Roach checking a portable wire. In fact, many were checking portables, with no to little success however. Searches were returning spammy invalid responses.

"I think we need to call someone," another State Guard suggested.

"Well, you can make that call because I'm sure not," kicked back VD Guard Mustang. He had dealt with the Governor on tougher dilemmas and was hardly thrilled about explaining how they were not only lost and had lost contact with their Top Charge, but they had lost tubs, possibly some Guards, and were carrying UNAUTHORIZED PASSENGERS! Forget the other mix-ups and who was to blame, wasn't no way he was making that call!

"Besides," Mustang further noted. "This system has been built to get through the last Mohican. There absolutely is no reason to roam and try our luck. We can get back on track ourselves."

Mustang felt certain of this. He breathed the system. Swore by the system. Trusted the system... and had been lock, stock and barrelling on and on about the tubs. So he climbed right back into his Tank, fully operational because nothing had rammed it, and it had rammed nothing, when just as he started tinkering with the navigator, a stream of Tanks that had been lagging far, far behind approached.

"What is that," asked an alarmed Mosquito.

She was speaking of noise emanating from the trailing advancing Tanks traveling at excessive speeds. Sounded like tons of thunder decimating to oblivion ALL CREATION. Bugs looked around, and many dove for cover, but there was NO SOUND as strident as the shrill shriek of one bug.

"OH MY CRISIS—" this bug wailed, the VERY LAST sound made before impact. A roaring erruption and volley of flames impaled the convoy in one rolling motion. There were no survivors; to include Romeo, Obispo, Mercedes, the cute Butterfly and sexy Wasp, and ALL others that copped a ride on the convoy.

Operation; Horrendous Snag.

The Honorable Sir Kingpin Yahinus Blackspan was chilling in the O-ring with his usual posse; Tiramisu, KFC and Starbucks; and oh, Falaffal was present too. They were catching replays of the County Officials exiting the Black Mound when the Breaking Broadcast broke in.

MAJOR EXPLOSIONS AT THE SOUTHERN BORDER ON THE BANKS OF SNAKE RIVER scrolled across the tube.

"What the jevil," scowled Starbucks. He was about to make a snarky remark about an especially mismatched Official exiting the Black Mound wearing a sleepy look and mohawk turned backwards. First of all, the mohawk didn't go with the uniform and neither did the accolade dangling from his left breastplate. Starbucks knew this because once upon a time, before rising up the ranks to advise Kingpins, he used to be a Warden in the County. Wardens never wore Mohawks. Only Judicials. Also, six-clove leafs were never pinned on Wardens, and certainly never dangled off a uniform. That accolade belonged on the Chief who also looked and dressed strange.

Except the broadcast cut Starbucks remarks short. "We better get the SSS on this," said Falaffal speaking of the broadcast...and the Special Security Squad.

WaWa groaned, "aah, that's Chiquamonga's problem. I don't know why these pundits think we care about other Sects mess anyway."

"Because it happened at the dividing line," Falaffal scoffed. "For all we know the blast could be directed at us," he nearly screamed. Over the course of WaWa's reign he'd been getting mighty fed up at WaWa and his lackadaisical attitude over important Colony affairs.

"Settle down Falaff," WaWa chuckled. "You get so worked up about this stuff. Not our bugs, not our Raid. Everything isn't always a big conspiracy!"

WaWa disabled the News Blast cable and got back to replaying the recording they'd been watching. "Hahaha," he went on laughing, gesturing at one of the Officials with his mullet hanging low. "What's that thing hanging out of his lickers," he howled loud, clicking his whiskers.

Tiramisu leaned closer to the tube. "That's drool," he replied, inciting the Kingpin to laugh even louder. "...And I think a lollipop (pacifier)," he added.

"Those buggers are sauced up," yelped WaWa, still heavily amused. "All of 'em! Look at 'em!" He continued jostling around like this when his node rang. "Yahinus here," he said into the widget, chuckles still riding his vocals.

"We got us a snag Yuckainus," said Superior Analyst Rushmore. And he hadn't screwed up WaWa's name on purpose. Rushmore just had a speech impediment. He had issues pronouncing 'yah'. It always came out sounding like Yuck! "I just received confirmation that those Officials that left the Black Mound are in fact imposters," he continued.

WaWa raised up. Of course he heard Rushmore all right, but wasn't really sure. "Come again," he asked with both antennas raised high.

"I SAID THOSE OFFICIALS THAT JUST GOT RELEASED ARE IN FACT IMPOSTERS," Rushmore repeated.

"But how," WaWa asked quixotically amused.

"—I SAID THOSE—"

"—All right! I heard you," snapped WaWa. "What else do you have?"

"I.SAID.THOSE—"

"—Did you NOT just hear me tell you to watch that tone! Now, I SAID I HEARD YOU! What I want to know is WHAT ELSE do you have for me!?!"

There was a ruffled muffle noise coming through the node. Sounded like Rushmore rustling with scribes, perhaps trying to read from it. WaWa waited.

"...We got one babbling Judicial... and a Chief being treated for seepage... plus two Wardens missing their CENTs (common sense), and another splayed out on a flatbed due to being fleeced by his Queen for not recognizing her," Rushmore rattled off.

"What!?! Where are you getting this intel," fumed an irritated WaWa. He hated hearing about problems. That's what the Palace's Internal Workers were hired and paid to do. His Job was to appear chill at all times and look Kingly, so that his FLASH (photo)-OPs came out perfect. Rushmore was raining on that parade.

"I'm at the INFIRMARY," shouted Rushmore.

"Whoa joka, DID NOT I JUST TELL YOU TO WATCH THEM LICKERS," yelled WaWa. "And what is your backflap doing at an INFIRMARY ANYWAY!?! ARE YOU SICK!?!"

"NO YUCKHINNY! I'M NO JOKA! I'M NOT SICK! AND—"

—And WaWa ended the call. He didn't have time for all that. He wasn't about foolishness under his brella (command/Palace/rule). He returned back to watching the replays, about to lean in closer when the tube switched back over to the explosion. "What the—" He looked over at each of his Advisers; Tiramisu, KFC, Starbucks, Falaffal and a few more perched behind his Top Line.

"How did that happen," he asked as if one of them had switched the channel.

"What do you mean," snarled Falaffal. "It does that when something of terrific importance is being ignored!"

Say what they wanted about WaWa behind his backplate, but three things HE WAS NOT. A Fluke. A Flake. Or a Flag. "Are you a Wire Wonka," he asked Falaffal, giving him no chance to respond before ordering him to go get a Wire Pro that could make the tube do what he commanded it to do.

Meanwhile, as WaWa and his Advisors focused on wondering what was wrong with the tube, way on the other side of the Colony, down near Providence Hill, was Nectar Paloompa Oompha in a Crucifixion Chamber under inquest by the IGI (Infirmary General Inspector). The Inspector was grilling Paloompa Oompha about the Chief's (her bowwow's/spouse... aka Chief County) critical injuries.

"That's right!" Oompha boiled, bursting into the Infirmary lit up. "You skippin' right I parted his gondola straight from his connector and'll do it again... zipping around here praising every bug but me... havin' the AUDACITY to act like he don't know me," she angrily lamented.

The IGI were concerned, but not too alarmed. Sounded like a typical jilted Nectar learning sweeter Nectars were catching her Guarantor's favor too. It was a common occurrence, though rarely did jilted

Nectars readily and enthusiastically admit to illegally correcting their Guarantor's bad manners via leathal measures. She could be curbed, barbed and bricked forever.

But then Warden Weuber rolled in, in a stat situation too, with his Nectar flipping out behind the ambulatory. "A Sect betta' hep him...Befo' I crush him some mo' and put him below the LAVA LAYER!"

AS SHE SO CLAIMED, NEVER EVER had her Guarantor behaved so depraved!

"First I thought he was trying to get frisky, given how long we'd been apart on account of his so called Official business. But when he started seeping all over my Grove, and I told him to straighten up, and he acted like I was 'da paid polyp, I CREASED HIM in crillions and then called Y'ALL!"

Warden Weuber was there upon scooped up and whisked away by critical services who put him in an Infirmary Bay... as more and more Wardens and Officials were wheeled in, in similar conditions with their Nectars crying behind the rolling in stretchers.

"They must be missing their CENTs (common sense)," one Nectar told an IGI that started grilling her too.

"Yeah! I think I even saw mine's firball pop out," remembered another Nectar.

"Well, I sure hope you Inspectors figure out what in Sambussy Crisis is going on," belted another salty Nectar...ALL speaking as if they had every right to handle the indecorous behavior they witnessed... AS THEY HAD!

CHAPTER 5

Escape Manifesto.

The challenge was real. For one, NO ANT in the Black Mound REALLY WANTED TO LEAVE. The catechism however, was the diversity within the Ant population in the Mound.

The Security Delegates; the Elites (Combat, Coach, Almighty, Amen and a few other Elders ruled the PACK, ensuring safety, which included forcing the Head Chancellor, the Highest Ranking Ant in the compound into hiding. Yet, in terms of size they paled in comparison to the bulk of Ants residing in the community; Antes (egg-holders) and Workers (both egg-holders and non-egg-holders) who had the least power taking on the basic care and feeding needs of the ENTIRE GROUP. By far, they were the MOST MULTI-LAYERED subsect, a sharp contrast to the Captains... the kernel of kibitz keeping this large class intellectually intact.

"I'm just ready to quid pro GO," one Captain announced.

"Well...you just say the WORD 'cause I'm right behind you, right on out of here," another Captain lopped on. Stories swishing around the Wire were NO JOKE! The bizarre tales polluting the WIRES claimed County Officials had been stalked, kidnapped, drugged, bribed, besmirched, tortured, held hostage and tormented by every alliance from Head Ant Czars, to Tycoons and Oligarchs, when no such coalition even existed in Ant regimes. Where the stories came from took a wilder imagination than the News Agencies that created the FAKE NEWS.

"LOOK, no bug is quid pro GOING NOWHERE," FuFu objected. "If this Mound is in peril, then SO ARE WE. So let's focus on a strategy to secure OUR safety!"

And this was the REAL dilemma for Captains. It wasn't easy waltzing into Ant Mounds. Scholars in particular, and most Ants at Senior Levels had to be recommended. The HEADS—the Chancellors—usually did the vetting. So the Captains couldn't just up and go, not with the stories swirling around. They needed to speak with the Head Chancellor and get his blessing to leave. But the Chancellor was absent, hidden away to prevent his destruction, and they left under the behest of a churlish leadership they sorely DID NOT TRUST.

"We've got to plan," FuFu explained to Fessy, and close cohorts; Doc and Mum & Macho (aka M&M), a Captain capable of turning herself into 23 species. They were in the KIA pit, in a TOP SECRET chamber where they held private talks. So their voices were low but not unanimated.

"Well, I think we should find a way out of here," M&M insisted. "We're in a lot of danger."

"Oh, that's easy enough for you to say," Doc said skittish. "You can just skip on out of here... sight unseen."

"Hey...hey," FuFu interjected. "How about WE first find a way to meet with the Chancellor—"

"—But I don't know if we have that much time," M&M replied.

"Yeah, I hoped we would've had more time," Doc somewhat agreed. "Guess I didn't count on their Nectars being bothered by lunacy!"

"Hahahaha," Fessy burst out laughing. "Yeah! But wait until them Meddies open that Chief's mullet and get a load of his firball! Hahaha! I sure don't want to be hanging around here when they do!"

"Whoa...wait a tick..." FuFu droned, still mellow toned but leaning in. "What's up with his firball?"

"Hey! I didn't have nothing to do with it," Fessy continued laughing throwing up a couple of whiskers.

FuFu kept quiet. And Doc wasn't showing much reaction either, other than focusing on an untenable space. Parts of the story was already being Aired, not very accurately albeit. Colony Wires were wrapped up in investigating why County Officials had gone to the Black Mound in the first place, as Ant Wires clogged their Lines speculating...and joking... (in some respects correctly), how 'the Black Ants' likely 'hooked *them* up'... on DOPE... as meanwhile City, State and local Officials criticized Chief County's decision to infiltrate the Black Mound WITHOUT JURIDICAL AUTHORIZATION or PROPER BACKUP. The stories running macro wild were creating havoc around the Colony... a fine time to take their time (as FuFu cited), scoping out a salvageable escape plan.

"Tell you what," Fessy went on teasing. "When them MEs (Medical Experts) carve into them bugs, we better hope they don't find that brat's bang-bang in there," and he rolled over laughing.

Now FuFu was alarmed. "What BRAT," he asked not amused. He knew about the swapping firball operations, but was under the impression no healthy Ant specimens were compromised; especially none of the Kiddies.

"Aah, don't worry about it," Doc groused, lifting his marbles off the void. "It'll probably take a while before it comes to that. Bugs knew the Chief and his Offies were a bunch of radical guzzlers. And NO BUG will miss a few misplaced kiddie firballs."

FuFu was NOT ONLY NOT satisfied. He was shocked! "Exactly how were these operations carried out," he asked fully alert.

"Look...let's just agree the BRAT won't be gettin' underneath any whiskers anymore."

That was Doc who never before was bothered by kids persistently getting in his way. He stayed in the lab researching stuff...up until he was put in charge, with Elon's oversight, to fix up the Offies.

FuFu didn't even pretend he understood the technical stuff surrounding Doc's work. He only knew, like Elon, Combat and the rest of the Security Council that Official firballs were swapped out with healthy firballs from an extinct pile of bugs. This wasn't too controversial. It was fairly common for hurt bugs to mend injuries by swapping out ruined parts. What wasn't uncommon, and more so than uncommon but anarchic in a way that might decimate the Ant Mound without the help of Colonial Officials, was stuffing precious Ant parts in foreign bugs.

"By Crisis," FuFu sighed. "We can't let this get out."

"...Or maybe we can..." Fessy offered. "I saw one of the Antes carting that BRAT to the coop the other dreg. Da' BRAT was drunk as funk! Stunk up the WHOLE Rotunda," he chuckled.

"But how is that going to help when this hits the Air," FuFu fussed. "Combat already doesn't trust us. He will cream us when this comes out."

"Look, we're getting ahead of this thing," M&M slipped in. "Why not get one of our Tech gurus to take out the Grid until the reports blow over?"

"Wait..." Doc jumped in. "...Before we go rogue and get too extreme, I have something better," he said before explaining the procedure he performed on the Offies, and how when he ran out of healthy firballs he decided to use the Kids that kept getting in his way. "What I'm saying is," he delved on, "...Elon was supposed to be the oversight. But of instead of getting that BRAT out of my way, he was busy looking the other way. So I just scooped up the kid, shot him up, unzipped him, snipped him, and switched and zipped him back up. It was done and over in a zing. I say WE blame ELON!"

"WoW," FuFu sighed. "That's pretty good. I like it. I'm onboard," he said.

"...Wasn't like the Com wasn't pressuring US to hurry up," Fessy added.

"This is going to be REALLY interesting," M&M signed on too.

"Actually, I think we should get a meritorious ribbon for them operations," Doc concluded. "At least them corrupt Officials are in tact...for the most part anyway," he wryly chuckled. "...AND that BRAT is no longer a whining pest. He's now a CHIEF!"

"Look, I want you all to find a place to hide," FuFu suddenly said. "I think I have an idea."

The other three... Fessy, Doc or M&M... didn't have a chance to so much as part their lickers before FuFu had exited the KIA. He headed straight for the Warpit, giddy with anticipation about how Combat was going to take this news. He anticipated attitude but was more sure he had the WarLord just where he always wanted him.

He met Combat inside a tight bungalow behind the Warpit inspecting mini blasters, perhaps not the best occasion to interrupt him...BUT OH WELL.... too late to change directions and turn back now. The DICE was in the middle of a ROLL.

"Look, I've just received some intel," he began looking down, trying his best to appear uber humble and obliging. He couldn't see Combat's expression, but imagined the mercenary WarLord staring at him with disdain.

Combat didn't speak. Didn't even look up. He appeared as aloof and dispassionate as the blaster he cosseted. For a tick FuFu was relieved and got a little comfortable...until he asked if he'd seen Elon.

WarLord's mullet popped up then! His marbles too. "Why," he asked, gripping the mini blaster in an improper fashion.

"Well... because a Confidential Informant has come forward with some critical intel," FuFu replied, very apathetically, but quite deliberately.

Dread washed over Combat INSTANTLY. He went from dark, to darker, to a complete wash out. "What are you telling me," he angrily spat.

"You want to speak to Elon about that BRAT... I mean that kid Pukey," he replied clearing his trake to correct the variations of respect he was trying to show the WarLord. "...It's possible the Elder may have damaged the kid," he added.

Combat's tentacles almost STAR ANISE came alive, flopping over his marbles impossible to miss. He looked at FuFu like he wanted to permanently damage him but summoned a barrage of Warriors instead.

"Follow me to the B-pit," he ordered the Warriors, before shoving FuFu aside. "...Don't go no sam-blasted-where," he turned, hurling the most of his vitriol at the fake struck FuFu.

"Copy that," FuFu muttered. Like where else was he going? He was stuck. Even if he returned to the KIA pit.

Combat stormed off, looking every bit bound to find Elon and get to the bottom of what happened to Pokey, when a few strides into his angry strut he abruptly spun around and ordered FuFu to follow him.

The lot of them; Combat, the Warriors and FuFu marched single file around the compound... up and down corridors and through Chambers supposedly searching for Elon. It was hard to tell the true intent of this search because Combat wasn't asking any of the bugs they passed about Elon, or interacting with them in any way, shape, fashion or form.

Funny... as in EXTREMELY COMICAL...Combat would march into a Chamber, and stop at a bug...be it an Ante, Soldier, Worker, Kid or whoever, and stare, then glare, grunt and then just move along.

It was bizarre, especially as the search ended up in the one place Elon would least likely be; the KIA pit where Captains were busy reading, researching, studying... basically doing what Captains normally did.

Suddenly it was here Combat decided to speak. "Where's Elon," he snapped at an unbothered Captain.

The Captain didn't respond. He didn't even look up. Actually none of the Captains paid the WarLord... and his TRAIN of nomad looking Warriors... a flick of notice. They barely acknowledged FuFu with more than a quick double-take blink... and that was only in very few insignificant cases.

So Combat repeated himself. "I said where's Doc," he barreled.

Still no answers. All mullets down, nothing but total silence ensued.

"Alright, since none of y'all smarty bugs don't want to talk, I have something for ya'," he sneered.

"SOLDIERS!" he shouted at Warriors lined up behind him. "FIND ELON! Search every crumb and crevice in this sweat pit until you find that samgussie!"

The Warriors leaped into action, though from the outset it was clear they were confused. Was it Elon or Doc he was looking for? Elders didn't (usually) work in the KIA. But frightened by the command and their inability to interrupt or ask questions they commenced grabbing Captains and shaking them down as if Elon ...or Doc would fall out.

"ARE YOU DOC!?!" one Warrior asked a frail pale Captain in a menacing tone.

"Check the Chambers," Combat yelled when the shaken Captain nodded in the negative he was not DOC. "And why would you ask a SAMBOLT you know good and well wasn't Elon...IF HE WAS ELON," he yelled at the distressed Warrior.

"But—" a brave Warrior tried to speak up.

"—No BUTS," Combat shouted back. "Elon is in this pit and I want him found NOW!"

In whatever OASIS Combat traveled in this speck of interval, it was clear to FuFu the WarLord was on a DYSFUNCTIONAL POWERTRIP. This was NOT expected.

Combat continued, yelling and screaming crazy orders until FuFu spoke up. "Listen up Caps, the War-Lord wants us to help him find Elon," he said. "If you have seen—"

"—Hol'up," Combat interrupted. "I didn't ask for your help. Of all these SAMCLUSKY know-it-alls in here, YOUR HELP is least needed!" If he especially hated FuFu before, he detrimentally despised him at this juncture.

Immediately he ordered his Warriors to brick the Captains...ALL OF THEM. "All except YOU," he snarled at FuFu. "I want you to stay with me. I got some more questions for your know-it-all backflap. I wanna see how much you really know," he sneered.

This became the glitch in FuFu's soft-boiled ad-hoc plan he hadn't tempered with his confidants. Despite his familiarity with the WarLord's erratic behavior, he expected the promenading narcissist to find Elon in a haste... and drag him to a coronation to officiate a social cruxifiction.

Instead, it was he (FuFu) hustled off to a hub deep inside the Warpit where no witnesses existed to be cornered, pinned between a sawing mill and a shell crusher, and interrogated vigorously.

"Now tell me what happened to Elon," Combat

harked...the most rhetorical question that required tumultuous excavating to candidly answer.

"That's what I came to ask you," FuFu pleaded.

"Don't try to turn this around," Combat argued back. "You said he did something to OUR young bug... so YOU...or ONE of THEM... must be hiding him!"

How the WarLord arrived at this conclusion sapped FuFu's imagery. First, what was this bit about OUR!?! When the REAL OFFICIALS came for THEM, it was guaranteed they would be hauled off as ONE COALITION. And since WHEN did he give a flimflam about one of them BRATS...to this extent!?!

"Honestly," FuFu quibbled, his voice stuck in his trake rattling. "We want to find him as much as you," he explained watching Combat turn on a saw and gun it. "...But I know for a fact the kid is alive," he blurted... more focused on the revving up saw. "If you let me out I can confirm this," he said sweaty.

That did it. Combat turned off the saw. "I'ma put you in the cage with the others, but you've got ten counts to tell me where Elon is," he snarled. "If I don't get what I want by ten, you'll lose a cappin' until everySect of y'all are gone!"

The Scramble.

In the Brick Captains gathered around FuFu wanting a digest on what was going on.

"Why'd they lock us up," one asked.

"Don't worry, we're going to get out of here," he muttered, outright lying while counting off two digits as he tabulated his next move. "First I need to know if any of you have seen Elon?"

"I heard him bragging about going to the Pedi," he heard over his rear. He turned around and there, lo and a feral wazoo, was M&M!

"What are you doing in here!?!"

Usually egg-holders and non-egg-holders were held in separate Bricks. The practice was adopted errs ago, after Marshalls (on the East side of the Knavish seas) dumped a bunch of bugs in a hole, only to return after a lavish meal to find the captives had populated in numbers... AND SIZE! The Marshalls were never heard from again, sending a clear message to other Custodians to NEVER MIX captives!

"Decided to stay," M&M chuckled answering FuFu. "...In case OUR bugs needed company."

A few Captains chuckled. A collection of Larva was already piling up in a corner. FuFu ignored it. The Marshall trick may have worked in the past, but it wasn't conclusive a population explosion could exhaust a stockpile of Blasters. Besides, he was on count six. "Well, where's Fessy and Doc?"

"Not sure," replied M&M. "But I can check—"

"—No! We're going to need you in here," FuFu shot back. And again a few Captains chuckled. They didn't know FuFu's quip wasn't the pun they thought. Few knew of M&M's Hallmark Gift. She actually was admitted into the Academy as Novelone. A training exercise later, after passing out and carted off to the Infirmary, Doc (feret BLOWN) discovered her ambidextrous nature. He renamed her M&M and UP-GRADED her status to TOP SECRET. But aside from her spying skill, she had no real superpowers.

"Have it your way," M&M replied with a shrug. "You know they sent some Tanks over here to wipe us out," she laughed...intel she, like the rest got from a WIRE during the escort to the Brick, rather than from her spying shenanigans.

"Yeah, heard that too," FuFu ruefully replied, the count down to T-minus NET ZERO being at the forefront of his preoccupations.

"Well, did you know they wounded up in Snake River at the Border," she chuckled.

No. He missed that part. Though he wasn't as toggled by that Calypso failure, as he was by the gravid gait of the WarLord's cumbersome hulk moving towards their crypt.

"—You got an answer for me," asked the MAD WarLord. He wasn't yet in full view but soon would be.

"What answer does he want," whispered M&M.

"...Said he's going to dust off one of us (at a time) until he gets Elon back," FuFu whispered back.

"I don't heeeaaar YOU," Combat teased.

"He's gone...He left..." FuFu shouted out.

The crushing drag stopped. "What do you mean he's gone," the WarLord said with enough pause to easily be mistaken for a gasp.

Captains, now dutifully frightened, spied at each other. Was this chassis of vitriolicism going to take one of them out because they couldn't produce Elon? Which one would he choose first?

FuFu started to reply when the overly dressed WarLord suddenly appeared. In a wisp Captains curled and shrunk, like how Spiders deflected attacks. M&M recoiled too. She slipped into one of her guises, safely undetected by distractions kindled by the WarLord's presence.

"You were saying," Combat snarled through the mesh, taking excess pleasure running his cobalt marbles over the Captains, inspecting each and every-Sect with excess revulsion. He didn't get to assault M&M though. She hid among the Larva pile he missed seeing, climbing as he glare, up a corner of the wall.

"Elon's in the Pedicle," FuFu replied, like a true leader and (to his ULTRA surprise) as he watched the WarLord look as if he had swallowed a boulder. His marbles turned from cobalt to rhubarb, and his shell buckled and bubbled. This was the absolute worst possible news the WarLord could get. Oh dear Crisis, what NOW? The Head Chancellor was in the Pedi too!

Suddenly M&M popped out of the Larva. Not one Captain, except FuFu, noticed.

"Maybe you shouldn't have told him that," she whispered to FuFu while Captains busily straightened up their inconvenient flubs. "I had to," FuFu replied. "He could've offed one of us if I hadn't."

"But we could've ambushed him," intervened a scrawny Captain with stellar instinct, but NO sinew.

FuFu looked over at the flimsy power broker and waited for him to figure out the lunacy of his bid. One backswipe and the wind the blow produced would've been enough to conk him out. He hadn't even seen M&M do her disappearing act, and he was parked directly in front of her.

"Thy word is mightier than the sword," FuFu told the scrawny Captain.

"Well, I disagree. Those Warbugs never gave us the respect we deserve! I say it's time to put forth thy sword. There's enough of us in here to take him out," argued the LIGHTFOOT Swell of Instinct.

Annoying as this impossible campaign echoed, Captain Scrawny was not altogether off track. On the other side of the compound at that very instance Combat was screaming 'MAYDREG!'

"Be jawgit," he was telling his Senior Leadership, "...Elon might be gibbing it up with the Chance," he huffed. "We've got to—"

"—I just talked to Chance," Brother Almighty interjected. "He didn't sound distressed."

Combat paused. "Well, get him on the node!"

Almighty made the call, and was waiting for a bug to answer when Elder Igotthis dashed into the Warpit. "We got a issue in the Tike Pit," he announced obviously panicked.

The Elders, to include Almighty, followed by the WarLord leaped to their whiskers and hauled out of the Warpit. In a shake they were in the Tike Pit looking at an undamaged Pokey quietly reading in what was really a Tike Infirmary. Kiddies ended up here when their conditions required monitoring. Usually it was for physical reasons, but in Pokey's case it was mostly cognoscible.

Right away, before asking Pokey one question, the trio knew they were approaching an intolerably altered kid. He looked (kind of) normal, and acted (sort of) typical, as any posturing was common for this queer kid, except in this instance his different was a different kind of different. Parked behind a durable block of charcoal (kid desk) diligently reading a scribe titled 'How to Dismantle Large Mounds and Get Away With It' was enough evidence to ascertain trouble on the horizon.

Combat almost lost his witheralls when he saw what the brat was reading. He snatched the digest out of the tike's whiskers and threw it against a wall. "What in Crisis is going on here," he barked as Pokey simply picked up another 'How To' digest. This one was: 'How to Destroy a WarLord!'

Combat snatched that digest too... and the next one Pokey attempted to reach for as well. The stack of destructive scribes climbed roof-top high.

"Where'd these scribes come from," Combat fumed, off his rocker looking around as he swatted at the entire stack.

"They've always been in here," replied a jittery Worker wringing her whiskets. "They were here when I first arrived."

This was news to Combat. For bugs he passed every single dreg to be reading this smut was one thing. But to learn these type traitor optics had been among their presence was ENTIRELY another thing. 'Should bury 'em all..." he grunted.

"I want this entire PIT searched," he barked aloud. "Every Worker I want thoroughly grilled for treason," he angrily lopped on before turning to the Worker. "What happened to him!?! Is he on meds!?!"

The frightened Worker shook her musk and twisted her whiskets tighter. Pokey wasn't on any meds. "Nothins' wrong with him..." she replied.

"What do you mean 'nothins' wrong with him," yelped Combat. "Why is he in here then!?!"

"Cabbies brought him—"

"—Cabbies!?! Who's that!?!"

"This is your fault," Pokey inserted, popping up to spray Combat in the mullet with more venom. "You're in hot sand now! You and your Blackie bugs are gonna pay!"

Combat twisted left, then right, unsure where to turn or what to say...or do. Elders surrounding him on all sides had no clue either.

"What happened," Combat ended up screaming at the kid, recoiled by Pokey's blunt force wicked breath. It reeked of illicit libations.

Without waiting for the kid's next pissy-tart retort he spun around and screamed at the terrified Worker, asking why Pokey smelled so bad. "He stinks to longoria!"

"He came to us sauced up like that..." shivered the Worker.

"Well, the puke is totally hammered," argued Combat. "You mean noBug knew this EITHER!?!"

The Worker looked about. She needed a boss of her class to come forward and deal with the issue. She only worked there. She had NO SAY. She knew nothing about the little tike, except he'd been the easiest kid to look after on her shift. He kept his sniffer stuffed in the illicit scribes.

Combat swiveled swiftly, as if the kid he was looking for was hidden somewhere, because this bug indeed WAS NOT Pokey. He resembled the little goof in that he was still a brat, exhibiting grotesque mannerisms and parodying much of the same boorish semantics. But overall, he had encountered a whole 'nother bug.

"Did you EVER get the Head Chancellor on the node," he barked at Almighty.

"Well...no..." Almighty stammered.

"Well what are you waiting on," yelled Combat. "CALL HIM! I want every crevice of this Mound searched," he bellowed.

The Elders scattered, moving in rapid circles. They had no idea what they were looking for because the WarLord never elaborated.

"Something foul definitely is in FULL BLOOM," the WarLord plowed on. "Leave NO STONE unturned. Search everybug! AND BLOCK ALL ACCESS TO THE TUNNELS," he raved on like a wounded screeching out loud demonic Cicada.

The Search.

Warriors sectioned off in groups and scrambled in all directions. They still didn't know exactly who (or what) they were looking for, but were armed with a free pass to curb and brick ANY ANT (beneath their stature of course) NOT COMPLYING WITH THE ORDER...vague as it was. This meant Worker Ants (SPECIFICALLY) were in trouble.

The 5th Squadron, led by Warrior CHOPPED, headed straight for the Pantry, AND NOT TO EAT!

There'd been an elongated beef between the 5th Squadron and Workers in the Pantry. The stir started over a Dallie, but the overall entanglement involved status and jealousy. Despite neither side having generated much prosperity and both in the same age bracket, all that empowered one group over the other was Combat authorizing the Warriors ultimate authority to wield those lethal BLASTERS.

Naturally when the 5th Squadron stormed the Pantry on this nefarious hunt, Workers were justifiably on edge.

"What ch'all lookin' for?" asked one egg-holder Worker. Wasn't much in there, BUT skifts of edibles and plenty of egg-holder Workers and Dallies.

"MOVE ASIDE," CHOPPED told the Worker, pushing her aside to go after who he really came for. Before non-egg-holder Workers were protected by general Law and Order, but recent developments changed all that.

YET BAM! That's all it took. Warriors may have flashed more power working for the WarLord, but Workers were no pansies. They often laughed at, and made mockeries of the Warriors every time they saw one trotting around exhibiting their corny metals and purplish uniforms. Even their dinky little blasters didn't chump them. If a Warrior got puffed up, if or when one was insulted, they wouldn't wait to crush the bug and take whatever punishment as a sort of rite of passage.

Poppa didn't flinch. "Look, she only wanted to know how we—"—and before he finished his sentence CHOPPED POUNCED INTO ACTION.

"—Bug, SHOW ME YOUR DIGITS! NOW!"

This was NO KIND OF WAY to treat an OG. Poppa was an OG. He'd been working in the Mound for many dinurals. He was a good Worker. Very well respected. Totally Harmless. His only offense was wanting to know how he could assist the Warrior.

Worker NoBluff saw this and wasn't amused. He wasn't about to let this slight go...BLASTER or NO Blaster. And there were plenty Blasters aimed at him.

"YO Bug, who you dissin' like 'dat," NoBluff spewed. "You betta' come correct or —"

"—OR WHAT," belted Warrior FLAY stepping forward to use his ONE TIME TO SHINE.

Under usual conditions Flay stayed in back rows. He was one of Warriors on the latter row when the Offies burst into the pit. But now here he was running up on NoBluff with his mini-Blaster ...and the WarLord's BOLO.

NoBluff just looked at Flay, marble to marble, basically waiting for him to blink. Being a lot younger than Poppa, and in pretty good shape he put Flay down midway into his blink.

Warriors of the 5th Squadron came from all directions to tackle NoBluff. All hit the DIRT in one vociferous RUSH. Crates of barley and berries and all kinds of nonperishable digestibles crashed to the dirt drawing a crowd of Antes into the Scullery.

"What in a Dear Adoration Crisis is going on in here," Ante Jumpy gasped. Nothing to this magnitude had ever occurred before. Normally brushes between non-egg-holders of any class took place out of sight of egg-holders. And never ever had Warriors barged into the Pantry, (HER PANTRY), brashly thumping on HER Workers!

"Get back," shouted Warrior CUTTHROAT; his Blaster RAISED...and POINTED right at Jumpy.

"I KNOW YOU AIN'T—" —And she whipped out a whacker and there flew CUTTHROAT'S helmet, while his lower half remained where he'd taken his final step.

"...But we have orders to bring any Bug to the WarLord that might have something to do with—" and Warrior CIAO stopped there because he'd forgotten Elon's name.

CHOPPED brushing himself off after rising up off NoBluff filled Ante Jumpy in. "We're looking for Elon," he timidly tendered.

"What," huffed Ante Jumpy, out of air after that vicious whack. "Why would Elon be in here?"

CHOPPED was about to respond, just as ANTE

JUST stormed in. She took one look at the Pantry and another look at the Warrior's helmet on her Cilantro, plus Poppa on the ground ...along with the lower half of the Warrior ...and went ballistic.

"I don't know what in a bejevil is going on but this Pantry better get back in order," she fumed. "And just what in JELLO do you think you're doing," she spat at Flay trying to put ties on Poppa.

"But we have orders to—"

—Just picked up a Wasp drumstick and conked Flay over his mullet. "Release him this very speck," she snarled. "Have YOU LOST your EVER FORSAKEN Mullet!?!"

Recorded in the Black Annuals, Black Antes didn't play. They stayed in their lanes AND FIERCELY PROTECTED THEIR TURF.

"Release him," CHOPPED ordered Flay with his whiskers raised in retreat. Though they had stormed the Scullery believing the Blasters was all the back-up necessary, apparently NOT they realized.

"I apologize Ante," CHOPPED said, doing his best to display good manners. "It was the WarLord that ordered us to come in here and—"

"—And ransack my Scullery and fleck with MY Help," she fussed. "I better not find out y'all been in here stealing MY goods and besmirching MY HELP and Dolls!!!"

"No. No goods were taken. I promise—"

"—Oh HUSH UP! Betta' not have taken anything outta here," Just fussed. "Now get over there and apologize to Poppa!"

"Who?"

"The bug you threw in the dirt," she hurled.

"But—"

"But nothing," Just snapped. "Apologize to Poppa right NOW and then pick up 'dem links and get outta' my Scullery before I tie y'all up myself!"

The Warriors obeyed. They apologized to the OG and noiselessly left the Scullery without further incident.

"We need to let the WarLord know about this," cooed Ante Woo. "Poppa could've been hurt!"

"...And NoBy (NoBluff) too," added a Dallie soft on the young bug.

"Naa, I'm good," NoBluff said brushing off the blow. "But them wobbles gonna need your concern when I catch up to them later on," he added.

"Hush up," Ante Just scolded NoBluff. "You're not catching up to noSect later," she said snatching off her wrapper (apron) before turning to Ante Hard. "Lock up after I leave out and make sure noBug gets in here. I'm 'bout to go find Comb!"

Just left out and Hard locked up...and those in the Scullery got to gossiping once they heard the last click of the lock.

"I can't believe them wobbles bust up in here like that," cackled a Dallie.

"I can," sassed another Dallie. "Have y'all been watching the Wire!?"

"No Doll," replied Ante Busy. "We've been in here making sure everyBug gets fed!"

"Well, maybe you should," smarted back the Dallie. "Word around the Hill is they about to roll us over!"

"Doll, I don't know where you got that rollin' big lie but you better watch who you smarten' off at!"

Basic protocol dictated and practiced within Black Ant compounds across the Galaxy was young egg-holders never spoke down to elder egg-holders, no matter how gorgeous. Imemine churning out these brazen Dolls flouting tradition were an irritant. Take Pokey for instance. He wasn't an egg-holder, but he was another example of a brazen irritant. Youngins like them weren't in play in the past.

Whatever the case, the Doll wasn't the only bug following WIREs, unlike others either too busy, too distracted or uncaring to heed hearsay.

"She's talking about those Tanks that blew up in Snake Lake," added Ante Bitter. "I got a link from a kuda (friend) that said she heard Governor State was on his way over here to apologize to the Chance."

"You mean the Governor BLEW UP!?!" shrieked Ante Nevermind.

"Oh Crisis, y'all bugging," laughed Ante Giggle clicking on her node. "If he BLEW UP then why is he on the Wire talking about the Tanks that BLEW UP?" And she shared her node, showing a live interview of State talking about the tragedy.

"Well...y'all can believe what you want," the Doll sulked. "...But I know a bug that was talking to one of the bugs in one of the Tanks when it blew up. Y'all betta' recognize and respect!"

Most ignored the gossip, even though the Doll was referring to Maz (City's Maz) who heard from a Reporter giving her the scoop about the impending visit. Overall, reports conflicted, the reason opinions in the Mound clashed.

"I'll tell you one thing," Ante Busy interjected. "None of that had anything to do with them Warbugs bursting in here like they did. Poppa or NoBy coulda' really been hurt!"

No bug commented, not even NoBluff. Things had taken a laborious turn. Were looking REAL. AND SERIOUS. All it took was looking around the Pantry.

"Why don't you get that thing off them weeds and toss it out," Hard ordered a Dallie. But she leaned away and recoiled.

"Ewww! I'm NOT TOUCHING THAT THING!" And she skirted behind NoBluff.

"Look, I'll toss the thing," he said. "You just go find some more Cilantro."

Crossing the Line.

As Just stormed around looking for Combat, Combat stormed around looking for Elon... and Doc too. He hadn't forgotten that creodont. Flashbacking on those operations he remembered the mealy looking bug well. He hated HIM. Like he hated ALL Scholars thinking their thoughts mattered.

"Where you at, bug," Coach asked, calling from his node.

"In the Tunnel...headed to the Pedi ," Combat replied, hanging onto the Lyft's whisk-handles as if on a joy ride. The Warrior had the pedal stuck to the metal and was driving without headlights!

"Well, I've got Just here. There's a problem in the Scullery," Coach said.

OH Crisis NO! "Where's Good? Is she okay," he asked worried.

"Good?" Coach asked perplexed.

"GOOD," Combat spat, annoyed at both Coach's dumbfoundedness and the Warrior's illicit driving. "Come on Bru', catch up," he spat, angry about having to distinguish which Bru he was speaking to as the Lyft swerved wildly responding to the Warrior's input making the pedal...and metal... do calisthenics it was NOT designed to do.

"Well, I haven't seen Good," Coach carefully replied. "Last I heard, she was vacaying in..."

"—Oh, good," Combat sighed heavily. Good was the last Ante he wanted to deal with at this point. He was so relieved he ended the call without bothering to hear about the crisis going on in the Scullery.

Little was he aware, as the Lyft came to a raggidy barbaric impasse, Good was a smidgen away, in the Pedicle (Pedi) at that very instance.

"Who trained you on how to drive this thing," Combat grumbled at the Warrior. "I want that gophers doodle because I think you just destroyed mines! You drive worse than Hooverdam," he scoffed, hopping out of the Lyft to confront Warrior Guards blocking access to the Pedi.

"Have any transports come thru here in the last ...say... last few dongs," he asked a trio of WGs.

"NO...No...nooo..." stuttered the trio, on guard themselves, automatically believing they'd done something wrong.

"I mean ANY transports at all," Combat more precisely clarified. "...Even deliveries," he added.

"Ugh well..." the trio continued stammering. They had to consult their log, a long scribe scarily not well maintained.

"...Well, next delivery is scheduled in a dong," replied one WG, electing not to explain how so grisly mismanaged the log was. Combat would have crushed and grinded the trio to minced dust before figuring out JUST MAYBE one delivery had been made within the time being investigated.

"Great," Combat replied nonetheless. "Make sure you call my node when that delivery arrives," he ordered. "I want to inspect it before it leaves this checkpoint! IS THAT CLEAR!?!"

"CLEAR," replied the trio.

Combat turned around and ordered the reckless driving Warrior to return to the compound, as MEANWHILE, Good was in the Pedi indulging in a not so rosy-cozy convo with Fessy and Doc...AND ELON!

"How'd y'all get here," Good asked when she saw the three on the other side of the Pedi-jam.

The Pedicle was the safest and most elegant annex to the Mound, where the Head Chancellor and his Queen had been stashed. It took ASYLUM-Level authorization, Security Codes, Temporary Passes... or being Head Chancellor, his Queen...or Good to get in the Pedi. So how did Elon, Fessy and Doc get access?

They took a BIG RISK hitching a lift on a BFT (Bug Food Transport). Using his Elder Clout Elon bribed the driver upon learning FuFu had left the KIA (without informing Doc and Fessy of his plans), only telling them to hide. Irrespective of the story Doc and Fessy fed him, he was desperate to meet with the Chancellor, but omitted retelling this much detail to Good. She'd never catch on.

"We caught a lift," was what he volunteered, abruptly interrupted by Doc (as well) desperate to meet with the Chancellor.

"The entire Mound is about to be flushed," Doc gushed. "I just learned they've stashed the Captains," he added. "Bricked them all... and probably planning an escape that likely won't include any of us!"

This was BIG TECH intelligence Doc and Fessy had siphoned and piecemealed during their meeting with Elon. It was only by fluke...and much determined talking that Elon hadn't interrupted their meeting and answered that first check-up call from Combat. NO TELLING what would've happened if he had!

Neverthless, Good WAS aghast. "You mean they bricked THEM ALL!? WHY!?!" She'd never been a fan of Captains, but this would be a BOMBSHELL for the Chancellor. He relied on their intellect. "If the Chance gets wind of this he's going to—"

"—Good!" Elon snapped. "The mound is UNDER ATTACK! It is on the CUSP of complete annihilation! We are ALL about to be wiped OUT! The Chancellor MUST HEAR ABOUT THIS!"

"Sssh! Lower your tone," Good hissed. "WE are currently in the safest part of the mound," she said, fumbling around searching for her node. "Let me call Comby and—"

"—No Good, you can't..." Elon said, delicately clutching her recently manicured whiskets. "Because there's more..."

Good was looking at what he was trying to tell her ALL wrong. He couldn't blame her though, because she, like EVERYBUG in the Mound...and in the Colony for that matter... had never experienced REAL WAR. She was envisioning a decorous struggle where a few terse WORDS and odd mishaps would end the scuffle and things magically return to normal.

"Look, is there a News Wire in this Chateau?" he asked when he could foresee WORDS were not likely to get through to her.

"I'm not sure," she replied flummoxed. "You know Our Chancellor isn't a fan of News Tubes. He only subscribes to matte films..."

Fessy groaned loudly. This was a MAJOR part of Good's and... save for the Scholars of the Galaxy... the ENTIRE POPULATION's INCOMPREHENSION ISSUE. IGNORANCE! They ALL subscribed to so much soft infotainment that they knew so very little.

"Don't pay him any attention," Elon said. "You know how impatient Scholars are," he added to keep Good from losing her patience as well. "We just need to get a feed running in here so that you all can see what's going on..."

"But, I already told you Chance doesn't watch that stuff. We can't disturb him with this. That's what he relies on HIS Captains for—"

"—And I already told you Combat Bricked ALL the Captains!"

Good's pearls enlarged...and pulsated. In that square of a tick it was hard to determine if she was detrimentally angry, implausibly scared, or decidedly insulted.

"Look, we don't have much choice," Elon sighed, glancing over at Fessy and Doc closely monitoring the exchange. "We have to let the Chance know what's going on. The kiddies are in jeopardy. One is still in the Infirmary—"

DEEP GASP! "What? Who? Which one..." Good softly shrieked after buckling slightly.

"He'll be okay," Elon continued. "They have him sucking on fructose to keep him calm..."

"Wait!?!" Good exclaimed, her voice still low, but really shrill. "What do you mean THEY have a kid on fructose!?! Fructose is for serial boozers! Who's THIS THEY!? And WHO'S THE KID!?!"

"I'm not sure but the WarLord is upping the search for the kid's bang-bang," Elon openly lied.

"—Pokey!?! Are you talking about Pokeymon?"

"You know I don't know—"

—And Good let out a wail shrill enough to bring the recessing Queen out of her divan in great haste. She burst in the vestibule covered in jewels, moving like a twirling Blasiere (chandelier).

"Twhat...Twhat...Twhat in a Galaxy is spindling in here," so cried the Queen.

Except for Good's deplorable wailing, No Bug spoke. Perhaps it would be this noise that ejected the Chancellor from his hiding? Elon, Fessy and Doc could only wonder and hope.

Sorely it wasn't to be so. Suddenly Good turned off the waterworks and opened her yap. "—I'll be a Jicknsickle cocknbeetle," she shrieked. "I'll hear NO MORE OF THIS! Take me back! Take me back RIGHT SINBLICKETY NOW!"

Here Comes Good.

The Black Mound was designed in the shape of a three-pronged fork by an excrutiatingly brilliant DREAMER long since dissolved. He never imagined one dreg it would hold a prodigious legend, or a colony of Black Ants. He solely built the fortress (turned fork) out of a propagating desire to infiltrate ultimate comfort and security.

Inspecting the structure from the outside... and above...its design was so camouflaged that the annexed wings couldn't be detected. Many presumed the Black Ants lived beside a decaying amphibian. Perhaps an Octopus? Bugs had to be inside to see its adroit design; the long connective veins wrapping the compound, serving as Tunnels to its winged outlets. There were dozens of wings, but only TWO MAJOR appendages attached to the main compound.

The Left Wing was rarely used. The environment was so hostile that it was only used to bury its pariahs...or train Cadets on how to survive Doomsy events; floods, volcanos, footbombs and the sorts... along with one crucial perk. The East Wing.

The East Wing's single security measure was how the Left Wing kept it so hidden...and protected.

The Pedicle's mossy covered roof and fashionable unintentional glass ceilings, along with its jewel studed walls, sepia sand floors, and bulbous ballrooms bragged a haven beyond measure. There was enough space in this wing that each class of Ants (in a crisis) could hunker down its entire clan comfortably.

But evacuations were rare. In fact, there'd never been an emergency serious enough to use the place. Other than Workers and Senior Elders, only the Head Chancellor and his Queen used the premises on the regular. So the Queen made it her call to juice up the interior, adding frivolous artifacts and details so few got to see... much less enjoy.

And yet, the long, dark and dangerous path getting to ...and from... the Pedi was heavily guarded and patrolled. PFTs used it to bring necessities, and Warriors used it to provide transportation for Workers and Guards. This was the path (vein) Good fled to (without proper authorization) to confront Combat about the lewd rumors she heard.

"Maybe one of us should go with her," Fessy

said having misgivings about inciting Good to bolt off looking for the WarLord.

"Aww...she'll be alright," Elon grimly chuckled. "She's tough," he huffed.

But it wasn't what Warriors Buttercup and IronChef believed. They were playing Mob Control when the alarms rang, screaming unauthorized movement had been detected. In a tick they spotted Good running in the Tunnel...in front of what appeared to be a shadow chasing her.

"Oh my—" Buttercup gasped, abandoning the spoctacallas he used to see Good. "I'ma go get her," he panicked, hopping up headed for the Pedi.

"Wait! No!" IronChef called after him. "I think we should contact the WarLord first!"

Nothing like this had happened before. There were NO RULES. The only time the alarm ever rang was during drills. So to hear the screaming whistle slicing up the thick air, didn't permit the WGs to do what they regularly did; call the Guard Shack nearest to where they spotted the WarLord's pet favorite, running.

Snatching and switching cables to disconnect their Mob Control game (a distraction that could cost them dearly), they scrambled preparing to report the situation.

"Yeah, what's up," they heard Combat bark.

"Umm," IronChef stumbled, frightened for so many reasons. First and foremost were the screaming whistles and bells confiscating his words. And just as he started to speak, the call suddenly lost connection.

"What did you do," IronChef panicked.

"I don't know...All I did was turn off the game," Buttercup replied just as panicked.

"You must've pulled the wrong cable—" IronChef was in midst of saying when Combat's voice burst through the speaker.

"What the jevil is going on over there," Combat barked angrier.

"Umm...ummm..." IronChef stammered. "I think something is chasing Good," he replied.

"Patch me in," Combat ordered, wanting to see what was going on in the Shack. Something sounded off. And it was. BUSTED! He caught them scrambling to collect their Mob Control toys.

"What are you two doing," he barked, clicking codes into his node to bypass what IronChef and Buttercup were up to, in exchange for a glimpse inside the Tunnel.

Right away Combat dropped the call and did what the dimwit Mob Control players should've done. He called the Front Shack and demanded a brief.

"What's GOING ON," he yelled.

Caught UNREADY WG Rosemary stumbled like IronChef and Buttercup had. "Umm...well...I just got Good and—"

"You GOT GOOD," Combat seethed. "What do you mean you got her. Where was she!?!"

"Well, she was trying to get to you—"

"BRING HER HERE," he EXPLODED so fumed he forgot to explain the logistics of bringing her to wherever he planned to see her.

So frantic Rosemary and her comrade Cumin (who actually chased Good down and brought her to the Front Shack), scrambled to coordinate a Lyft.

It took a while breaking the RED TAPE however... prompting a belligerent follow up call when NO GOOD materialized. "WHERE IS SHE," Combat SCREAMED into the node.

"We're waiting on APPROVAL from Command 960 for a Lyft," Rosemary nervously replied.

Only then Combat realized his mistake. Though back down he DID NOT. "A Transport will be there in a tick. BE READY," he demanded.

That's all Good wanted, which the heroic jog through the Tunnel cut the RED TAPE exponentially. A Lyft was on its way in a jiff.

Combat sent an Acorn Leaf; the equivalent of a hearse, nothing he'd ever send for the Chancellor, but not the worst mode of transportation considering how depleted she was running that last whisket to the Front Shack. SHE WAS BEAT!

Limply waving in a roundabout fashion she was loaded onto the Acorn and driven at nano speeds back to the compound.

"Are you sure you're gonna be okay," WG Oven asked sprawled out Good.

BUT LOOK AT HER! WHAT DID HE THINK!?! She almost committed an unintentional suicide. She couldn't even speak, talking in squid cant. They were a janket away from the main compound when Combat finally called.

"Where are you," he asked Oven, keeping tabs on the info flow. After learning about the Scullery Affair, AND Elon...and Doc still loose, he banned the Tubes and had ALL WIRES turned off. Controlling the flow of information was his top priority.

"Almost at the Infirmary—"

"—THE INFIRM—" The WarLord liked to have BLOWN HIS STACK!!!

Who in a Houdini did this Warrior Guard think he was!?! "Were NOT YOU SPECIFICALLY TOLD TO BRING HER STRAIGHT TO ME," he shouted, before softening his tone. Other Warriors and Elders were in his presence. If Good required urgent medical care, he wouldn't want to be viewed as that callous.

"Bring her to my pad," he gently tendered. "I'll have medics meet us here," he added for the benefit of the eavesdroppers surrounding him. But once he moved away from his listening audience he called the Infirmary and summoned Formaldahide to his patch.

Formaldahide was a defrocked defamed Researcher that came to opprobrium by inspecting what would happen if...before APPALLING bugs with what happened when. She was the only foreign bug (Wasp) allowed in the compound... given there was NO WAY Ants could get a chemscope for next to zero!

Oven arrived at Combat's patch with an alert Good. She burst into the pad wanting to know straight up ONE, and ONLY ONE THING!

"WHERE'S POKEYMON," she growled, baring tiny sharp scissors.

Disarmed, Combat coolly turned around. "Why are you concerned about Pokey," he asked.

"What do you mean why am I concerned about Poke!?! WHY WOULDN'T I BE CONCERNED... YOU and YOUR WAR MONGERS only been trying to abuse these kids since the dreg you came onboard!!!"

"Good...Good—"

"—Don't YOU DARE Good ME! I will tear this Moun—"

"—HEY! Hold on," Combat interrupted, raising a whisker to put an instant halt to the insults. "Poke is fine," he explained, cuing Formaldahide to hold off on subduing the excitable Ante. "In fact," and he turned to Warrior Cannabis, "do me a favor bug and bring Pokey here."

Cannabis left out and Good settled down... and Formaldahide moved further back. Tepidly settled they waited for Pokey.

"See Good, I already told y'all, you have to be careful about listening to ALL THAT gossip," Combat lectured, it not occurring to him that she had been in the Pedi...with NO ACCESS TO WIRES.

"The Mound is perfectly safe and sound," he carried on, making it clear he had everything under control. But Good listened, herself having forgotten WHO fed her this so-called gossip.

And then, before it occurred to her what was going on, Pokey high-hoofed it in the pit acting like they ALL were strangers in his midst.

"Oh my GOODNESS, look at him," Good cooed. Workers in the Infirmary, of course on instructions of Combat, spiffed up the kid. He was bathed and dressed in age-appropriate Cadet armor, and sprayed with a lavender scent to cover the licentious libations smell that followed him around like a bad hangover. Workers still weren't able to completely rid him of the natural nasty disposition that had accompanied the old Chief. But they were able to spiff up the little tike to acceptable norms.

"He looks so cute," Good carried on, ignoring the distance Pokey maintained between her and him. She wrapped her whiskets around him anyway.

"...And he smells so sweet," she sang, glancing up at Combat to apologize for assuming the worst.

"How've you been sweetie," she asked Pokey, marveling how nicely he fit in his uniform. He looked darling, almost like a Maple Moth, though he made no pretense of what he thought about his old Ante.

Pokey stared back, looking like he wanted to puke. During the time he spent in detox, he drank more than the originial Chief. "Well, I'll be better when they let me out of that can," he spat.

Good gasped as Combat moved forward. "And you will," he spewed. "Soon as you pass that exam we'll pin on your Wings and let you FLY!" And he meant this in more ways than one. He had very special plans for the brat.

Pokey started to argue. "But YOU—"—and his argument was cut short.

"—DO YOU WANT THOSE WINGS, OR NOT," Combat barked in a voice that mellowed Pokey out.

Good looked up. "Oh Comby, you all have always been so hard on him. Don't be so—"

"—HUSH YO' SMACK you old wainch," Pokey bleeted. "I wouldn't be—"

"—HEY!" Combat barked. "That's two Deuces for sharping off at your Ante!" And before Pokey's next mellow wore off he hooked a whisker around his miniscule snapper (neck) and ushered him towards Cannabis. It looked like a gentle gesture, but was anything but. Combat had pinched Pokey so expertly that the kid failed to cry out. And had Good looked closer she would've seen his mullet flip over and heard his snapper crack. The kid was hurt.

Cannabis escorted Pokey out, like how puppet strings were pulled to make them dance. For the rest of the trip back to the Infirmary Pokey had to be carried, though Good saw none of that.

"He really deserves that promotion," Combat passionately told Good. "It hasn't been easy working with him though," he reminded her. "You know how willful that little TIKE can be..."

"...Oh, I know," Good sighed. "I can't believe I was thinking so crazy."

It got pitch stone quiet here. No bug spoke. Not Coach. Not Almighty, nor Amen or any other bug in the pit. They now knew the collective truth.

"I must apologize," Good cooed on. "I have to admit being really concerned, but after seeing little Pokeymon I feel MUCH better," she sighed relieved.

Again, no bug spoke up...readily. No bug was eager to expose the low down on the state of affairs in the Mound. It was why Combat didn't ask if she'd heard OR SEEN Elon...or Doc. He didn't want her ants raised anymore than they had been. But this didn't preclude her from bringing up these names.

"...I am so sorry," she impishly giggled. "Elon really had me going with—"

Combat stiffened. "—Wait. ...What? When did you speak to Elon?"

CHAPTER 6

Presentation.

The IGIN (Infirmary General Inspector's Nest) reached out to WaWa. "Look, a Federal Investigation needs to be opened immediately," was how the IGI greeted the Kingpin.

"Who is this," WaWa asked indignant. "And how did you—"

"—Look here BaBa, I know this isn't your thing, BUT! ...WE HAVE A COLONIAL PROBLEM!"

WaWa was about to get righteous with the IGI but Starbucks interrupted him, rushing into the O-ring waving a scribe.

WaWa lowered the widget and tried to read and hear what Starbucks was showing and telling him. A Border Chaos, Possible Coup, Cover up...among a few other crisises was included in this Show & Tell.

"Look IG, I have to get back at cha'," WaWa told his caller.

The IGI quixotically opted to hang tight, as WaWa and Starbucks pow-wowed over the 'No End In Sight' catastrophes. Tampering with Official Property was a serious offense, but would have to wait until that entanglement could receive the attention it deserved.

"Look, I'ma need a speech writer to prepare an Address because there's NO WAY on a Sandusky Hill

I'll ever believe Black Ants are trying to overtake the Colony," WaWa extrapolated at the conclusion of his tight meeting with Starbucks.

Problem was, Starbucks believed WaWa was too naive and trusting. He wanted to unleash Colony Troops on the Black Mound to KILL all the brawls in ONE CLEAN SWIPE!

But WaWa pumped the BIG NO BRAKES for being ON RECORD for EXTERMINATING bugs he (kind of) considered kin.

So he went on and summoned Top Scribe Ghost ...and Tiramisu for oversight... to help conjure up a Top Notch Speech.

"Make sure my accomplishments are weaved in that speech," he told Ghost. "It's—"

"—Aww, no bug is gonna care about your past accolades," intercepted Starbucks letting loose a big yawn. "Bugs are getting CRUSHED... Careers are CAVING...AND THE ENTIRE COLONY wants to know what you're gonna do about them Black Coups!"

In other words, Starbucks...and Tiramisu too, wanted to know what WaWa planned to do about THE PRESENT!!!

"Whoa..." WaWa semi chuckled. "'Dem bugs don't have enough assets to pull off a Coup, much less run a Colony...even if by a WILD fluke they declared themselves successful."

"You never know," Starbucks slipped in.

"I DO KNOW," WaWa hit back. "I know Black Elder Antlers are 40 chimongas long and they can—"

"—Phewww," Tiramisu whistled. "Black Elders are THAT STACKED!?!"

The conversation skided over to the surplus endowments of Black Elders before zipping back to the topic on the plank. The TALKING POINTS for the speech, which Ghost had finally come up with and presented for feedback.

"I like it, WaWa said in barely a glance, fully on board with telling bugs 'to knock it off.' If they didn't, he would... that being knock off helmets.

"Whoa...hang on here," Starbucks cut in. "We need to address those 172 Officials that entered the Black Mound but only 122 came out."

"I call cheese-whiz on that," WaWa exclaimed. "If a hun'ned and some chips were released, then they ALL were let go," he argued.

"How can you say that if only—"

"—I can and I just did," WaWa replied. "Why would those bugs release some and not ALL!?! Doesn't make sense. Somebug is lying..."

"...Or stoned," Tiramisu chuckled.

"Yeah, I'm going with what we have," WaWa agreed. "That's one of the largest, most respected Mounds in the Colony, probably Galaxy. SirDreamer designed and built that compound," he recounted, about to delve into more Black Mound History before Starbucks (uninterested in hearing a braggadocious long citation) cut him off.

"How about promising an investigation," Starbucks interjected. "At least it'll look like we care!"

And that's what happened. WaWa appeared on Colony Wires, during normal meals when viewership was highest, and in his extremely debonair drone bedazzled a kaleidoscope of bugs, almost like RMDG the 200th had during his popular reign of stupefaction.

"Dearest Colony Plebs," WaWa began, speaking in an elegant snail's pace, hemorrhaging words about how the inequities of available dirt led to unsheltered bugs... and the harsh realities of Tarantulas taking over Passels...along with the explosive hardships the rising cost of Collards (his favorite food) caused. But behind the Green Wick (camera tube) Starbucks frantically waved, hailing a SOS, desperately trying to get WaWa to SHUT UP! Or change the topic!

But forever the salacious elocutionist WaWa was, he continued on... hooking and snookering Colony Plebs in his BIG Poetic Style on the lack of safe brine (beer...his favorite beverage), and the HORRORS of jalopy fumes and foot assaults, making sly ambiguous remarks about benign groups using allegatious lexicons and fictitious monkish apologues rooted in sordid duplicitous racket scapes abetting, knavering and beknighting untold clusters of Insectivores. Ah... his fettering of... and pandering to syllogisms was a chore and a marvel.

Calm, cool, collected and extra poetic, he sold the tripe to the Plebs anyway, and none more so than to his sightless kin kicking stones along to stash his mission... and be herald all in one for having done so.

Starbucks was almost in rhythmic exodus by the time WaWa got around to the purpose of this cinematic show.

"Frankly," WaWa began and summarized in conclusion, "We must respect the GreatExodus and Killorbekilled periods by honoring their sacrifices..." and he broke here, more accidental than intentional. He forgot what page of the scribe he'd been reading.

"...Well," he ended up admitting, "NoSect is expected to remember everything... BUT, I promise one thing," he yelled without warning, being an apostle of sending BIG MESSAGES. "There will be A FULL INVESTIGATION into what's occurring over there on Providence Hill. —Stay Well. Be Safe." And with that he waved, grinned, and dissolved from the Tube.

Plebs were Fast, Furiously, AND Sound Asleep by then though, that being ALL EXCEPT for Combat who was SHOCKED out of his ghoard! The WarLord wanted WaWa's whole essence...and not in a decent way. There'd been no pressure on him to rehash all those terribly boring stories, and yet he dispatched all those dispassionate implausible promises anyway!

The Call for Help.

Constantinople City was laid back on a wharf, swaying and sort of downloading from the runaround caused by the felonious billboard situation the busted Chief and his crony Boss created when his node rang.

"We have a problem," was how the IGI opened his greeting. "Where are you? We need you!"

The Constantinople lifted up. Who was WE? He had no problems. At the moment HE was chilling. "Who is this?" he asked annoyed.

"It's Stonebug. I'm the IGI for the IGIN," the bug replied. "I'm the Chief Medical Examiner for the Colony," he explained to ensure City knew the clout he was hearing from, and the seriousness of the call. "We must get WaWa out of the Palace—ASAP!"

City didn't doubt that. WaWa was a nuisance and a prop...a mere imposter CROWNED without ONE LEGIT VOTE. He definitely didn't get his vote. But City was curious about this IGIN.

Infirmary General Inspector's Nest was the regulatory board that investigated serious medical allegations. And (no help from WaWa) Stonebug was in possession of files that had explored and exploited the paraphernalias of the released County Officials. "Where are you?" he asked. "I'm sending a Dragonfly by to pick you up."

Whoa...hold up. City didn't come right out and express this, but he and Maz had discussed the rising climate around the ENTIRE Providence calamity. The Offies, (first and foremost) should have never rushed the Black Ants as they had. But the fact that they had didn't confiscate the objective compensation so rightfully earned and deserved. As far as they (City and Maz) were concerned, THE DIRTY DEED WAS DONE AND OVER. CASE CLOSED.

"Well, whatcha expect me to do," City asked

anyway. He always learned to hold his FINAL opinion until all the goulash had been poured.

"Kingpin," Stonebug flatly replied. "We want to put the Colony Back On Track (C-BOT), AND believe you CAN DO IT!

"DOING WHAT," he asked straight up!

"KINGPIN," Stonebug replied like what else?

City accepted, without dither. They (him & the IGI) met in a huge Can annexed to the Palace. It looked kind of sketchy, but then the entire proposal came off shifty. After the whole billboard affair it didn't take much to be suspicious. He could've taken a sip of the Bee juice offered, and awoke to learn he'd been WRONGFULLY sentenced to a guillotine.

But his concerns were postponed, at least for a tick. "You are OUR Great Orange Hope," Stonebug openly spelled out. "With the way you've run your city, if you can't help US, the Colony is DOOMED!"

WoW! That was an incredible endorsement. City always knew that much, but coming from a bug that he'd never met, let alone had never been to HIS CITY, it sounded CAMPAIGN RICH!

And Stonebug wasn't done. He had only begun, detailing what was needed, and how the Kingpin role was expected to be fulfilled. "WE NEED A BIG BUG LIKE YOU, that looks mean and isn't afraid to Shake Things Up, AND MAKE US CLASSY AGAIN!"

"I'm IN," City replied. Shucks, looking MEAN and being UNAFRAID wasn't an ACT. Stonebug could have saved his wind.

"Good," Stonebug tendered anyway. "Truth be told, I always marveled your resolve after that yarble over the removal of them billboards," he chuckled. "Takes REAL yawn to do what you did..."

City refrained from responding because not only had he NOT DONE ANYTHING, but the service he provided for the city, he did because he liked nice clean safe grounds. The same way he rescued MAZ was the same way he attended to all matters. Being a decent bug didn't require applause. On the other side, praising him as Stonebug had, still ruffled his wings. It didn't, however, stop him from allowing the lying sack of bile to continue explaining the Kingpin job.

"We need sturdy bugs ABLE and WILLING to take orders and fall on stakes for us," Stonebug went on, to City's increasing consternation. "We need loyalty, PLUS STRENGTH able to take pain and keep cool too," the sad crumb yammered on.

City meanwhile listened. Certainly sounded like an assignment prior Kingpins had taken on, dorkily. It was common knowledge Kingpins weren't the geniuses drafting policies and enforcing rules. But if the cooky bug perceived this would be how he operated in the Palace, he was exorbitantly WRONG!

"Here's the deal," Stonebug whistled, leaning in to really level with City. "We have evidence those PC (Providence County) Chief's firballs were tampered with, completely removed in fact, and we haven't been able to get a sable statement from YOUR BOSS to confirm, or deny, circulating rumors."

"Ump," City hummed. His Boss couldn't confirm if his own firball was intact. The bug, like his heavy brine drinking bud, were BOTH losers on the SAME TEAM. But he refrained from speaking out. Afterall, he could care less about what was (or wasn't) found inside those bugs. His marble was on getting inside the Palace...TO PUT A HALT TO THIS NONSENSE!

"Look," Stonebug continued, oblivious to City's lack of response. "We're putting faith in you that by giving you the HIGHEST PLATFORM to rule from, YOU WILL get the JOB DONE."

"Bug, you have my WORD I will GET THE JOB DONE," City readily assured the IGI. And he wasn't schmoozing THE BIG GUY either. He really meant it.

Maz was concerned when she heard about this arrangement. "Something's not right," she projected, as if City hadn't already come to this conclusion.

"I know jell well something's up," he replied. "But think about it," he also slid in. "We will finally get to oust the poet laureate."

Maz lit up. "You mean I'll get to kick him out?"

City chuckled. Maz especially disliked WaWa. She blamed him for trying to outslick poor Plebs on an Infirmary packet as if he was trying to help anybug but those in the Palace. She called him a SELLOUT and looked forward to being a part of his dragout, which happened to be why City chuckled. "I'm afraid it doesn't exactly work like that," he told his most staunch supporter, always ready and set on go. "It's a process," he explained.

"What kind of process?" she needed details, as set on go as she was, A HACKED CONSPIRACY THEORIST she was NOT!

City had to get back to her. Though it hardly mattered how the laureate poet left out, and his being all too familiar (like every other bug) about the level of CORRUPTION going on in the Palace, he needed to get the lowdown himself.

Stonebug's response surprised him however. He had NO IDEA of the CHESS GAMES played in the Palace.

"Your appointment will be effective once we get our final payment," Stonebug explained. "We lost rolls of hills on that last one," he greedily chuckled.

"You mean you expect ME TO PAY!?!"

"Oh no," Stonebug quickly replied after clearing his trake. "I just have to take care of our Galaxy brokers," he sleezily explained, gesturing like run-of-the-hill common lowdown law-breakers. "That xinhahn cost us a mint," he laughed. "But don't worry... we have our bets on you! You're gonna recoup OUR LOSS!"

Before Stonebug even made that confession, City knew he didn't like this sella. His glaring lack of concern for the countless Plebs the Palace claimed to serve was so abnoxious he was fit for a grinding mash then and there.

"—Yeah, umm...tell me something," City butted in, cutting the Chess Player off as he bragged on his stale checkmates. "So what was in those kooks y'all cut open?"

Stonebug burst out laughing. "This is between us," he said moving in closer, even though they were alone. "We HAVE NO IDEA," and he burst out laughing again. "But this is how the GAME works. We make up stuff and then pin the stuff on the bug standing on the wrong spot."

Big and fiery orange MAD as City was, he went on and stomached the lousy joke, laughing ridiculously loud. "So, how long do you think it'll be before you can take care of that payment?"

Stonebug thought a tick. "You know what. I have an idea," he replied pulling out his node.

"Hey! GOAT," he bruleed into the node, winking at City. "It's been confirmed," he bellowed, his tone full of spritz. "Blacky has to go!"

The GOAT on the other end replied, and the game player replied back. "Yeah, did you catch his Wire on Air?"

"Yeah, we learned he's in on it," continued the corrupt bug. "He's got to be siding with them. Don't even want to investigate," he piled on... speaking of evidence he couldn't even corroborate.

"So we decided to turn this thing over to City," Stonebug drove on, the EXACT point when it became clear who the GOAT on the other end was.

STATE!

"—OH NO! Gotta stop ya' there," State said LOUD AND CLEAR. "Don't mention that name to me!

He don't have my vote for nothing! Over my dried and dusty caracass! I WILL LEVEL HIS PLACE before I let that dreck Kingpin over ME," he protested.

"But why not," Stonebug asked (acting) jarred, enjoying the charade in excess.

"Because, HE'S UNFIT," retorted State. "He isn't even competent enough to remove billboards and accept the fallout!"

"Is that all," Stonebug pressed on amused.

"You need more," State raged. "I thought the Palace only Kingpinned SCAPEGOATS!!!"

"Well, I have City here with me," Stonebug said, HUGE GRIN smeared over his mullet.

"Hey there Govvy," City grinned, leaning into the node and waving. This wasn't a visual call so State didn't see the wave, but the wave nonetheless counted as a karmatic part of a Tragic Comedy about to play out in a MAJOR theatre.

State choked, strangling as he decided if he should swallow, take a breath, or just flip over the Chess Board. In the end he kind of selected all three. "I want YOU in my Nest—"

"—Hey, Hey, Hey..." Stonebug chuckled. "How about taking it down a notch. We don't want to run the risk of losing the whole kit and caboodle..."

"Go on," State grunted, begrudgingly going along with the call. "So exactly how do you suggest WE," he snarkily inserted, "NOT LOSE the Palace!?"

"Well, for one you can help us come up with a TALKING POINT for this Billboard controversary," Stonebug tossed out as a teaser.

"WHY!?!" State slammed back. He obviously was a terrible Chess Player... and a sore loser to boot.

"Because..." City piped in anyway. "Either way YOU LOSE!"

"Hmp," State muttered back. "I'd sure like to see the size of your shooter!"

The Vienna Gambit.

Whereas State had NO OTHER VIABLE OPTIONS, BUT TO 'HELP OUT', the Constantinople had endless prospects.

"Look, I can't afford to go with you on this iffy venture," NuGro said outright. "You know I have a large lair to feed." In other words this new gamble could mess with her city chips (paycheck). Politicking was for bugs that had more wiggle room to spend in Bricks, or Infirmaries, OR WORSE.

"I gotcha'," City replied. Though he (too) had a high intolerance for being permanently disabled, he also had NO FEAR of going down with his spurs on.

But he didn't leave the city out to dry and die. In fact, he put NuGro in his spot, giving her his city chips and all. "You know how I roll and what needs to be done around here," he told her prior to departing. "Just hit me up if you get ANY PUSHBACK WHATSOEVER!"

Of course, Maz had NO DESIRE to hang back, waiting on her Ceboo's *possible* return. Not that she feared losing her idol's fidelity to a long-term (or) possible permanent distant relationship, she followed City to watch his BACK! And he didn't object.

"Just know there are A LOT of AMBITIOUS TREASONISTS squatting in the Palace," he warned, electing NOT to sugarcoat the issue. "They will do ANY and everything in their power to ruin you," he also told her in NO uncertain gratuitous terms.

"GOOD," Maz replied. "Let 'em BRING IT! All I hope is they are bringing their BEST!"

And BAM! Just like that, they rolled up in the Palace, BEFORE Stonebug made his final payment, and ushered everybug...one by one...starting with WaWa... OUT OF THE GRAND PALACE! Stonebug was livid when he heard, rescinding his offer immediately!

"You don't run this Palace. WE DO," Stonebug fumed. But City only mocked him, knowing it was over and done. It was too late. The deal had been cut. The IG had made a deal with the Jevil that to his grave misfortune could not be returned.

"But if you're concerned about that payment," laughed City, "...I'm sure whoever you owe will still take your walnuts!"

AGH! How dare the traitor get traitored! And yet still, the terrible Chess Player didn't squander a tick. He scribed a missive titled, 'The Complete and Unbiased Trilogy of Exterminating Black Ants'. The plagerized anthology was credited to City, the new "Kingpin", and passed straight UP to CONGRESS.

SHOCKED Congress batted the missive around until Media bugs intercepted and reinterpreted its precepts for Pleb consumption.

NOT ONLY Gobsmacked, Plebs were horrified and rightfully ANGRY hearing the details about how WaWa had been ousted and this NEW Insecturists (RACIST) had not only installed himself Kingpin, but planned to destroy ALL LOWER CLASS BUGS, Black Ants CROWNING the List!

The Trilogy however, from go was bizarre. Not only had City entered the Palace WITH MAZ... a Black Ant, BUT CITY WAS A GRASSHOPPER. By default, and historically framed, both of a minority class could NOT be Insecturists. And while true, THEY had removed WaWa from the Palace, BOTH served MORE underclass bugs than ANY bugs that had ever served in the Palace. PERIODT.

Nevertheless, upon devouring this propaganda, Insecturist haters branded City 'Orange'... 'the Big O' ...and '20' (coinciding to the number of Insecturists given a trial date for MAJOR ABUSES).

This was the inauguration "20" and his on edge thermantidote Maz received, reciprocated in kind by getting rid of the IG ASAP! "He MUST be held liable for stirring this hurricane of HATE," Maz contended. "His ROT HAS TO GO!"

"Well, what do you propose I do?" City asked amused, obviously not because he didn't have plans of his own. He just wanted to entertain her "process."

Incensed about the ruthless Trilogy Stonebug blamed on HER CEBOO she wanted him to make a public apology on Live Wire before the Plebs, BEFORE personally CRUSHING HIM HERSELF!

"Alright," replied City, now officially Kingpin YE (Your Excellence). "Let's set it up!"

Perfect. Maz set the meeting for 005.75, in the Press Chamber, and invited Press to capture the broadcast. Stonebug arrived first, VERY EARLY, at about 004.35, a significant chunk of dings ahead of schedule.

"Excuse me," Maz said looking up, not knowing Stonebug from a fleck of dust. "Who are you!?!"

"I didn't come here to see you..." he growled, never completing the breadth of his hostility.

BOOM! Stonebug was there one tick, the next tick he was described by actual clean up Workers as a large gloopy stain on the ground.

That was an accident...as in NOT the plan. The Press...and YE...(and most of all Plebs) looked forward to the recantation...and sniveling apology. In the end what all got was a so-called partisan investigation the IGIN (Stonebug's team) opened, that failed when no bug could produce the IG.

"You know what," Maz quietly said to YE. "We should go on and gloop 'em ALL."

"Naw..." sighed YE. "We got enough conspiracy theorists out there. We'll just take troublemakers out as they are identified!"

No sooner said than a Roach appeared, touting he oversaw the most gelationous and rottenous click of all Palace Workers and Associates: THE (IROT)! The Independent Review of Terminations.

"I'm here to speak to 20 about his letting the ENTIRE IGIN UNIT GO," he huffed hurriedly-like, as if having to introduce himself was wasted energy.

"Who?" Maz asked. She was just getting used to her Ceboo's NEW handle; YE. The insidious, nasty vilifying tags hadn't yet caught on.

"Listen," snapped the Roach. "I'm here on a very critical situation. NOW get up off your Black—"

"—Off my what," Maz interrupted. "You want to start your insult over again!?!"

The IR, uninterested in giving Maz the same benefit of doubt, elected not to repeat himself. So he shouted. "DO YOU KNOW WHO I AM!?!"

And Maz shouted right back. "NO! Do you know WHO I AM!?!"

A Better Colony, A Long Way Off.

The NEW Kingpin's sweeping oustings, a practice of all incoming regimes, albeit of course, not exercised in as exacting a manner, FUELED speculation. Why was WaWa ousted WITHOUT a Formal Ceremony ...and WHAT HAPPENED TO THE IG!?!

Many of the Plebs had a point of view. WaWa himself, and those that were in his regime, bounced around hypothesis. They'd been bought out, similar to how WaWa was brought in, was the overall theory, though none could agree by who. There were so many backstabbers it was hard to tell. Those that were inside the IGIN agreed, with one caveat. They KNEW WHO the buyer was, but didn't know where the buyer was. Outside of this circle, Plebs were all over a map about the dealings internal to the Palace. All sorts of conspiracy theories consumed common bugs. Only Maz and YE understood the full picture.

Maz and YE lowered the sashes and commenced setting up the Palace in their way, again no different than any other incoming regime. Vo5 (a Roach they worked with in the city) replaced Stonebug. And NO, Vo5 knew nothing about medical issues. He was a Tank mechanic for cripes sakes, but got the job because his proficiency maintaining city vehicles was the next best thing to being a surgeon.

And Casper too. He joined the Palace regime in a similiar vetting process as Vo5. He had been there with the 'old' City climbing that dreadful pole to (by order) remove those damning billboards. There was NO doubt he'd make A Fine Top Security Advisor. No nonsense was getting by him EVER AGAIN.

Except the NEW Kingpin YE...and his 'might as well be' running mate MAZ, had racked up 173 OPEN investigations against them. BRIBERY. HIGH-WAY ROBBERY. ADULTERY. SORCERY. AND SUSPECTED MUTINY were among the TOP LITANY of CRIMES ascribed to this regime. Now Casper could squash any bug in his space, but this many threats was hard to make disappear. The best he could come up with was UNPLUGGING from the system sending those rancid transmissions. Let them trolls come talk that SMACK in his space!

"Just make sure, NO MATTER WHAT," YE warned, "NO OUTSIDE BUG gets to SECOND BASE!"

Getting to second base was equal to getting inside the Palace, which Casper WANTED to happen. "Well, I'm trying to separate the trolls from the bugs that hope to MAKE MY DREG," he bounced back. "My skiff (in box) is at capacity he complained.

So YE called a Top Tech Guru and told him to hook Casper up. "I want the image of anybug in his skiff to pop up on our CCCs (Closed Caption Cams)," he ordered.

Within ticks of being set up, the CCCs jammed.

Too many pings. Threats and complaints and inquiries and LAW SUITS poured in from every crevice and crack across the Colony...and Galaxy! Every bug OUT-SIDE the Palace wanted a piece of YE...and his regime. Treason. Trafficking. Pilfering Poor Plebs. Besmirching Egg-holders (all ages). Embarrassment. Ego-Jacking. Unbecoming of a Kingpin...the Plebs were coming for the new Kingpin's throne!

And yet, all that and YE was never more in control and powerful. "The creed of strong leaders," he pontified in one of many speeches he gave. "Plebs don't want shakers and fakers, like past Kingpins," he blasted, condeming the historical nature of wasteful investigations that dragged on and on and on.

"They want ICEBERGS...LIKE ME," he semi-chuckled, for he never was one to laugh at his own jokes. "They want a DINO to say 'NO MORE," he orated into a megaphone heard across the Colony. "They want the wasteful abuses to STOP, so WE ALL can enjoy normal pleasures',...and I'll tell you something else," he lopped on to this particularly damning speech full of vain congratulations, truths, and needling insults. "I just broke WIDE OPEN the plot that was meant to destroy our GREAT COLONY!"

This was the ONLY time during his reign when no bug spoke, waiting for what he would say next.

"What in a holly-jolly," gasped Plebs when the wait turned into dregs.

"How did that raw onion get in the Palace in the first place," wondered many.

"HE'S CRAZY!" contended Media bugs, angered by YE leaving Plebs hanging. "He's trying to gaslight us, to deflect them investigations against him!"

The prior regime and old IG's started seeing him as a plain old FOOL. "He won't last past a Tik-ToK (the usual Kingpin term)," WaWa scoffed. "It's but a matter of time!"

And not that the past regime under WaWa didn't try to speed up this 'matter of time'. They tried really hard to get YE on those damning speeches. Mentioning 'plot' was a Felony, and an IMPEACHABLE offense, which YE fired off 'plot' every time he used the word "I".

And yet, actually getting the GRASSHOPPER for this infraction was near impossible. A hearing conducted by Congress meant Congress Reps had to visit the Palace, thus get BY CASPER... and or Maz, which just wasn't happening.

Once the Cam was fixed, and up and running, Casper and Maz relentlessly traced troll flyers and communications, placing ALL threats at the Top of TERROR Lists. Congress was number one on 1,239 dockets. So unless a Congress Rep wanted to take a chance entering the Palace, and not exiting, there would be NO hearing.

And yet, even with the IRON security around YE, his inability to ignore HATEFUL and SCORNFUL CRITICS became his greatest THREAT. Regularly blasting IFs (Instant Flyers) to combat the problem, along with delivering those immobilizing speeches only increased problems. HATE for him started growing everywhere, to include inside the Palace.

CHAPTER 7

BuzzKill.

While 20 may have performed like a ROCK STAR in the city, Ants in the Black Mound couldn't get over the Trilogy. It wasn't uncommon for a bug to receive Solar Recognition and start acting like they were un-dustable.

Combat called an URGENT MEETING. His Top Senior Leaders and Elders met in the Warpit with a Consultant he hired to gather intel into the impact of what 20's installation might mean for the Mound.

"Aww...Nall," Elder Shonuff scoffed when the Consultant (who had worked in WaWa's regime) confirmed 20 INDEED had scribed the 'Trilogy'! "Dey out to get us. 'Dey settin' it UP! We got to get out of here NOW," he charged.

The pit got quiet. Enormously silent. It was true. If that Trilogy had been authored by 20, they were as done as WaWa... or rather Stongebug!

"Hold up," interposed the Consultant, whisker raised, objecting to Shonuff's point. "You don't want to make any sudden moves. It'll attract attention... make you look guilty...like you've done something."

More silence and blank looks. How clueless was this Consultant!?! Had he NOT detected they indeed had DONE SOMETHING!?! Even if he believed every lie they told him, how could he ignore the Offie visit?

"What you bugs need is an EXIT strategy...and a contingency plan," continued the Consultant who's name (by-the-way) was DonWon.

"We already have an exit plan," Combat quickly tendered. "We only need you to toss out some alternate plans."

"Well, if you've read that 'Trilogy'," which none of the Leaders had...(that typically was a job for the Captains which they had since bricked), "you should know rumor is you bugs are plotting a coup," the Don sort of chuckled.

Immediately Shonuff snorted. "RUMORS," he grumbled, interrupted by Elder Almighty.

"Well, if that rumor is in there about us, what's to say the whole thing ain't but one BIG RUMOR!"

"Because 20 scribed it," replied the Don.

A few...Almighty, Amen and Coach... didn't believe 20 had scribed the 'Trilogy'. They had sources still inside the city that said the missive was a BIG LIE to make Plebs turn against the Kingpin.

BUT Combat DID, and he shut done the speculation right away. "Look, the bug is a traitor and we've got to figure this out," he said. "Now let's here what the Don proposes!"

"What I suggest you do, is immediately start releasing some of your bugs in small groups...so that it's not too noticeable."

Shonuff groaned even louder. "And what," he lamented. "Leave us in here like patsies!?!"

"...Just hang tight," Combat said, extending a whisker to cool Shonuff down. "What else you got," he asked the Don.

"Well you could also build a contingency with the city because we know 20 is still—"

"—WHOA! Whoa..." Shonuff cut right in. "Bug, you gon' have to speak plain-Ant to us," he groused. "It sounds like you trying to get us LYNCHED!"

"How about we pause for scripture," injected Pastor Amen. "Sounds like—"

"—Aww Pastor, no disrespect," Combat intervened. "We really don't have time for the prayers. If you don't mind I'd appreciate it if you could just pray silently that them buckles ain't in the pedi right now, convincing Good to bring out the Chance!"

That reminded him. He interrupted the powwow to pull out his node. "What's the 411," he asked one of the Warriors in charge of returning Good to the Pedicle.

"So far copesthetic," sighed the Warrior, sounding quite a bit bored. So far they had been camped outside the Pedi for dings (weeks) after returning Good. "Haven't heard or seen any movement since we got here," he said.

"Good," Combat replied. "Stay-at-ease until I call back," he said, disconnecting the call to pluck up the Head Chancellor. It took several attempts but Good finally picked up.

"Hello...' she sang in her restful voice.

"Yeah, patch me through to the Chance," he said as if he was going to ask if he was hot or cold.

"Comby," Good shrieked. "You know the Chance doesn't like to be disturbed when he's bathing!"

The Head Elder maintained a detailed schedule, which all the Seniors memorized back and forth and upside down. But of course with the escalating situation Combat ignored the routine.

"Good, we're at a RED CODE 1. PLEASE put me through to the Chance," he squeezed through near sealed closed lickers.

"What's going on? What's a red one," she innocently asked.

Combat almost lost his stack but managed to keep it together. This was the problem with coddling bugs like Good and the Royals. They were oblivious!

"Good," he coolly...and very slowly articulated. "Shipment sent the wrong exclir. If Chance uses that stuff while bathing, his antlers could fall off and you don't want to be—"

—Say No More. She plugged in the Chancellor before he could finish explaining in graphic detail how loud and long and piercing the Queen's cries would be if she saw her King without his crown.

When the Head Chancellor picked up, Combat spared him few frills as well. "How've you been?"

"Oh, I've been—" the Head Chancellor started to reply, sounding like perfumed air floating by.

"—I'm sending in a beeper," Combat cut in, not really concerned about the Chancellor's feelings. The bug was a pain. He would've preferred not having to make the call at all. "Listen, take the Beeper and I'll call back with instructions in a tick," he rattled.

"Wait...what's going on? Is everything—"

"—Ugh...I'm working on something over here," Combat cut in again. For the past few dings he'd been making this call to keep a pulse on the Chancellor's mood. So far so good. After Doc and Elon shook up Good with their histrionics, he was concerned they'd find a way to shake up the Chancellor too. That's all he needed. An old gangly musty creature dragging back to the compound to funk up the area with his tired WeShallOverCome lackluster wisdom.

"Oh, okay... just—"

—Click. Combat ended the call. It wasn't only that the Don had been (sort of) eavesdropping in on this conversation, along with his team, all tapping their whiskers waiting to get back to the meeting, but he really did have many stokes in the embers. Trying to gage the response of having released the Offies, against the constant movement in the County, City, State and Palace, plus leading his Warriors was getting mighty natty.

"A'ight, here's what we're gonna do," Combat began, relieved the Head Chancellor wasn't stressing. "I want you to scribe up some options for us," he said to the Don before turning to Shonuff. "And I want you and Almighty to work with Coach to flush out Doc and Elon!"

"Wait," Amen interjected for the manyeth time. "We MUST pray before closing this meeting," he insisted.

"GEEZ," Combat huffed. "ALRIGHT PREACH! Give it to us, PASTOR!!!"

"...Bugs, bow your helmets," Amen said before Combat got irritated again and changed his mind.

"Oh Crisis, give us traveling grace and mercy as you send us on our missions to—"

BRRRRRRNNNG!!! "—Yeah, hello!"

"Hey! Say...You think you can send over some Whopliftas (construction workers) to build a canvass (deck) onto our rock-a-away? I meant to tell you the last time we talked but—"

"—Yeah...yeah..." the WarLord replied not so obliging. The Head Chancellor's sense of danger was astounding. "Anything else," Combat asked irked.

"Well, I was wondering if I needed to wait at the jam for the beeper because it hasn't arrived—"

"—No!" Combat shouted before lowering his voice. "I mean, I'll call when it's ready..."

"Oh, okay... because I—"

—Click. "Let me straighten this out before I have to put him down too," Combat joked with the Leaders (and Don) watching. A tick later he was on his node ordering one of the Warriors outside the Pedi.

"Listen, I need you to take your Alert beeper to the Head Chancellor. Have whoever answers the jam call me to confirm." He was about to end the call when he added, "...oh, hey! Let me know if you see Elon or a Captain hanging around!"

DonWon's sprouts (brows) spiked. "I wouldn't make any critical moves before you see my options," he warned.

"How 'bout this," Combat retorted. "How 'bout leaving me your options and let me DECIDE how and when I make MY moves."

At this very moment Combat was getting testy with the consultant, Good was welcoming the Warrior inside. "—Oh my goodness," she teased. "I didn't know you Warbugs were still out here. How long have you all been out here?"

"I have instructions to deliver a beeper to the Head Chancellor," replied the frightened Warrior. In addition to the order Combat gave him, he was under strict orders to NEVER ENGAGE WITH OFF DUTY BUGS WHILE ON DUTY!

"Oh, there's no need for that type formality around here," Good laughed off. "You want a bite to eat?" And before he could decline she rushed by him, headed to the Warmobi where he heard her asking the Warriors if they wanted a bite to eat as well, gidily ignoring the command he'd been sent to deliver. Quickly the situation got more awkward.

"Come on in," Good went on, pulling Warriors out of the mobi. "I'm sure it'll be fine," she insisted, gaily talking about how safe the area was, and how nothing ever happened and so forth and so on.

And the Warriors took her up on the offer, entering the Pedicle where so few bugs had ever been. Other than the Chancellor, his Queen and Good (obviously), plus a few Elders like Combat, Coach and Amen... only Workers assigned to various labor duties had ever ventured deep inside the Pedicle.

Good called out to the Queen. She idolized company too, and came running to the front. "Come... come," she wooed, opening her winged mandibles and wrapping them around as many Warriors as she could.

She would smooze a stack of Tarantulas she was so starved for an audience. "Have a cushion...can I get you dants something juicy to sip?"

The Warriors declined, so scared they dared to move further than the entranceway. Instead they squoze together and huddled around each other. If Combat saw this, or caught a whiff of this orgy, they'd be demoted and dusted without trial.

"Come on in," Good urged anyway, nudging and pushing them deeper into the Pedi. "Don't worry about that mean 'ole WarLord! MY SAY TRUMPS HIS!"

NOT TRUE AT ALL! The Warrior holding the beeper was so terrified that he grabbed the Queen and proceeded to ask for the Chancellor, until she fainted on him. Good almost passed out too. No bug, ABSOLUTELY NO BUG EVER TOUCHED THE QUEEN! NEVER!!! Only Her Majesty touched Her!

"Oh My Word," gasped Good. "What have you done!?!"

"The WarLord commanded you call him so that I can deliver this beeper to Our Chancellor," bleated the worked up Warrior. He was a wreck.

"But where's your training? Have you no sense? Don't you know you're NOT supposed to touch THE QUEEN!?"

"Give it to me," Good snapped, speaking of the beeper...reaching for the gadge as she fanned the disoriented Queen trying to wake up.

Seeing this the Warriors scrambled out of the Pedicle, all except the Warrior holding the beeper. "Sorry," he said. "I didn't know what to do."

"So you touch the Queen," Good said flustered. "I sure hope you don't lose your shell over this..."

"Well, I won't..." stammered the Warrior. "If you don't say anything..."

Suddenly the Queen was fully awake, asking what happened. "You dozed on me Yahqu," Good halfway chuckled, while looking over at the Warrior to pass him a dirty glare.

"Well, my...my..." sighed the Queen fixing her bauble and looking around. "I seem to recall a group of young Soldiers in here."

"No Yahqu. It's only me and this Warrior."

"Oh," she said getting up, about to stagger off. "Well, see if a bussbug will fetch him something to drink."

"Oh, that won't be necessary," Good said. "He's only here to make a delivery—"

"—and check for Elon and the Captains," the Warrior timidly added.

The Queen suddenly came to a DEAD STOP. "Ooo!" she huffed. "I'm sure they're resting," she said bitterly. While Good was away checking on Pokey she had a very disturbing conversation with those bugs. "Let's not disturb them," she added. "Now, if you would fetch that youngin' a drink and let him be on his way, I'd be ever so delighted!"

Good acquiesced. "I sure hope this doesn't get back to Comby," she whispered to the Warrior.

Good? Or Bad?

The WarLord had much to contend with, the reason he almost forgot about the Warriors he assigned to the Pedicle. But the Warriors hadn't forgotten about him. They were worried sick about the visit INSIDE the Pedi.

"Look, if we just don't say anything there's nothing to fear," said one logical Warrior. This would be the one ordered to deliver the beeper to the Head Chancellor.

"But you touched the Queen," gawked another Warrior. He had been in the mobi for a while and still looked like he was seeing the Queen fall.

"So what," argued the beeper Warrior, also known as Warrior1 or W1. "You wouldn't have known had you not gotten out of the mobe too. It's not only me that went against code."

"Yeah, that's true," sighed another Warrior. "WarLord is gonna pop us ALL on this for sure..."

"BUT ONLY IF HE FINDS OUT," W1 reminded them. "Let's just be cool!"

W1 called Combat to let him know the mission was complete. "Assignment done," he told a confused WarLord.

"What assignment!?!" Combat snarled.

"Umm..." Warrior1 stammered. "You asked me to give the Head—"

"—Oh, yeah..." Combat suddenly remembered. "Did you happen to see Elon or one of the Captains?"

"Umm...no," W1 replied. "The Queen said—"

"—The Queen said..." Combat muttered, sounding both nonplussed and angry. "What in the Jevil were you doing in there talking to the QUEEN!?!"

"Well, she offered to give us—"

"—GIVE US!?!" There was no mistaken the WarLord was 100% ANGRY!!!

"Well...ummm..."

"...What in the jekyll happened!?!" For a tick the WarLord was sincerely stumped...until it occurred to him, Good never called, which propelled him to fire off a volley of questions. "Where was Good!? And why didn't she call for confirmation? Who let you in?"

He was HOT! Didn't even allow the Warrior to respond. "—YOU ARE DONE!!!" he screamed. "Get back HERE NOW!"

Combat called Good. There was no telling what might've gone awry, but was convinced his orders had not been followed as instructed. For whatever reason Good chose NOT to call, assured him no good deed had been done. Crisis forbid he took off. Because it was an option! A regular Soldier talking to a Queen could land him (as WarLord) before a firing squad!

"Oh, Comby I invited them in here," Good said. "In fact, I forced them in here. That was so cruel to have them sitting out there all that time without anything to eat or drink!"

"Good. There's a mini Scullery in the Mobi," Combat said as if he was speaking to a kid. "And you didn't even bother to call me to confirm I sent them!"

"Awwl Comby, who wants to eat that mess—"

"—Good! They're WARRIORS!!! Not your play pods. They—"

"—Oh Comby, those rules are plain silly! You shouldn't be making those poor bugs go through that hyper battlewar whoha! It's ridiculous! That's why Elon and them don't want to go back there! You have them scared to Junipers!!!"

"Oh really," Combat coolly replied. "Well, I'll have you to know...since y'all don't have Tubes to know what's taking place on these wires... but Our Mound is under attack by the Palace."

"Say what," Good mumbled.

"Yeah, and I probably should also let you know that your favorite Kingpin... 'while you've been laid out vacaying' ...has been dragged out of the Palace by his whiskers and stripped of the crown."

"WHAT?!? OH MY WORD! Who—how—when did this happen!?!"

"Like I said... WHILE YOU'VE BEEN CHILLING IN OBLIVION!!!"

"I'm coming back—"

"—No Good," he urgently said. "You're better off where you are. There's nothing you can do right now anyway."

She started sobbing. HORRIFIED! WaWa was her idol. He was her promise everything would be okay and they not have to leave the Mound. She would've never let Pokey show out as he had, if WaWa wasn't Kingpin. This was awful news. JUST DREADFUL!

"Well, who's Kingpin?"

"You won't believe it," Combat replied.

"Why? Who is it?

"They call him '20', but you know him as City."

Silence.

"Good. Stay there," Combat ordered. "Do not exit the Pedi UNDER NO CIRCUMSTANCE. I'm sending transportation for you."

Under normal circumstances she would have been in the pantry joshing with Workers and cooks, or trying to delight His Queen with a new taste, or more likely, prepping a departing meal. But she was too distraught for that type merriment. Packing up a sort of 'last meal' to take back to the compound to share with the other Antes, or alerting the Captains and Elon who'd been spending inordinates amount of time on the lakes with their scribes, and wires, and antmade tools were not in her sights.

Instead she clutched a few essentials...a Babylon and her Babylon-like Bubbles tape, and made her way to the Lyft Area. A short distance away she noted an odd sighting. The Chancellor and His Queen were whisked away in their Gold Leaf. She considered asking the driver, a young Warrior not loaded with gobs of accolades, how he (and others) were taking the ousting of the Kingpin. But even the lowest on the WarLord's roll kept his lickers SEALED SHUT, and marbles on the dark ahead.

So she stayed silent too, watching moss sicles, cobwebs and ash whiz by...the same articles she saw whenever she was in the tunnel. The terrain appeared normal...until the Lyft stopped at the main port.

Trepidation consumed her at once. The area was cordoned off, which beyond the barriers were Ants as far as the sight could see.

"What's going on," she gasped, not expecting an answer, nor expecting gushes of Ants to engulf the mobile. Antes, Dallies, Kiddies, Elders...and troves of Workers and Warriors clobbered around them.

"Oh Crisis Comby," she fretted as soon as he emerged from the mob. "What's going on? Where did all these bugs come from?"

"Shift change," he replied, brushing aside bugs trying to speak to her.

"Well, I thought for a tick I got famous and nobug told me," she teased. "I can get used to this!"

"Well don't," Combat huffed. He was indebted to her, but not her wishy-washiness. "They're on their way to the Forum," he snarled, escorting her through a throng, with the help of Warriors clearing a path.

The noise and chaos was so great that she was unable to isolate the bits from the boulders. At each twist and turn bugs shouted pleas at her. Gnarly suppositions, and blenchy too. One bug begged to be her whisket washer.

"In all my dregs I've never seen it like this," she said addled, almost comatose by the frenzy. "But why would you bring the Chance and his Majesty into this mess..." she sighed.

"Chance wanted some upgrades done," Combat gruffly replied adding... "...but don't worry! I'm sending them right back soon as the whopliftas finish!"

"But—"

—Suddenly Just appeared, front and center. "All jevil has broken loose since you've been away," she scoffed noisily, both whiskets fixed to her sideplates, wasting NO TIME displaying her displeasure. "I've been trying to reach you for dregs," she argued before Combat broke up the chat.

"—Will you please let Good get situated before pounding her with your gossip!"

"Oh, Comby I'm fine," Good said. She needed

to talk...to ANYBUG but HIM... just to balance the haywire happening around her. "So what's been going on in the Scullery?"

But Just's lickers went limp. She stopped talking and glared at Combat. "Comby is right," she replied in a cagey tone contrary to the leer dulling her mullet. "It can wait. Call me when you get settled." And she turned, disappearing into the crowd.

"Comby, will you please tell me what's going on here? Just has never bit her licker."

"Everything's fine—"

"—RIGHT NOW Comby," she warned, seeing over his arch Almighty grinning salaciously.

"Good. First get settled. I promise. We'll talk. In fact, a meeting is scheduled in..." and he checked his node. "...Oh, in another few dings."

"Well, I want to know right now if YOU really bricked those Captains!?!"

"Why would I do that!?!" he limply chuckled. "I thought I already told you... we had to infirmarize them after getting infected from one of THEIR 'gone bad' lab tests. They're safe NOW," he maintained.

Good WAS NOT SOLD. She turned her pearls into lasers and aimed them straight at him. The fuzzies started dispersing, making her even more leery as of the wishy-washy baloney replies.

"Well, what is the deal with sending that many bugs to the Forum!?!" The Forum was only used for major announcements, thus it had never been used.

"Some Mites escaped the Yard (zoo)," he lied with ease. "Yeah," he continued, deflecting the lasers aimed at him. "If you need to know something, just ask us. Don't listen to unofficial sources. They'll lead you up a shamrock."

"Well, I have a question," she snarled. "Are you trying to OVERTHROW the Colony, OR just throw US UNDER THE DIRT!?!"

Who's the Traitor?

Not the greatest secret, but less aired was the snug attraction Senior Elders had for Good. No one readily admitted it, and for many charry reasons... most effervescent, Good wasn't interested. She especially shared NO thirst for Almighty, over his skis thrilled Combat assigned him to escort, because she wasn't the only egg-holder he had his feelers on.

"You know I was twigged out when I learned you went on vacay without me," he jostled, sticking to her back whiskets like a pesky kid.

"Ugh!" she moaned disgusted. Just annoying. A hundred percent pest! Like a Tick that won't let go.

"Would you mind dropping back a skip," she hissed, jabbing him in his soft spot. "In fact, now that I'm SAFE, you can leave!"

"Oh no," Almighty grinned greedy-marbled and thrasher starved. "Can't do that," he groveled. Sticking on her wasn't all for her safety... or his score list. He had orders to stay with her until the WarLord announced 'they' were in the clear.

"WHY!?!" Good asked appoyed; meaning both apprehensive and annoyed. Already, learning about WaWa's ousting...along with the unusual activity at the Entry Port and Combat's explanation, on top of Just's strange behavior unpacked UNRIVALED surmise something wasn't right.

Almighty declined to answer, simply hitting her back with "Because," as he continued grinning and sogging up his soppers.

Irritated to cruella with his DRIP, DRIP glee she told him if he didn't come clean she had a rolodex of suitors who would.

"Look, I've been ordered to stay with you until the coast is clear," he replied a little less pesky. "A lot is going on I can't—"

"—No! You looka' here," Good bit back, HARD. "I don't care what your mission is! If you don't tell me RIGHT THIS INSTANCE why you are here, I'm going to throw you RIGHT OUTTA HERE!"

Impossible. And Almighty knew it. Good was in no shape to handle a bug of his range. But he did drop back...a smidgen however, leaving just enough room to smack a widget (remote) out of her whiskets when she attempted to turn on the Tube. "No Tube," he ordered. "WarLord has banned the Tube!"

"What!?!" she near shrieked. A major portion of her stay in the Pedicle consisted of watching her Bubbles (Soap Operas). Forget WHY Combat banned the Tube, she would not survive a TICK if she missed the rest of the lowdown going down in Czaritza.

So, when Almighty took matters in his own whiskers, she used ALL DOZENS of her digits to poke the Elder sore in both marbles.

"AAAHHHHHH," he yelled curling backwards, MORE SO IN FEIGNED DEEP PAIN!

She ignored him and turned on the Tube. The Czaritza crew was scheduled to air soon, giving her a little time to make a stein of brew before reaching out to Just.

Except midway into fixing the brew he started to stir. Clearing his marbles, seemingly searching for her, she happened to notice the Tube blaring NEWS!

"Who's been in here messing with my GIGS (Channels)," she muttered pointing a widget (remote) at the Tube. TRESemmé, an anointed anchor Roaches slobbered over, and Black Antes threw projectiles at, filled the screen. She never watched this GIG. And SMUT Outlet never aired News on this GIG she liked more than her brew. This GIG barely broke in with commercials in lieu of the Bubbles.

"Good, turn off the Tube," Almighty listlessly ordered. He wasn't hurt, just crushed...and tired trying to woo her. "You shouldn't be seeing that," he said, giving up on the GOOD fight.

"But where is this," she asked distracted, unable to unhook her pearls off the humongous flames, and one bug she recognized. "Is that Peedy?"

"It's the Southern Border," Almighty replied. "And Yes," he added somberly. "That was Peedy."

"But What Happened?"

"It happened while you were away," Almighty explained. "It's a WAR going on. That's why I'm here..."

"A WAR," Good asked, looking around stunned. There hadn't been A WAR since WeShallOverCome. Suddenly that crazy rant Elon, Doc and Fessy tried unsuccessfully selling her...and the Queen... filled the gaping hole she'd fallen into looking for the 'old' compound... both in concert latterly dismissed. NOW A WAR. And not that Peedy was unblemished in his outside dealings, he certainly didn't deserve to be set aflame. "Well, what is Comby planning to do about all this," she whispered.

"Well, that's why I'm here. We're supposed to meet a little later—"

"—OH NO! I'm not waiting 'til later, when we're in here being blown to bits!"

She headed straight for the EXIT, stopped by Almighty...and a crackly buzz emanating from the Tube. On screen was another anchor she recognized. Her name was Stormy Weatha. She was an anchor for WBBA (We'sBeBlackAlways) presenting facts about this WAR from the Black angle.

"The DEADLINE LOOMS," reported Stormy, perched upright on her cushy branch, looking peachy happy and cute as usual. "If Leaders at the Black Mound don't turn over their Chancellor, '20' plans to BLOW THEM ALL OUT OF THE GALAXY!"

"Oh luscious forbid..." Good hissed. She didn't care for Stormy either. Like the rest of them (the anchors that being), they were marvelous at goading hysterics they liked to soothe withe their brand of therapy. Right after promulgating her dismal crushing report she was going to move on CANCELLING the obvious farse concern she showed for bugs caught up in this WAR, to extrapolate about her pet silkworm and her trauma making beauty logs (appointments). Outrageous! Next to TREACHERY!!!

"AWFUL," Good muttered horrified. She again headed for the exit, and again was stopped by strapping Almighty.

"Good, please," he begged...for more reasons than his honest concern for her. "That's why the WarLord banned the Tubes," he explained. "You don't want to alarm other bugs...it might cause panic."

"LOOK AT ME!!!" she shrieked, her mullet just about pressed into his. In another setting he would've been in sleep euphoria.

"DO I LOOK PANICKED!?!"

Once more he looked into her pearls...deep and warmly...despite holding onto her a little too tight to call this embrace affectionate.

"TOO LATE BUG! I'm already PANICKED!"

She started to break free but Almighty held on tight. "—Good," he sternly but coolly said, effectively stopping her. "THERE'S MORE..."

She stopped resisting and paused, and slowly pirouetted around. What ELSE could there be?

"Everybug can't go, Good..."

"What!?! Why!?! What are you talking about? Are you saying HE is planning to leave all these bugs behind...the ones that have been so loyal to US over the eons!?!"

"No, I'm saying there's only space for those on the main roster."

"What main roster? What are you saying?"

"I'm saying the Chance is not invited..."

CHAPTER 8

'He Shall Not Be Moved.

20 refused to budge. Pledging allegiance to a position he had no desire to abandon, he realized he could do a lot for the Colony. He didn't ignore issues like WaWa, nor was a DIVISIVE WAR MONGER like the Founding torrents of RMDG Kings. To his lengthy scribe of merits, he built and led a solvent city for many dinurals. It's government was flush. He employed the best and brightest. And they came in all statuses and classes. Communities built under his governance were flush. They lived on velveteen sand. The troposphere above was clean. Their edibles fresh. Their young healthy and its Plebs happy. He could do the same for the Colony; THE SOLE REASON he was installed Kingpin in the first place.

But he moved into the Palace to ANARCHY. He discovered he had adversaries, and plenty of them. Criticisms and grievances piled up, stacking sky high, beginning with skeptism about how he gained access to the throne. WaWa and his regime's ousting played third fiddle to Stonebug's cryptic disappearance, and the subsequent dismantling of the entire IGIN.

He addressed none of those concerns. Instead he mined for more enemies. He wanted to discover them all, yanking up his greatest thorns by the claws-full, solely using his fantastic brutal semantics.

"The Kumquat MUST BE eradicated NOW," he bluntly declared. "Get rid of the Kumquat and every-sect gets to exist WONDERFULLY!"

The lament set off the IGs ousted from the IGIN. What...or who was this KUMQUAT? It didn't sound like he was speaking of Ticks, Lice, Gnats and the ICKY sorts...among the germiest of all classes. No, those bugs lived in his GREAT city. Sounded like he was referring to A COLOSSAL set back. He was trying to take the Colony back to Crawler periods, where he could mass exterminate bugs he reserved as his enemies. Bugs he hoarded an arsenal of SLURS to cripple. The KUMQUAT, which of course was them!

So, once more the IG's dusted off the MEGA-Fat Trilogy and stuffed the missive with more propaganda to CONCLUSIVELY PROVE why 20 should BE REMOVED from the Palace IMMEDIATELY.

The Trilogy lived on, reminding MEDIA about how inept, corrupt, and dangerous a Kingpin 20 was, and MEDIA regurgitated the reminder to Plebs telling them they could be this KUMQUAT! And of course the Plebs bought the LIE, believed it, repeated it, and so forth and so on lived the message.

So 20 did what he did best. He shredded the IG's...and he shredded them in one speech.

"First, arguing with bugs you can't tell their front from their back is a total waste. Don't subscribe," 20 replied via a COLONYWIDE speech.

Cries streaming from every corner and crevice were shattering. It was terrible how 20 described the much respected IGs, especially Ph. Xanax. Plebs slammed 20, pitching him and his speeches in an orbit of ferocious condemnation.

But care, 20 DID NOT. In fact, he got worse, if this was even attainable.

He called WaWa (who he nicknamed) YaYa, A GRAND-STAND TRAITOR! All you Sects know YaYa was NOT doing his duty," he lamented in one speech. "Treason is not welcomed in OUR GREAT COLONY of THEE," he added, infuriating WaWa's admirers who blasted ALL OVER Black Medias, 20's implication in removing the billboards, and thus his complicity in covering up this corruption...aka the real Treasonist.

Anchor Stormy Weatha led the pack reining in an insidious HATE for 20 using the BLACK MEDIA as her courier. Being a big proponent of the Black Mound, she swung that Trilogy like a baton, citing NO BACK UP and Researching NADA, calling the NEW Kingpin EVERY NAMED ICIST but the ONE in HIS IMAGE! Quickly she became Maz's ARCH Numero Uno ENEMY. How dare that SKANKaDANK MAGGOT try to char her Ceboo!

FACTS FIRST. Orange was not orange, but a soft melon color. He was descendant of the Lord Howe Island Phasmids (basically Lobsters) morphed into the Beetle family before splintering off into a host of breeds, Roaches among the species. Thus by CREED, he DID NOT discriminate. This meant HE WAS NOT AN ICIST... AND certainly NOT a filthy one given how meticulous he was about the habitats where he lived and worked. The accoutrements in the Palace were so detestable to him that he decided not to live there... barely worked there. IN FACT, most of his meetings were held in his Groloppa Compound.

Orange spared NO EXPENSE lighting into Stormy Weatha like a Sharp Sheet of High Voltage. "Whatever bug told Crummy she was an anchor and tossed her a widget, is guilty of attempted mutiny," he matter-of-factly extrapolated across quazoolla kilowatts traveling in sub-zero speeds.

"She, and her ilk, should've never been freed off the Hacienda they hailed from. She is a disgrace to her trace and will only bear pome to those who rely on anything that urps from those slurpers."

Plebs went wild. Those that enjoyed YE's brand of retaliatory subversion laughed hardest. And those that didn't, the Media premier, condemned him, describing his antics as incredibly divisive...among many other grisly things they had to say about him.

However, the probe into what happened to Stonebug became most PROBLEMATIC. IG, Ph. Xanax relentlessly scoured for the truth. He drummed up scornful scores of allegations, none relevant to Stonebug's whereabouts, yet he whipped up these amusing investigations on this thin shred of nothing and hurled them with all he had at YE, and thus Maz.

And still, the New Kingpin was not phased. He bit back harder. "IF THAT BUG ISN'T ROLLING WITH THE DUST, HE SHOULD BE," he countered. "And if, and or when that bug is located, both he and Funky Storm WILL BE held accountable and severely dealt with. I PROMISE...

...You'll never hear from Crummy or her wacko cronies ever again, NOT THAT THEY'D BE MISSED, because they are delusional and offer nothing to us DECENT law-bading Sects," he strummed on, as well making it ULTRA CLEAR, "THIS IS NO THREAT. I ASSURE YOU, IT'S A PROMISE!'

Ok. So the WORD CHOICE elements inserted in YE's speeches were an issue. The hieroglyphs he used to describe the colorful bugs obstructing his pledge to Plebs who wanted what his city had, and the incorrect chattel he borrowed to push back HATERS, fueled his greatest problem... a problem he was only too grateful to have Maz fielding on his behalf. Lots of oops and ouches resulted from her help too.

Being even less empathetic, Maz usually left nothing to redress once she finished mushing off brand and out of shape opinions. She enjoyed taking this heat in fact; arriving at the Press Booth after EVERY major scourge, claws out and READY!

One dreg, after a particularly busy session cleaning up for the Big 20, a little huffy media bug appeared in the Press kit. He, like so many before him, wanted to know the whereabouts of Stonebug. Maz gracefully blew an invisible nuclei off her over arch (shoulder) and replied like she had so many times before. 'She didn't know.'

But a little mighty Cheerio decided to go for extras. He asked if it was true if SHE, HERSELF had smashed Stonebug.

Politely, which was highly unusual for Maz, she offered to answer him after the Presser...alone...in the O-ring. Little Cheerio took her up on this offer ...toting along his equipment...ALL OF IT... the bulbs, flashes, lots of cabling and wires, everything he'd need to insure her confession reached the furthest corners of the Galaxy... and Beyond.

But he never left the Palace.

There was a little puddle to clean up after his visit however, but not as much gloop as Stonebug left behind. But then, Stonebug was larger, so it pretty much answered for the lesser mess, and why that time around there was no cause to call in Clean Up Workers that might later turn into snitches.

As it panned out, little tooter Cheerio was in lockstep with Miss Cootie, ex-Secretary for Chief County. And Miss Cootie was quite perturbed; not only over losing her job over the Chief losing his job, but most vexed by YE NOT being held accountable for his past...and present actions. Instead of being ghosted...and quite literally so...like the Chief and Stonebug...and now Cheerio, and by the way... WHERE WAS STATE, HE was PROMOTED to KINGPIN!

And YE's audacities didn't end there. He, as well, according to Miss Cootie, had the YARN to blow off the Pleb's questions, cover up possible crimes, and then send out that big black bug to clean up his dirt.

So, after Reporter Cheerio's disappearance, Miss Cootie Founded TOO (Take Out Orange). She met with bugs that felt like her (many Reporters and those City and State Nectars cheated out of a mate), and together they conspired to get 20.

Miss Cootie led the charge, electing Pinochle (a disgruntled County Official Nectar)...and Scrappy, (a WBBA Reporter) to help BRING DOWN 20. The plan was to get inside the Palace and FORCE 20 to besmirch one of them. Originally they wanted to solicit Stormy Weatha to trap the Kingpin, but feared she would be recognized since 20 HATED HER so.

Interestingly enough, Miss Cootie was almost recognized herself. Maz remembered her voice, when she worked for Chief County. But fortunately, (for Miss Cootie) she didn't recall what Cootie looked like given they never met mug to mug.

"Isn't it a shame what's happening on the Hill," Miss Cootie asked Maz in passing one dreg.

Maz paused. What was Cootie doing out of her lane!?! And frankly, why in a DNANG did SHE (a Roach) give a ratty-patooty about a society of bugs HER POLLS could care LESS about!?!

"Absolutely NOT," Maz clicked back. "Thanks to OUR Kingpin those Plebs are doing just fine!"

"But did you hear about its County and State?" Miss Cootie's pearls bloomed and twirled. "I am so surprised you haven't heard what happened."

"And what happened?" Maz shot back. She was testing Cootie. BIG TIME!

"Their Nests were HIJACKED, and Officials KIDNAPPED! By those Blacc..." and she sucked up her whisket and turned a grayish color herself.

The Palace Speaker, and obviously Black bug snarled. "Don't start none won't be none!"

Maz strutted off, leaving Miss Cootie licking her wounds...and seeking comfort from the other two infiltrators that had tweazed their way in the Palace; Pinochle and Scrappy.

"Oh, that sounds just AWFUL how HIS Press Speaker spoke to you," Pinochle cooed.

"Well, I THINK his INACTION SHOULD BE ACTIONABLE," Scrappy protested.

The three whipped up another Palace Trilogy, this time simply titled: 'Get 20.'

Accordingly, a mountain was made from a mole hill and YE accused of EVERY besmirchable offense known to the eons of time. He had assaulted, assailed, defiled, besieged, contaminated, depreciated, invalidated, vulgarized, pulverized, collasped, crippled and permanently blemished Cootie's spirit. And TOO had a trove of TOOERS to confirm this!

"Who in the formaldehyde is Scabby and Peetruffle anyway," YE growled irked.

"Ceboo, you don't need to be concerned about them lotuses and all that chiffonade they slinging," Maz replied. "Let me deal with them lotuses!"

Lotus was a horrible epithet and YE did laugh. But he also was concerned and had good reason to be. Even if Maz could handle the three responsible authors of 'Get 20', which she in fact did, flushing the floosies and their gripes out of the Palace, this ugly mantra all the same had infected the O-ring.

The COC (Colony of Courts) embraced the squalid propaganda. THEY BELIEVED THEM! "20's success running a city does not transmorgrify his routine and regular assault on 'OTHER' bugs," a COC Adjunct belabored on the same dais where HE had raised a whisker and SWORE TO TELL THE WHOLE TRUTH AND NOTHING BUT THE WHOLE TRUTH!

It was a racket for sure, but didn't preclude the COC, and HOB (House of Buccaneers), and SCOO (Security Council of Outcasts and Outlaws) AGAINST RULING 20 HAD TO GO!

For creases upon creases (hours) this band of Palace Overseers toiled tirelessly to scoot YE ...and his running MATE out of the O-ring.

They begged and pleaded. They spread more rumors and more LIES. They tried tricks and treats. And then they waited... for a prime opportunity when Maz was out and about visiting kin, and YE was where he was usually, hanging out in his Groloppa Compound.

While away from the Palace the lower ranking regime inside the O-ring were gaslit and put under Bricks, and the LOCKS changed. Maz returned unable to access the O-ring.

So YE DID NOT GO WILLINGLY. He took to a PODIUM and gave his greatest SPEECH Of ALL!

"These Leeches, these SLUGS and SLIME have cheated you Plebs out of a GREAT FUTURE! For the FIRST TIME since the reign of Kingpins, We The Plebs have been LOCKED OUT of a choice to choose the Leader WE WANT to govern our great Colony. The COC, the HOB, and the SCOO... among others... have unjustifiably and diabolically DECLARED WAR on US," he projected. "But if YOU WANT the Palace back, YOU MUST TAKE IT BACK!"

YE, in fact, called on bugs to take back the Palace, and many so angered AGREED! They circled him, waved banners, CRIED, PRAYED, and by the end of his speech capitulated to the summons.

"Bring it On!!!" a VERY worked up crowd roared. Maz was out there. She was among the incensed protesters hurling sticks ...kicking in jams and frightening some VERY FEARFUL, but disgraceful bugs that assumed it would be a breeze stealing the Palace.

"HE SHALL NOT BE MOVED," Maz screamed at SCABs (Security Council Arresting Bugs). Before doing some real grisly damage to a few SCABs she was carried away, dragged off to a REAL BRICK, tossed in, the jam slammed, and key discarded!

The Cheese.

IT WAS BROUGHT AND WASN'T A THING YE could do about it...for the interim of time that being.

The shake down all happened so fast. One dreg YE was on top, in the Palace raising Kane calling his adversaries unsavory names and setting ablaze Miss Cootie and Scrabble's shenanigans. The next dreg he was locked out and somehow a SooZxY in the O-ring redecorating.

WHO SooZxY was, noSect knew. She wasn't there before, suddenly now she was. But NO protests were heard. Inside the Palace was quiet, except for lingering wails about how awful and disgusting a King-pin 20 had been. The COC, HOB, SCOO, CONGRESS and indexes of lawscribes affectionately called the DREAM TEAM assumed control, mentioning nothing of SooZxY's presence, yet tirelessly explaining how much Clean Up it was going to take getting rid of ALL traces of 20. Oh, THEY SO HATED HIM. Couldn't shake HIM. Get beyond HIM. The name-calling bugged them more than his supposed besmirchings and other crimes. Perhaps this was why they readily ignored SooZxY; the ONLY real crime in this mix.

The glittery red Beeish-looking creature communicated entirely in stings Colony Plebs DID NOT UNDERSTAND. In the beginning her presence was just foreign...and slightly IN THE WAY!

But before long, once 20 seemed long gone and far away, SooZxy ...and her inability to answer questions properly...started raising suspicions. The SBC (Special Bug Crusher) was contacted by an unnamed and redacted Source, and given specific orders. "The Palace appears to have been hijacked by a foreign entity! We need YOUR SPECIAL SECURITY BUGS (SSBs) to REMOVE THE THREAT!"

So, entrenched on those clear-cut unambiguous

instructions the SSBs arranged an Oval Rally. It took place at the BOOB (Bug's Official Offsite Bungalow), a sumptuous sprawling compound where Colony formals and banquets were ordinarily held.

SSB (Special Security Bug) Pepperjack led the meeting. "It has come to my attention that we have a problem in the Palace," he began. "CBs (Congress Bugs) have lost track of 20. It is unclear whether he is being held HOSTAGE, or merely ABANDONED his post. But it is OUR MISSION to FIND HIM..." and he added, "EXISTING OR NOT!" (This meant DEAD or ALIVE).

NoBug replied. Only grumbles rumbled around the BOOB. Few cared about the HUGE orange Grasshopper, or the big Black Ante he consecrated to push bugs around. The HIJACKING synopsis eluded them. Like REALLY? So what. The IN and OUT recaps were getting old...and BORING. There'd been so many, each different...with its unique twisted conspiracies and controversies.

"Well, what's the assignment," SSB Muenster asked after a deep long yawn.

"We're going to storm the Palace," Pepperjack replied. "We have intelligence that a suspicious perp dressed in a glittery red Beeish-looking outfit—"

"—WAIT. WHAT!?!" That was SSB Brie, a thin stringy Cricket with pearls so enormously large that she tipped over ...(a lot) when she so much as batted her pearls. Thing was, she, like every other SSB that ever SAW 20 up close, or far away, KNEW he would NEVER wear glitter or hide in a Beeish costume, if by a bizarre miracle he could fit in one. And he NEVER EVER would transpose his HE, for a SHE!

So Brie stopped the meeting before the Brine started flowing. "We can't trifle with that bug's whatabouts! That's the FIRST RULE in the ROCC," she squealed, referencing the Rules of Colony Conflict.

"But why not," Pepperjack asked, as if he hadn't read one word in a SSM (Special Security Manual), or hadn't witnessed prior incidents involving SooZxY roaming the Palace and getting in the way, OR...and this was a big ONE, as if he DID NOT know 20!

"Aww...come on Pep," groaned Gorgonzola. "We ain't tryin' to go up in the Challis and frisk that bug looking for 20!"

"Yeah gee," inserted Mascarpone. "I've done a lot of iffy search and seizers, and even seen a lot more, but this one cracks the nut!"

"Alright! Alright," huffed frustrated Pepperjack. "How about this..."

The sober bugs buzzed up waiting for their treat. "How 'bout all bugs agnostic to following YOUR MARCHING orders, GET LOST! Do not even go to collect your last cannoli (paycheck)."

The mood changed exponentially after this heat. Most bugs, even SSBs, needed their cannolis, and would do anything to get it. That's how approximately 25,000 SSBs, comprising of both algorithms (egg-holders and non-egg-holders) ended up in Tanks rolling over to an eerie looking Palace located at 30000 Colonization Palace.

It was early when they got there, but not so eerily early that no bug wouldn't be up and about. Workers...and all types of guards serviced the mega structure from light to dark.

"What do you think is going on in there," asked Mascarpone, who had seen most of it, and done the rest. The place looked completely empty.

"I don't know," whispered Gorgonzola crouching and crawling, and pulling down his vapor visor.

"HELLLOO," Pepperjack called out, his voice bouncing off walls inside the Palace. "We're Special Agents deputized to extract existential threats," he recited by rote.

The Palace however, wasn't as truly empty as it seemed. First off, SooZxY indeed was still in there. The 25,000 SSBs just missed her...sound asleep in a corner of the O-Ring looking much like Tick toot. One SSB saw the toot, and cursorily questioned how a Worker had missed it, but ultimately ignored it.

But what none of the SSBs could miss was Baba Ganoush's, Head SSBBI (Supreme Security Bureau of Bug Intelligence), voice streaming through intercoms.

Unbeknownst to Pepperjack and his thousands of SSBs, his own voice was being amplified throughout auxillary field Nests. Bugs in the HOUSE, the COC, the HOB, the SCOO, CONGRESS, and the SSBBI all heard him... LOUD AND CLEAR! Even the DREAM TEAM heard him.

"If you don't EXIT the Palace RIGHT NOW, I will turn these pipes on FULL BLAST," seethed Baba Ganoush.

25,000 (or more) bugs had only ticks to get through 116 exit points. They had no time to codify an orderly evacuation, much less deliberate what Baba was unleashing on them, and why he was disseminating such an inflexible message during an impossible mission...yet they did.

"What pipes?"

"But why would he turn them on?"

"Are you sure WE have orders to be in here!?!"

"No, what we need to be discussing is what's in them pipes," said Gorgonzola, already well protected with his visors down.

SSB Leaders got THE point, especially since gasses had begun rising from the ground. In the few remaining ticks left, 25,000 bugs managed to escape the Palace with NO fatalities, and few injuries. It was an awfully close call, whichever way the situation was later examined. The bugs couldn't get beyond the the WHY...and WHO gave the FIRST Order?

AIRING LIVE ON BLITZ, the Top Anchor in the Colony (#1 Lead Spot at Blitz; a rumored super FAKE News Outlet), Cokenasmile, also known as Coke, attempted to answer questions Plebs...and SSBs had about the Palace entanglements.

"Just in," reported Coke, propped upright and a-line straight, and clean as an oil slick, "one of OUR oldest institutions has finally come down," he said with a semi big smile.

"What the—" —the echo resounding around the Colony.

The oldest institution had finally come down?

What institution? For the Palace was NOT an institution, but rather the Pleb's HOUSE! And likewise it was NEITHER the oldest. Many Royal Palaces had been built, originally to house its most elite. Over time these Palaces were opened up to ALLOW elites of other classes (beyond the Roaches) to Serve and Rule from...and to ASSIST in administering carrying out these Rules and Laws and Service from. This was how bugs like WaWa (for one), and YE (for another) gained access to the throne. And it was where the various outfits housed their Agencies: the COC and HOB, and SCOO, and CONGRESS, and HOUSE, and even the SSBBI!

But did Coke seem to KNOW or CARE? Nope. His job was to EXCITE and ENTERTAIN, and that he did with excruciating passion. Where he lacked facts, he made up for in roundabout guesses that didn't require proper clearances and approvals. Lam-blasting the SSBBI for entering the Palace without authority was NOT ONLY within his PROTECTED FREE SPEECH RIGHT, it was within his ELEMENT... and DESIRE.

"Over 100,000 Troops, 'unleashed' by SSBBI, entered the Palace, and according to Sources, without authorization, to reinstall '20'!"

Absurd. And listeners promptly called Blitz on

AIR to impart their takes. "Where did you get your facts!?!" grieved the first caller. "FACTS FIRST, it was the SSB and NOT the SSBBI that entered the Palace. And neither the SSB nor SSBBI have that many Troops COMBINED. In fact, the SSBBI has 0, as in ZERO Troops, and the other unit has only 20% of that wide number you gave, which lends to the real questionable elements of your so-called reporting...

...When was YE ever ousted to be in a position to be reinstalled, AND HOW DO YOU KNOW WHO UNLEASHED OR AUTHORIZED WHAT!?!"

Coke had no comeback. He smiled for a while, and took in a lot of air for another while, seeming unable to close his lickers. And when he finally conjured up the gumption to reply, he had so little to say.

"Hmm, you bring up good points," he replied. "I, myself, never counted the Troops in each outfit, but I do rely on OUR sources," he added. "Like if you can't trust your sources, then who can you trust?"

The New Regime.

The REAL DEAL. There was no '20' in the Palace. Once the DYE settled, (DYE used to fumigate the old Kingpin's hubris), HIS ESSENCE was totally obliterated.

A New Regime marched in... led by none other than good old Tiramasu. For the most part, Plebs were relieved seeing him stroll in. Most hoped this would put a period on a tumultuous reign. The name-calling and turgid speeches and bugs that kept disappearing, or getting ousted... there'd been just entirely too much disruption.

But gone as 20 visually seemed to be, and Love or Hate him, it was as if his ousted fumes had been blown out into the Colony. His dust was everywhere. And there were no underground pipes to move this inchoate miasma along.

But at least the prism wasn't in the Palace, which odd enough, the glittery little Red Beeish-looking SooZxY still was. She continued with her busy work, redecorating the O-Rings in earnest, albeit of questionable taste.

Problems started immediately. Outside of the mysterious SooZxY, the bigger sphinx was the chalky blume polluting the Colony. The Plebs didn't know how it had gotten there, or what should or could be done about it, but became extremely unsettled with how the new Kingpin chose to deal with it.

Methodically he ordered Colony-wide SWEEPING MANDATES! "We're getting rid of that plague... not letting ANY hydra meant to destroy us, take us down! I won't allow it," he angrily retorted, his mullet trapped in an assortment of folds. This was how he earned the tag, TLM (Tough Little Mope).

Like the weight of iron concrete he came down FULL FORCE on ALL Plebs with MANDATES, sparing no prisioners. He pummeled them ALL. Black bugs. Poor bugs. Sick bugs. Young bugs. Without warning or explanation he CLOSED Trade Squares ALL OVER THE COLONY, indefinitely. He CLOSED habitats for Kiddies. He ordered CURFEWS, and made it illegal to be out in public without proper approval. He as well ordered INVOLUNTARY EXAMINATIONS and PUNISHED ANY bug that disagreed with his modern Dictatorship.

Instantly it became US against THEM. Agree with his MANDATES, and that bug was Sterling. But those that disagreed, they were 20s. Didn't matter if the bug liked 20 or not.

ONLY bugs working in the Palace, or one of the annexes; the HOUSE, COC, CONGRESS, and etcetera were spared his havoc. And Oh, SooZxY. Nothing of this magnitude had ever occurred before. NOT in ANY ERA. Not even in Crawler periods!

As a result, an unprecedented CRIME SPREE ensued. Bugs lost it. Went wild. Had nothing to lose. Looting, riots, barbings, curbings, besmirchings, dustings, desperation and depression SOARED!

The MEDIA tried to memorialize the unrest, which may have not been as troubling had the annexes not started falling apart. The COC stopped speaking to the HOUSE and CONGRESS. And SSBBI (after the Palace ruse) collided with them ALL...to include the Dream Team!

Secrecy, conspiracies, pandemonium and mob rule flourished, which SooZxY in the mix DID NOT HELP. Who was this little Red minx anyways? Where had she come from? Admins especially wanted to know. Even if they liked her cheesy-chintzy taste, which they HATED, normally they redecorated the O-rings themselves. Except there she was, enlightening whopliftas on her redecorating agenda ...without consulting them. They were enraged!!!

So, on behalf of Admins griping about SooZxY and her aggressive remodeling offenses, Frittata (a HOUSE bug) went to see TLM. "Look, we have to do something about little Zooky," he explained. "The Admins are in there about to rip her apart!"

"Agheewe benpeedjaredday soweg ahh," TLM sighed deeply, winded trying to explain himself.

That's when bugs inside the Palace really saw something very wrong with the Kingpin, more so than his usual cantankerous self.

It became impossible to converse with him. Mumbling, stuttering, fumbling and bumbling around, semi-conscious, mostly fast asleep, he fast became a running JOKE. Even the MEDIA, on the bursa (PAID), couldn't avoid capturing his gaffes. A faint breeze would topple him over, sending him rolling over their widgets where his awkward tumble would accidentally be filmed.

The time he rolled into a Soldier and ended on his back, BEFORE GALAXY-WIDE WIRES, rolling around but refusing the Soldier's help, that clip ran for dregs, until the embarrassing fall off his Gold Flyer went volcanic (viral).

The fact that he drooled into widgets, wore bibs at meal-time and wrappers during long meetings, his tumbling gaffes and his mumbling speeches increasingly became intolerably painful to ignore, (1000% worse than 20's most grisly tirade). It left CONGRESS with no choice but to order a DESIST and CEASE filming him...hoping to conceal the double mystery occupying the Palace.

CHAPTER 9

Gettin' Good!

As the Colony reeled in turmoil, Almighty hightailed it after Good. He assumed she was headed for Combat, so he took a short cut hoping to circumvent her trip and prevent a combative situation altogether.

But somehow he missed her. It was either that or she was moving slower than he assumed and hadn't reached the cut off point yet.

"Hey...hey..." he said, breaking up a brouhaha between a group of Warriors about to brawl over an incident having to do with the Brick.

"Look, where are you bugs supposed to be," he asked snatching up a particularly feisty one, really peeved about whatever the incident.

"It was HIS FAULT," yelled one Warrior; the one not being restrained from the one Almighty had snatched up.

But Almighty didn't have time for this spat, likely (he assumed) a silly matter having to do more so with pride than anything urgent he needed to contend with right away, such as finding Good.

"Look, I want y'all to go guard the Scullery," he told the unrestrained more calmer Warriors. "And I want y'all to help me with something," he ordered the Warrior he had snatched up, and the few remaining acting as worked up as the one he held up in the air. "I need to find Good."

"I just saw Good go that way," replied WB13, (Warrior Brick-3rd Tier)... meaning this Warrior was assigned to the Brick-1st shift, third level.

Immediately Almighty panicked, and for more reasons than a few. His levels were already above the norm just chasing after Good. So his anxiety wasn't lessened seeing WB13 point in a direction opposite where he was headed. And this revelation all dawned on him at the same time he realized these WB's were supposed to be in the Brick guarding the Captains.

Teetering between deciding if he should head off in the direction where the Warrior pointed, or the Brick where he was just learning the Captains had escaped, his Security Node cackled. It was none other than Combat.

"Yeah, what's up," Almighty wheezed into the node as his marbles swung wildly around, looking out for either Good or Captains.

"Where are you," Combat barked. "You've got to get in here. We gotta get outta here. WE GOT TO GO! I heard the Hill is about to take a HIT!!!"

Things were escalating, perilously FAST. They were supposed to be voting on their next move. But now the WarLord was talking about just going!

"Ugh...ugh..." Almighty stalled, looking around, AND missing FuFu cutting clear across his path.

"WHERE ARE YOU," Combat shouted again. On his end he heard quite a bit of interesting background activity.

"I'm in the corridor—"

"—What are you doing there," Combat belted. "Where's Good!?!"

Almighty ducked. A torpedoing ligger (Ant limb), narrowly missed hitting him. In those few ticks, between running after Good and bumping into and stopping the Warriors, the corridor had turned into a WAR ZONE. It had gotten so bad, the connection between him and Combat was lost.

"Listen, I want y'all to get EVERY bug out of these corridors and into the Forum," Almighty quickly rattled off no longer stuttering. "...Then LOCK and BARRICADE it," he ordered, about to move on before remembering ONE MORE THING.

"...BLAST ANY CAPTAIN you find...AND you have my EXPLICIT PERMISSION to PUT DOWN any other bug that gives you the slightest trouble!"

Now he was angry. He knew he had to report back to Combat, and he had lost track of Good. So he left the Warriors with his parting deadly order and headed for the Warpit where he assumed Good already was, in there giving the WarLord a full lobe of grief.

But as he neared the pit he didn't hear sounds typical of a crier good at complaining. What he heard instead was compartments being opened and slammed shut, and muffled conversation.

Combat looked up. "Where were you? Where's Good," he asked in one fluid sentence.

"She said she was coming here," Almighty lied before adding "...and she took off."

He didn't miss a beat. "Pass me that crate," Combat said to Coach as if a flurry of calls weren't pinging his node and alarms weren't shaking the pit.

"Well, where're you gonna put it? We don't want to be over—"

"—Just give it to me," Combat snapped. "Looks like we're gonna be light a load since I don't see Good," and he looked up at Almighty to give him his best unhappy grimace.

"Look, she wasn't having it," Almighty replied. "The bugs are out there tearing up the compound."

"It's alright," Combat sighed. "We don't need her. We'll be out of here in a jiff anyway."

"And I CAN'T WAIT," cheered Coach.

"Yeah, well...you might wanna pump 'da jollies," Combat inserted. "First we need to make sure this pep can do what them jargonnit Cappins boasted it can do," he scoffed.

Almighty hung back surprised. Combat wasn't jostling around. He was actually going to put this last resort plan into action; a plan that quite honestly none of the bugs ever believed would be deployed during their time above soil.

"I'm not convinced those fake scholars wouldn't take ultra pleasure in seeing us crash and singe," Combat continued scoffing, shoving the crate deep inside the peppito (fancy Jet) it had taken one of FuFu's teams dinurals to build.

"Look, so long as we make it by the 'Round Ups' I'm cool..." was how Coach summed up his concern. The 'Round Ups' had been stirred by the QUARANTINES AND MANDATES. It used to be kids out in public without an Elder that could be rounded up and tossed in Bricks. But now this rule even applied to Elders. All bugs were required to carry scribes explaining who they were and where they were going.

"But are you sure that thing is really sound?" Almighty was now more than surprised. He was both concerned and SCARED!

He remembered the Captains working on the piece of tin, an aerodynamic contraption touted to be able to move in nano speeds. The Smartest bugs in the compound worked hard on this shiny projectile, and tested it regularly for flyability...using foreign bugs that wandered in the pit, or derelict Workers as CRASH simulators. Wasn't pretty. Many expired right outside the jam!

"Look Almighty, we don't have no more tricks. We're fresh out," Combat coolly replied, moving on to peek beneath the undercarriage and yank on coils. "But YOU ARE FREE to hang back," he added.

"Hey, I'm not trying to ambush the mission," Almighty offered, whiskers raised. "But I..."

"...BUT YOU ARE," Coach butted in, so giddy with jinks that worrying seemed ridiculous ...until he sternly added. "No more talk. We just got intel from the State that the Palace is gonna fry this place!"

"The State?!" Almighty echoed surprised.

"Not the State!" Coach snapped annoyed. "The State isn't gonna do—"

"—I know. I heard you," Almighty shot back. He wasn't questioning the possibility of such drastic action being levied against the Mound. It was the SOURCE he questioned.

True, the Palace had turned into ONE HUGE MESS and just might do such a thing. Wouldn't be the first time an entire Mound disappeared at the behest of orders from the Palace. But the Senior Leadership had far more reliable sources in the city, than in the State. Almighty just found this intel suspect. But Combat didn't refute it, and when Amen showed up, lugging extra weight adequate enough to tilt the tin with his mammoth Bablyon...the subject moved to another topic.

"HAMMERCI!!!" Amen gasped, falling into the Warpit like a libations hurricane. "Looks like Jantin out there!"

Jantin was a huge celebration Black Ants held once a yarn to acknowledge each gen's transition to Elderhood. The gala never got better, only worse.

"Yeah, we're celebrating early," Combat teased. "...Before your Kingpin wipes us out," he laughed.

But Amen, as pretty much usual, wasn't in the mood for laughing. "Well... I never seen anything like it! I don't know how you plan to corral that bunch for this trip," he said shaking his mullet.

"Well... we're not," Almighty flatly replied. It was a naughty quip, but it was his last shot.

"We're NOT," shrieked the Pastor, swiveling around to poll the looks circling him; Combat, Coach, Shonuff, Declare and a few other Elders that kept their marbles looking every which way but at him.

The Pastor opened his lickers to speak but Combat spoke first. "We're bailing," he said. "If we don't, we're fried."

"But...but...but what about the others? ...Good, the Chance—"

"—Uh Pastor," Declare slid in. "Put 'em on Your Prayer List!"

FACTS First.

While Combat was gunning the peppito, and Senior Leaders (namely Almighty), were putting their hope in Amen upsurping his best prayers, Good was in flight, headed to speak to the Head Chancellor.

Whether Combat had told the truth why he REALLY brought the Royals back, she was fortunate the Chancellor was NOT in the Pedicle! She would've never made it that far. She barely made it the 12ks (basically 50 yards) to the Majestic Chamber intact. She was a heaving wreck when she collapsed into the whiskers of the Guard securing the Trap Jam.

"You have to let me in here to speak to Chance," she panted at the Guard on duty. Like the Pedicle, few ever visited this area as well. Senior Leaders, Workers, Guards... and quite frankly...HER...were the exceptions. Truthfully, both places, gorgeous as they were, were uninspiring. Still, the Guard started to protest the visit.

"Well, I have to call—"

"—G! Open this thing..." Good panted, low on breath... "WE don't have time for that!"

"But—" and the next thing they BOTH knew, they were looking down the hole of a VERY long scope.

FuFu appeared STRAIGHT OUTTA NOwhere... jettisoning through background tyranny heard OVER alarms, a volition of super blasts... and pure out-right anarchy. He wasn't as low on air as Good, in spite of his troubles getting to the Chamber, and still able to make it perfectly clear he needed to speak with the Head Chancellor, URGENTLY!

"Open it!" he ordered, pointing a Blaster he confiscated from a Warrior, directly at the Guard. The jam was opened, and Good flew by him into the foyer screaming recklessly, "Yo' Chance! Yo Chance!"

Frantically she darted from basilica (dressy room) to basilica in search of the Chancellor. If any-Sect would hear her out, it would be him.

Rounding a corner she bumped into the Queen first, rushing out of a coffer (regular room). "What in the lorry—" gulped the Queen, only managing to remain upright by the Head Chancellor who caught her after exiting from another coffer, likely the washer, as he donned none of his Majestic wares. Actually he was naked, save for a fig shielding his essentials.

Conflicted by the rollicking cacophony the Chancellor naturally wanted to know in what arrears of Insect usury was going on.

Both started to answer at once; FuFu opening his lickers to speak, and Good garbling gaggles of words trying to explain the Pokey affair... the Tube's ban...WaWa's ousting ...20's Installation ...and the inexplicable and unheard of bricking Captains. "And DO YOU KNOW, COMBY AND THE TOPS are about to ABANDON US!?!"

"Wait. Slow down," the Chancellor urged. He couldn't make grains or cranola of her garble.

So, she tried to start over again, causing His Queen to buckle at each mention of WaWa's name. The Queen adored WaWa. She couldn't tolerate the rumor. At no time in her expanse above soil did she expect there'd EVER BE A BLACK ANT KINGPIN, and hearing he'd been so UNCEREMONIOUSLY OUSTED was beyond GRIEF. She had fainted four or five times before Good got to her real concern. "You've known for too long how much Comby wanted to covet your spot and take over the Mound," she upchucked. "Now I have proof he's trying to CONQUER the GALAXY!"

CLA-Boomp! His Queen passed out again, that time falling into the whiskets of loitering Workers hanging close by to pick up scoops.

"Oh, there must be an explanation," sighed the Chancellor. "Conquer the Galaxy..." he chuckled. "They can't possibly expect to survive—"

"—Your Highest Majesty, with all due respect I must disagree," FuFu interjected. "The problem is not about THEIR SURVIVABILITY, as it is OUR MISSION to stop these Lethal Blastings they have authorized," he explained non-panicked.

"Oh Crisis forbid," the Queen hissed clicking her lickers. And she dropped out again.

The Chancellor could not ignore Blasts heard from beyond the still ajar Trap Jam. Neither could he miss seeing bright flashes, nor not feel the walls shaking around them. "Well...where are the other Captains and how did you escape," he suspiciously asked, AFTER ordering a lone Guard watching the gossip unfold to lower his Blaster.

FuFu was unable to answer, and not because he didn't know where the other Captains were headed to, or HOW they escaped. To the contrary. His qualm was keeping CLASSIFIED INTEL CLASSIFIED. As it was, His Queen had connected with the ground over a dozen times. He definitely didn't want Good following her suit.

"We need YOUR presence to restore law and order in the Corridors," he told the Chancellor. "We'll be doomed if you don't go out there."

CHAPTER 10

PRIORITY, Numero Uno.

As the peppito soared above the noise pollution, YE was on another soaring jetpack concocting a strategy to take on the Palace, gut it, AND devain the bugs responsible for putting his ace-in-a-hole in a Brick and tossing the key!

Problem was, it had taken many dinurals to build his team to create an excellent city. So, while he had many supporters and able bugs to make the impossible possible for his city, the same bugs were unable to deliver similar results at the Palace level.

There were too many layers to unquilt; COC, the HOUSE, CONGRESS...and the list assailed on. His best bet was a Full on Mutiny...UNLESS...Crisis doing what Crisis did best, A HOLY WAR intervened.

To YE's convenience Plebs in the Palace were still trying to make sense of SooZxY spiffing up the O-Rings without explanation. She was the biggest RED distraction, ahead of the jillions of other noises; MANY NO small matters... such as his installation and ousting being premier.

"ADMIN needs to inform Plebs about what's really going on in here," Hormel, one of the HOUSE JDs (Habitat of Unlawful Scurrilous Events) said, speaking informally to a small group of COC (Colony of Courts) and CONGRESS bugs trolling the Palace.

"Why? How will that help," asked Blu, a CONGRESS bug in charge of reff'ing Palace brawls.

"Because if we can't come to a consensus about that Koo-Koo (SooZxy), the Colony is DOOMED!" spat Hormel.

"Not so," replied Swiss, another CONGRESS bug speaking in a loopy low lull. "Not if we just ignore her. It has never failed us before."

"Ugh, Swiss," Hormel kicked back. "How do you like your Rantula Wicks...with or without kojibang!?!"

Swiss looked around. "Huh?" He had not a clue what Hormel was talking about.

But Blu did. "Come on Bug, cut the cheese a lil slack," he told Hormel. "...BESIDES, if you really look at it, SLOW wins races too..."

"Well, that would be great if I liked that RED bug's taste, but fact is, she's NOT redecorating for OUR pleasure OR taste," Hormel snapped. "It's but a matter of time before she dusts us off TOO!"

"Look, a clean well-decorated Palace WILL NOT affect us," interjected Peaches from the COC, one of hundreds overseeing rulings on CONGRESS matters. "Only filthy bugs object!"

"...OR bugs that don't care about disappearing into a bunch of 0's," Hormel cracked back.

TLM and his party navigating around SooZxY, as if she were invisible, was like ignoring a GIANT FOOT stomping crusade across the Colony. Never before (in its history) had the Palace ignored those type threats. It was one of the few times when they linked up whisker to whisket, and took out the threat. NEVER EVER did they discount FOOT ASSAULTS! NEVER!!! They nearly called in Fort Vesuvius when YE switched out the IG, and cried nonstop throughout his nefarious divisive speeches. But Soo-Soo destroying the place? Officials just looked the other way.

"Well, the 'wait and sees' have the MAJORITY VOTE," cheered a COC bug, moving aside as SooZxY shooed them out of *her* way to plant a HUGE Bamboo

Stalk in the center of their Meeting. Interestingly enough, she only behaved like this whenever a group gathered. She'd insert her annoying self in the middle of the meeting and right away get busy tearing down a wall, or scrambling a Wire, or planting a distraction that almost always burgeoned a pit full of Fiddle Figs.

"Anydo, I'm sure TLM got us," added a bloated Moth about to hatch any dreg.

"Anydo?" teased a three-and-a-half liggered Spider. "You really think that frail bug got us!?!"

"Yeah, tuffy got us alright," scoffed a HOUSE bug so angered about the Kingpin's willfull disregard of SooZxY, that he did some digging. Turned out (so he uncovered), the 'ole prickly cactus was trying to sell out the Colony....as in CHANGE ITS NAME!

Of course those present assumed the HOUSE bug was referring to the Kingpin's MALIGNANT RULES imposed on ALL Plebs and his TUMULTUOUS fumbling around. It was NO secret, TLM needed guidance climbing and descending planks, and LITERALLY had to be carried to plinths (podiums) to deliver the WORST SPEECHES EVER ORATED.

Credit to his polemics Trade Squares stayed closed. NO ROAMING RULES, supposedly to abate lawlessness, despite a lack of authorities to enforce the NEW ordiances, CLASHED with SKETCHY DECREES MANDATING Plebs leave their domiciles to get 'INK STINGS' SUGGESTED by unvetted Phony Polyps...aka IPs (Infirmary Practitioners) claiming YE's odious installation, and the shady disappearance of Stonebug created a viral pestilence.

These MANDATES alarmed the Plebs, stirring UNPARALLELED divisiveness as it forced bugs to leave the safety of their habitats at the risk of encountering volatile rioters, or being cited, bricked or worse for breaking NO ROAMING RULES. Plebs decried the MANDATES were unclear, unjust and untenable. NO competent Official could justify it and TLM (most of ALL) couldn't explain it. Something was HOLISTICALLY AMISS, and VERY FEW Plebs were buying it.

NuGro was one such bug, (of course) inspired by YE already in an uproar over Maz's bricking. "I'm NOT PENALIZING OUR City Workers that DO NOT get INKED," she announced on LIVE WIRES!

City Workers would've been against the INK stinks regardless of NuGro's bold stance. Many had kin that fled Bowldusts, Buglugs and Mass Extinctions committed against them in other Territories. Knowing the precursors and having already been through the DRILL, they naturally ALL ON THEIR OWN braced for WAR!

But when Palace DEPLORABLES heard about NuGro, they injected an INSIDE EXECRABLE into the situation.

"Looks like Providence City ain't PAYING TO PLAY," lamented an execrable.

"Yeah, I hear that's YE's old grounds," scoffed another execrable. "I'll sic Alpha on them!"

Alpha was a COC Agent who didn't waver to call NuGro. "We can have you flicked off the landscape for shucking a Colony Order," she told the Interim Constantinople who didn't know her from a KNOCK-OFF DICTATOR.

"Umm Hmmm..." NuGro hummed unperturbed. The City Nest received troves of hostile calls from wimps attempting to bring down their wonderful city. So she blew off Alpha by laughing, "YEAH, YOU and WHAT ARTILLERY." Never (in ANY ERA), had there been a ROUND UP unleashed and enforced with the FURY of a GESTAPO.

Of course Agent Alpha could care less about what precedence was being set. She had orders. NO BUG WAS ABOVE THE LAW!

"Look, THIS IS A PALACE DIRECTIVE," she asserted against NuGro's need to know. "You are putting your Plebs at risk of being BRICKED!!!"

"Oh yeah," NuGro shot back. She had ORDERS too. "Well, if y'all that MAD and BAD, come on out here and see what you can do!"

"I don't have to take this disrespect," Alpha smacked back. "We'll have that entire city flicked off the Atlas! Try me and SEE!"

"Aww...chuckamazoo, chahole," NuGro laughed more. "Just bring your RAFT out here so we can take ALL you willywonkaclowns down!"

Alpha instantly severed the call and hurried this threat to the O-ring where TLM was NOT. He happened to be snoozing in a cooker (latrine), where he claimed to get his best work done. So since she (Alpha) couldn't go in a non-egg-holder cooker, she put Admin PsiFi up to the task.

He entered the cooker to personally deliver Alpha's scathing report. Now, he had to wake TLM up, and sort of like prop him up, to explain how NuGro of PROVIDENCE, possibly under YE's authority, not only was flagrantly DISCARDING the INK Rule, but she had detrimentally threatened THE PALACE!!!

TLM WOKE UP! Well, partly. "AH... jusama ju amashus ad'em jusa toja jusamajuz zusaha jist," he slurred, offering a gimp wave. "Zmazba jona juzza."

PsiFi understood NOT A SINGLE WORD. He did however, have a clue about what to do next... since he was in cahoots with WHO was really in charge.

He called GWiz Pâté, an ENORMOUS olive-colored Prayin' Mantis acting as Head of the SSBBI (Supreme Security Bureau of Bug Intelligence). One thing had become clear about TLM's posse. There was NONE. Koo-Koo had so switched out the layout in the Palace, through her marauding restorations, that the bugs were operating on utter DYSFUNCTION!

When GWiz Pâté got the call...and message, he sounded the ALARMS. The POP (Palace of Probes), the OC (Oversight Committee), the COP (Core Over-Lord Probes), the SSF (Special Security Force), and the SSBBI (Supreme Security Bureau of Bug Intel), among the lengthy scribe of regulars... COC, HOUSE, CONGRESS and etcetera and so forth and so on, GOT THE ALERT! The Palace was under ATTACK by ROTTEN PUTRID YE and his city Plebs.

"We've got to reduce this threat," Pâté told Hormel (in the HOUSE). "That gussie is actually trying to get back IN HERE!"

"But isn't that YOUR AOR (Area of Responsibility)? Shouldn't the SSBBI (HIS AGENCY) send in SSBs to REDUCE THE THREAT?"

"No!" Pâté flatly replied. "This one's on YOU!"

"Oh, really," Hormel replied. Though he came across respectful, he was NOT HAPPY. The gall with which Pâté delivered this odious order was as offensive as directing him...and HIS UNIT... to eat dust.

"We got us a situation," he told his Principals Kikkoman, Green Giant...and a GINORMOUS BLUE ROACH called Piranha. "Pâté wants us to DUST YE!"

"But hasn't he ALREADY been dusted," asked Kikkoman, a nice young naive Ladybug.

"—Don't fret it," Hormel replied. "This is going to be one for the ANNUALS! We're about to MAKE HISTORY HERE!"

BRIBERY ACCORDS.

Adding insult to injury Pâté called YE. LEAKING GALL like a water squall he opened his greeting by coolly demanding YE "GIVE US" (as in the Palace) Stonebug. "If YOU turn over the IG, or his whereabouts, we'll give you the location of your bug...and the key."

But YE wasn't FOR SALE. He snickered. "How about THIS. How about YOU come out here and get YOUR 'IB', and WE TAKE YOU, instead of the key."

Pâté didn't see YE's humor and the call ended as quickly and stringent as it began. Both returned to their TRADING CORNERS; Pâté offended and YE so outraged that he reached out to his inside Track, INSIDE THE PALACE. He called Piranha.

"Jevil to the Nevel," Piranha kicked off. "That schemer OUT RIGHT just CONTRACTED us to TAKE YOU OUT," he openly admitted. "...BUT..." he quickly lopped on, "...If he thinks for a SHAKE DOWN we're PAYING TO PLAY, he's in for one ABAFT ACCORD!"

YE (of course) liked hearing this. But he didn't become the greatest city enterpriser by putting ALL his creds in one cask. "You've always been a decent bug," he told Piranha. "...Because that moldy piece of cheese in the Palace is going to ROT the Colony."

"I definitely see it coming," Piranha confirmed. "There's a lot of rot in here doing some real damage but hang in there with us. WE GOT SOMETHING for Pâté and the BATTLESHIP stuff he's trying to pull."

Piranha returned to the HOUSE and relayed his talk with both Pâté and YE, to Hormel, Giant, and another GINORMOUS BUG called Pepperjack. They discussed how to procede.

"I say we present the rot with a Pilot program; let's call it GOWIPHO—"

"—WHADT!?! GWAPO," heckled Pepperjack.

"GOWIPHO," Piranha correctly pronounced. "Stands for Get Orange Where It Phases Him Out..." he soberly tendered.

"Alright...settle down," Hormel piped in. "And retract them scissors," he chuckled. "Actually I like it," he admitted, adding... "...Just remember... we're on the SAME TEAM. WE MUST GUT THE ROT from the Palace."

The HOUSE AGREED. And so Hormel briefed YE on the general points of the ROT REMOVAL pilot forged in warp speed. "We need you to get in front of as many WIRES as possible; BLITZ...TMZ...that Black WIRE...hit 'em all...as many as you can," he instructed. "Make sure you pile on the insults too..." not that YE needed encouragement in this lane.

Yet Hormel loaded up on schooling YE to be as foul and vile as possible. "DON'T LET UP! WE need to make sure EVERYBUG is locked in on you. We'll take care of the rest."

"Very good," YE simply replied. "...So long as I get that key..."

"Oh, you'll have the key..." Hormel replied. "We just want you back in the Palace to fix this MESS!"

It was ALL YE needed to hear. With him and Maz back in the fold, there was NO DOUBT once he was back on the Throne, he was going to do for the Colony what he'd done for Providence City. And those that disagreed, THEREAFTER would become HIS SWORN ENEMIES!

"Just keep our conversation tucked beneath your Front Plate," Hormel warned. "We don't need any sabotages."

YE connected with NuGro, still Interim city Constantinople. "Do me a favor," he told her. "Call up ALL the FAKE SNOOZERS and let them know I got goo-gobs of HIGHLY CLASSIFIED INTEL...on the SSBBI."

NuGro didn't ask why. She called an anchor from WBBA and had Crema, Cokenasmile and all the rest flocking to the Providence armed with Top Notch LIVE WIRES. They whipped out clickers and clappers (portable cameras and microphones) and shoved them beneath YE's lickers to catch EVERY DRIP that fell from his center orfice.

"But NO BUG likes you," a Reporter informed

the exiled Kingpin flanked by a REEF OF SUPPORT. "Why should WE believe you," she naively asked.

The ex-Kingpin bunted that question and those that followed [[AFTER]] telling the emaciated Media how the Palace had been HIGHJACKED and was about to be MANDATED into TOTAL ANNIHILATION.

"Shortly your Mounds, and Challises, and Webs and Honeycombs will CEASE TO EXIST," he told the hostile (and oblivious) anchors. "I'm only here to save ALL OF YOU from a RED BUG COUP operating under TLM's helm."

Of course he was speaking about SooZxY, but the Media returned to their portals cluess, echoing to OUTRAGED and SHOCKED Plebs clips of this exchange. By the time the HOUSE...Hormel, Pepperjack, Piranha and Giant met with Pâté to ask approval for GOWIPHO, they were exhilerated to learn there'd be NO waiting period.

"Pull out all the stops," Pâté FUMED. "Hit him so HARD, we never see or hear from him AGAIN!"

HOUSE Principals called an assembly ASAP. ALL BRANCHES of the Palace were invited; POP, COC, OC, CONGRESS, SSS, SSF, the SSBBI and of course the HOUSE. But NONE...NOT ONE bug from the other Branches attended. Of oodles and oodles of bugs that worked for the Palace in the auxillary units; Roaches, Spiders, Grasshoppers, Wasps, and Yellow Jackets...along with Flies, Fleas, Ants, Gnats, Mosquitos, and even Worms and Maggots...not a one saw it worth its while to so much as entertain WHY it was necessary TO GET YE! And many of their reasonings had NOTHING to do with NOT WANTING TO SEE YE GOT. They just didn't want to return to their Nests and find themselves LOCKED OUT. It was a grim prognosis. No Bug could trust No Bug.

And yet HOUSE bugs joined GET ORANGE, mostly because they had NO CHOICE. Any which way the PIE got sliced they were caught between a paradox and axiom... whether they went and returned with NO YE, and ESPECIALLY if they stayed behind and their cohorts returned WITH YE!

But they did try to get out of going...

"Is TLM aware of ANY OF THIS!?!" inquired Baklava.

"Just as aware and complicitory as I am here," Giant replied. A nerdy question deserved a nerdier reply. Of course TLM wasn't aware. TLM didn't know where the Throne was...or who held it!

"Listen..." Giant told his HOUSE bugs in monochromatic tone. "We're coming back with YE...and will exist Happily Ever After Thee."

Corny, but the lymric worked. It was ALL IN and WIN BIG, or GO BUST and go where bugs were sent to be cremated.

Headed For Ground Zero.

MAJOR ISSUE STARTING OUT. No Transportation.

The Trek was scheduled to consume 2 Whole Dregs...with NO STOPS. This proved problematic, not only from a somatic sense, but questionable for bugs plagued by nuisances such as excess weight.

Watermelon, a hefty Waterbug that worked in the Admin hem of the HOUSE, (in other words... in a clericalish capacity), was one of many bugs in the rear complaining. She, like the others, were IN NO SHAPE for even a minimal Trek.

"What I don't get is WHY if '*they*' so want YE, UP or DOWN so bad, they won't at least spring for some Leafs!?!"

"Gotta be positive," Garlic inserted. "Ever heard of cessing out the outcome you want to see?'"

"Ummm...No," fumed Watermelon. "But have

you heard of NOT eating the SMELL you don't want to smell like!?!"

Bugs burst out laughing, ALL but Watermelon who was REALLY peeved. In addition to the dastardly Trek Giant forced on ALL of the HOUSE bugs, it was the limericks to a cooky chant those obviously up Front had cooked up.

Here we go Movin' On, Rollin' Along
Singing Our Triumphant Song
About Rights and Wrongs
Weak and Strong
Bugs that do, and DON'T Belong
In the CollllLOW-NEE
For ShuuuuC-KA-NING
RESPONS-SA-BILL-LA-TEE
ACCOUNT-TA-BILL-LA-TEE!
Yeeezzz Sirree,
Cause We Looovvve
Our CollllLOW-NEE!

The song, sung with ZEST...up Front... peetered out by the time it reached the rear. But Watermelon wasn't the only bug (in the back) with a valid reason to complain. Paella, an albino Termite, hatched crippled. He never learned to use his liggers (feet). Literally he dragged around. And Paprika was due to hatch any tick. So she called 'up Front' and spoke to Hormel... explaining the predicament of those in the rear. He listened, and told her to contact Pâté, who told her to basically 'roll over and eat dirt.'

Now why would Pâté act this way when he not only approved the operation, but demanded it!? Those up Front knew why. Those in the rear only knew they were on a (short & quick) path to being fleeced if they didn't speak up. Already Paprika had dropped her litter. And Paella was so far behind he was no longer visible. Leaving Watermelon to use her last breath plopping down on a curb to relay to Hormel what Pâté had told her.

"We're NO USE to the HOUSE if we're NOT HEEERE..." she warned Hormel.

Why the Palace (alas TLM via Pâté) ...and even the HOUSE (via Hormel, Giant and others) gambled on bugs being too fearful (and UNDISCIPLINED) to EFFECTIVELY SPEAK OUT, amounted to spinning a COSTLY roulette. All it would take was ONE SPIN.

Dings later, true to the lapidarian accord between the HOUSE and the Palace, a decker squamate rolled up. Watermelon lost her cool when she saw the gondola. "This is totally unacceptable," she cried. Squamates were SNAKES, sliced in half, length-wise. The upper half was stacked on top of the bottom, and congealed Beetle Bugs were tucked, fastened and fixed beneath the long tubes to create mobility. Yet, the ghastly part was the carcass hadn't even been gutted.

"Crisis have some Mercy," Watermelon wailed. "I'm not riding in gunk and gook!" And she wasn't the only bug refusing to ride in SNAKE guts.

Rumbutan, an unusually quiet Locust, called a Dallie she knew quite well... in the Black Mound...since the convoy was headed that way. "Do you think you can have some bugs pick us up," she asked Jocund, one of many Ants she befriended back in their buttermilk (school) dregs.

"I might," Jocund replied. "But we kinda locked in here... Didn't you hear about the LOCKDOWNS!?"

Rumbutan had. But the convoy she traveled with were (of course) exempt. "Well, do you know anybug in the city who can get a pass to help us out? It would be great if they could actually send a Limo-Leaf. It's a lot of us out here."

Now here, Rumbutan was actually crossing a

rubicon. Depending on who Jocund beseeched on behalf of accommodating Palace bugs, could open a block of gouda. And the fact that 'up Front' and those in the Palace (monitoring the progress) knew nothing about this call, could open blocks of more gouda.

"Well, if you can hook us up, we might even be able to get you an assignment in the Palace... I mean we got a bug with us that just hatched a litter. We can't go any further..."

AN ASSIGNMENT AT THE PALACE!?! Was Rumbutan KIDDING!?! Jocund would jack a ride just for the fun of it... and perhaps a little viral bling! Her only problem was, THE LOCKDOWNS...and what was going down INSIDE THE BLACK MOUND!

"Lemme call you back," Jocund replied. "I'ma see what I can do to help y'all out!"

"We'll be right here," Rumbutan sang. "...On curb Woke, Inc.," she added. "Hurry..."

@BLACKSABOTAGE.

At this juncture FuFu had convinced the Chancellor to address distressed Ants corralled in the Forum by Combat. This was where Jocund happened to be when they (himself, the Chancellor, Good...and surprise-surprise... Elon, Doc and Fessy) arrived. His Queen, along with Workers, a few Guards and a Warrior were with them as well, but none of the latter accounted for the relief of having so much intellect in one space, at such a corrosive time, than a group of Captains.

For sure FuFu was elated, and not only because Doc, Fessy and Elon were alive and well, but because it freed up having to spend an enormous amount of time (they didn't have) force feeding a stubborn old Royal on what to tell the bugs. The HARD WORK had already been done.

The Chancellor however, cooled the hysteria on sight. He didn't have much to say, speaking about how preemptive it was for Warriors to handle the crisis as they had, BUT, all was well now that he was there. BIG YAWN. While he soothed over horrors many in the Forum had seen with their own marbles and pearls, Ants hurdled over each other trying to get into a lobe that mattered. Good was their top choice, though one of the Captains...or even His Queen still battling dropping out bouts would do.

That's how Jocund caught up with Good, who happend to be catching up with Just.

"Hey, one of my bubs is stuck out there on the grounds," she bubbled breathless, interrupting the Antes' catching up.

Good looked over at Jocund as if she'd crawled out of a sewer, a far more pleasant glare than the look Just gave her. Not long before the interruption Just was explaining how many Ant blasts she counted on the way to the Forum.

"What bub do you know outside," Good asked nonetheless. "How did she (or he) get there?"

And that's when a part of the Palace plot liked to have unfolded. "Well, she works for SS," Jocund ignorantly blurted. Rumbutan DID NOT work for the SS (Secret Security). Actually there was NO such unit. Close. But No. Her bub worked IN the HOUSE.

But the odd disclosure, in light of what the Ants had been through and were witnessing, didn't take much convincing to know this INTEL needed to be distributed to the Chancellor and Captains.

Just as Jocund had done, Good and Just cut into the Chancellor thanking a Warrior for his exemplary dedication and service for NOT offin' ONE of his own kin. "They're COMING," Good blurted, assuming on her own she had decoded the transcendent and was about to SAVE the MOUND!

"Who's coming," asked an incredibly naive Head Chancellor.

"The SS," Good replied frantic.

"Whoa...whoa," FuFu intercepted. The SS was a Foreign Squad that hadn't been active since before WeShallOverCome. He was a wannabe when the SS was kicking. "Where did you hear this?"

Meanwhile, on the other side of the corridor, Ants stuck in the Scullery were ALSO starved for information.

"NO! Please don't go Poppa," Ante Hope was telling the most Senior Worker among them offering to make the sacrilegious trip across the compound for information. "Just went out there and still hasn't returned," she cried.

Of course, after a thaumaturgic weaving and bobbing session, inclusive of bribes, chicanery and bludgeonings of her own making, Just forgot about bugs she left behind after hooking up with Good.

"We just have to be patient and wait this out," Hope said. "Crisis will make a way..."

"Well, I'm NOT waiting on hubble I can't see," Ante Jumpy fumed. "The Babalyon also says SOMETIMES EVEN CRISIS NEEDS HELP!"

"Well, you go right on out there and help Crisis like ALL the rest that left and still haven't returned," Ante Bitter snapped. "But you will be taking your tikes with you! It's too many in here as it is!"

Jumpy had a slew of kiddies, almost enough to make a Brigade. Wasn't no way she was getting far with that troop she hatched. So she settled down...for a bit, when it occurred to her Pokey was among this brood. He wasn't being a pest...THEN...but she, like EVERY Ante in the compound, knew was but a matter of time!

"Well, one of y'all gonna have to deal with that one," she spewed, speaking of Pokey who'd become even more troublesome since their MOUND tumbled.

"Maybe we should send his snarky carcinogenic tail out there," muttered a Worker wearing plenty of bruises from looking after Pokey. Prior to the Offie visit he mostly fell under Good's charge, but since his subsequent infirmary visits he'd become more a Ward of EVERY Ant's charge.

"Oh, please let's not," scoffed another Ante. "He'll liable get us ALL offed!"

"Not if we lock the Jam after he leaves," joked a Dallie.

"Well, considering the Jam is already locked I doubt it," chuckled another Worker. "From what I saw getting in here, they'll mow that Jam down!"

This Worker had narrowly made it to work. He had described true EVIL lurking in the corridors. "They're mowing down bugs like collecting souvvies!"

"I just wished we knew why," cooed Ante Woo.

"Because they're WARTHUGS...always have been," replied a Dallie. "I used to court one—"

—Suddenly Pokey put down the scribe he was reading... 'How to Sabotage Blackies'... and addressed Ante Nice...the sweetest of the Antes.

"Hey chippy," (an especially derogatory name) "...it's time for my libations," he spat.

"Ooo!" Ante Icy gasped. Actually quite a few Antes responded. Usually they did anyway. He'd become a particularly nasty creature as of recent.

"Let me at him," Ante Bitter growled, baring her scissors as Antes tried restraining her. "I'll give him his libations ALL RIGHT!"

Captains hearing the commotion came out of a corner, at first peeking around as if checking on how safe they might...or might not be. Like the Worker, they too narrowly made it to the Scullery. Warriors had been ordered to blast them ON SIGHT!

But the coast appeared clear, so they came out and Captain Flim-Flam spoke up. "I think we're good here," he said, getting empty gazes back. What did he mean by *they were good*?

"Chief, who's we," asked one of the Workers. There were at least five distinct classes among this group of Ants; the Antes... the Dallies... the Workers ...a few Warriors... plus the kiddies...and then there was them.

"I mean it looks like the coast is clear," Flim-Flam replied, that time eliciting a burst of cheers.

The bugs headed straight for the Jam. The Trap flung open and out they ran, stopping in their tracks as if they'd hit an electric barricade.

"Ah," gasped the first Ant out of the Trap.

Two others collapsed. There were more gasps and moans, followed by a series of long wails.

"Oh my Crisis," cried Ante Woo. "Help us Oh Crisis, please help us," she wailed too.

Ant parts littered the corridors. Shells covered the ground. Liggers and ligglets (basically limbs) were stuck to the walls and ceiling. Marbles and Pearls were everywhere. None in its proper orfice. The only bug parts nowhere to be seen were Warriors!

The scene that greeted them INDEED was horrific, but Poppa and Workers like him, plus dutiful Antes and insightful Captains helped them mount the horrors to get to the Forum. There they joined the other half of their population; among them, Good... FuFu...the Chancellor...and His Queen still periodically passing out.

If the occasion hadn't been what it was, it would've appeared a joyous reunion was in motion. For the first time ever the Classes intermingled. Antes, Dallies, Captains, Workers... and Warriors and Elders exchanged particulars of what they knew and heard. Jocund made herself front and center talking fast and loose about her bub working for the SS.

But the Ants circling her couldn't understand

why in a Crisis an SS would 1) be calling her about 2) being stranded. CLA-BLoop. That was His Queen. She could stand NO MORE of the stories, and had to be carried off for the final time to the Infirmary.

"What's your bub's name? Are you sure she works for the SS," Poppa asked beyond incredulous. No matter how pretty and sexy Dallies were, often mating up with the best at the Top of Species Chains, that type chain was rarely broken, even for a Dallie!

But Jocund was sure, circulating whispers among the other gossip being discussed. Not far from the SS talk was Just arguing with FuFu about having the unmitigated mutzfa to callously order Workers around. Snarling through gritted sharp scissors she told him off. JUST WHO DID HE THINK HE WAS!?! HOW DARE he send Workers off to clean up their own kin's remains!

"BUT WHERE IS OUR WARLORD?" asked the Chancellor.

No bug seemed to know. Not even the Warrior the Chancellor thanked for not offin' his own as the WarLord had (according to him) INSTRUCTED.

Ironic as it would be, at this precise moment their WarLord, and Senior Elders and Top Security, were trying to figure out why the fans mounted on each side of the Peppito were rotating backwards, INSTEAD of forward, making the contraption fly in circles. This wasn't supposed to happen, and the contraption certainly wasn't programmed to STOP mid-flight, but was exactly what occurred.

"Prepare to BAIL," Combat yelled. "...Because we are about to go DOOOWWNNNNN!!!"

The Chancellor, FuFu and selected others were headed back to the Chamber to discuss these optics ...and rumors... away from the noise when they heard and FELT the fantastic BOOM!

What was that?

No bug inside... OR OUTSIDE... the Mound had a good guess. All most knew, the sound was irregular ...AND FANTASTIC!

It wasn't until NuGro called, on behalf of YE, that the Chancellor and Captains' concerns grew to evervescent heights.

According to NuGro, ARMED Black Ants were aimlessly meandering around in public. AND THEY HAD MADE THE TERRORIST LIST. They were in THE # ONE SPOT!!!

Too flabbergasted to be sufficiently shocked, FuFu called YE directly. "We're hearing some awful reports we want clarified," he pointedly declared.

"Clarified," YE mocked. "I think you mean confirmed don't you?"

YE being of much higher rank, even as an ousted busted disrespected ex-Kingpin, wasn't corrected. FuFu wouldn't dare. "Well...we just heard an explos—"

"—My question is what in a beehive jinx are YOUR BUGS doing out in public... ARMED!?!"

FuFu had NO RESPONSE. He was only acting in ABSENCE of Security that abandoned them. He had NO ACCESS to ANY REPORTS, and he seriously doubted the Chancellor knew of any SARs (situational awareness reports) either.

"Let's not discuss this now," YE said. "But I suggest you collect your records to have an accurate count of every bug in that fleahole."

Again FuFu didn't correct the ex-Kingpin that time either. This was too serious a matter to quibble over petty panoplies. But he did warn the Chancellor. "Those Warriors may have really dug us a grave."

"Oh, I'm sure we'll work it out," replied the daft Chancellor. "We mustn't assume the worst."

Really, FuFu wasn't unsure of trouble lurking ahead. He was ABSOLUTELY SURE he wasn't assuming. They were in DEEP STRAIGHTS!

Politely he asked the Chancellor (calling for hot lattes) if he might know where the WarLord kept their records.

"My consul, that is your area. I've long stopped keeping up with those pitterlings."

'What a waffle,' muttered Fessy.

"Yeah, we might want to get to the Pedi," suggested FuFu.

Doc, Elon and Fessy who HAD the opportunity to visit the Pedicle unamimously VETOED the suggestion. "But why not," FuFu asked. The Pedi supposedly was the most secure Chamber in the Mound.

"There's no way I'm going to sink in that tub!" Doc forcefully submitted.

#INITTOWINIT.

As the Captains worked feverishly calling local areas for refuge to shelter their most vulnerable bugs, the few remaining Warriors kept guard, strictly for presentation and morale, over the entrance.

"I'm kind of antsy about what's going on here," said one Warrior. "Maybe we should take off like the others."

"WRONG," replied another Warrior. "I heard they're being dusted as we speak."

"Yeah, but do you really think they BLEW UP the Pal—"

—Suddenly the Trap chimed, announcing there was a visitor on the other side. The several Warriors milling around the Front pit turned and looked at each other. "Where's Cappin' FuFu," one asked.

"He ain't a Warbug," another scoffed.

"Well...then you open it," yet another nudged.

But the tough Warrior declined. Though he swiped at FuFu for not being one of them, he hid like an imposture himself. "Lemme go find the Cappin'," he actually said.

"We don't have time for that," urged the Warrior closest to the Trap. If the chime got any louder they'd require surgery to stop the ringing.

"Well, go on and open it then!"

"But what if it's—"

"—Wouldja' open the Trap already," scoffed another Warrior, readily in position to FIRE on any opposition.

"But... I'm outta amno," came back the reply.

"If you don't answer that RINGING, I'll use what's left in mine on YOU," snapped the Warrior.

The nervy Warrior obeyed. Gingerly opening the Trap revealed on the other side a HUGE Orange Grasshopper surrounded by a BLATOON of Soldiers. The Warrior's marbles grew almost as large as the Big Bug borrowing ALL OF THEIR thoughts!

YE didn't waste time. He crossed over the threshold and entered the Front pit. A few of his posse followed. "Geeze, what a DUMP," he huffed. "Where's your Leader?"

The Warriors faltered, all trying to be first to say nothing.

"Is this the way," YE tossed over his hulk, taking charge to find '*the Leader*'.

Actually, it was Firefly Redbug, a brilliantly lit up bug and YE's Chief IT GPS Specialist, that signaled the way to the Captains (making exit plans) ...and the Chancellor (sipping lattes).

"HELLO," YE greeted the diligently toiling Ants, his voice and heft breeching (in comparison) the small pit.

The Captains looked up, xylphone crescendo fashion, as the Chancellor popped up. "Why Hello... Welcome ...Please...Please come in," cheesed the out of touch Head Elder. "Can I get you ANYTHING?"

"Yeah, you can get me the JEVIL out of here," jostled the Big BRASH Bug with the BIGGER PERSONALITY playing along.

"You know... you keep a mighty NASTY place," YE continued with the OPEN and HONEST insults, as he casually observed the surroundings.

"Maybe that's why you bugs call this HELL HOLE a Pit, huh?" He wasn't kidding either. The litter he and his posse traversed getting from the Front of the Mound to this part confirmed his opinion.

"Well...we can meet in my Grand Suite," replied the Chancellor, his tendrils and antennas swaying and bobbing like they always did when he was excited... or nervous...or embarrassed.

"Oh no, that won't be necessary," YE waved off. "It's a lot cleaner in here," he added, finding the stained grounds (free of debris) and carved ceilings (free of dull lighting) more to his predilection. "I'm here to save some of your bugs, and actually this WHOLE COLONY. But I need you to come with me."

Up to this part of the exchange not a peep came from any bug, other than (of course) YE and the Chancellor. That changed when a surge of Antes, led by Good, stormed into the pit.

"What's going on in here," Good immediately wanted to know.

YE looked over his arch, one tendral raised, but otherwise unfazed. "TaTa, we're taking your king with us—"

—That did it. Just jumped in. First off, what curb did this tryalla trip over and fall in their SPACE talking so disrespectfully!?! "Ain't NOBUG in here ya' TaTa," she fumed. "You have some chutzpah coming in here besmirching us! That's why they kicked you off the throne—"

"Gee, she sure is revved up," YE laughed, about to strut off, the Chancellor slinking behind him.

"Wait," Good called out. "Where is he taking our Chance?" She spun around to look at FuFu, before swiveling around to see how Doc...and Fessy...and Elon were responding. All appeared complicit, as if they had set their poor gullible Chancellor up. She hooked onto her Chance, desperate to stop him when Just jumped in front of YE.

"YOU ICIST," she spat.

"Name-calling doesn't faze me," YE said. "I've been called worse," he added, continuing towards the way he had come.

"That's because Icist have no beater," argued Just, doing just enough to slow YE's gait, but unable to stop him. "I hope ALL YOU ICIST BURN IN HELL," she shouted, drawing bugs into the corridor.

"...And I hope ALL YOU ANTIGGERS (equal to niggers) decompose well in your sanctuary."

If Just lost it before, she REALLY LOST it hearing antigger. Others that heard the vitriol slur moved in closer, moaning and groaning and depicting visages of hurt too.

"How can you allow this," Good hissed at FuFu. "They've been so determined to eviscerate us," she continued. Since the beginning of the Ant Kingdom's arrival to the Colony the UPPER CLASS had enslaved and preyed on them.

Just, restrained by Antes trying to prevent an altercation, spewed similar rhetoric...shut down as YE reached the Trap. Slowly he turned around and just as unruffled as his entrance he told Just...and the bugs holding her, "I'm not your enemy. You, of all bugs should remember when I ran things. You got to enjoy your Flea Marketing and fabulous atrocities... and fried Beeswax, greasy Collards and lumpy jalopy," he reminded them. "We had no problems."

"Then why did you pull down the Billboards!?!" Good shot back. "You're just like the rest of them!"

"Look," FuFu apologetically began once YE left out. "He's really doing us a favor..."

"A FAVOR," shrieked Good, and gasped Just. "You call dragging Chance out of here a favor!?!"

"Good," FuFu softly continued. "Our Chance isn't being dragged anywhere." IN FACT...and quite to the contrary... the Chancellor was still in the Mound. Of course His Queen was STILL OUT COLD. When she came to, she was going to be fit for burial.

"I'll tell you what," FuFu went on... "How about I go with them? Will that make you feel better?"

"No! How about you go and the Chance stays here," she shot back. Yet, no matter how riled she protrayed herself to be, she couldn't ignore his look... and CALM. "I just don't see how you can let that ICIST take him," she sighed, the fight in her just about all gone.

"Look, let me show you ALL something," FuFu said, pulling out his node. He swiped left a number of times before clicking on a WIRE he knew the bugs knew nothing about. They enjoyed the social purviews of their nodes, only turning off familiar mediums when prompted...typically during Colony-wide EPIDEMICS. (i.e., the MANDATES...and the WARLORD'S TUBE BAN).

Antes clamored around FuFu's node watching a JET hurling out of a clear Nebula in MACH SPEEDS, hurdling towards land in a RAINBOW of FLAMES. In a phantasmagorical EXPLOSION it hit land!

Good looked away. Exploding fireballs wasn't her thing. She preferred the Bubbles. Saucy romance stories that made her happy. About to ask FuFu the point of showing this shattering film, her argument was excised by gasps. In mixed STUPOR and PANIC she read a Ticker Tape scrolling along the bottom of the node: **BLMO** (Black Mound) Operatives **RESPONSIBLE FOR BLOWING UP THE PALACE!**

For The Bugs.

At a loss, questions circling her like a swathe of unfed kids, Good looked at FuFu helpless. "Does this mean we're done?"

"No," FuFu replied, though Good had directed her question at Just. "It means we can't expect to be always sowing," he said.

"Well, seems like we've been doing a lot more reaping," she argued, still refusing to give in, despite the obvious disasters stacking up at the helm of their leaders. To her left, right behind her, Warriors held a private chat discussing their thoughts.

"I heard the whole SOS on my SIC (Secure Internal Communicator)," one said. "WarLord screamed the WHOLE way down!"

"Well...SERVES 'EM RIGHT!" scoffed another Warrior, angered like many.

"I just wished I'd never let Chance take them kids to the market," Good whispered, more to herself than out loud.

But Ante Woo heard her. "Don't blame yourself," she cooed. "We must keep our faith in Crisis. We'll get through this one too."

"I'll say one thing," Bitter muttered too. "YE was right about one thing."

The Antes looked up. What possibly could that Big Orange bug have been right about!?!

"This pit looks DISGUSTING!"

If it hadn't been for so much dark hanging around, the Antes might've chuckled. "How about we clean up and get these bugs buried," Ante Nice said. "Maybe it'll distract us from seeing the—"

—The Trap flung open. Again the Antes looked up... surprised... hopeful... and desperate. But it was only a city Soldier, anxious to get going. "Come on," he hissed at FuFu. "We have to GO!"

FuFu was busy tying up vital specifics before departing. The Chancellor needed his traveling perks; scribes, silk woven webs and materials only he thought he needed. He also wanted to smooch His Queen, still OUT COLD. She was going to be a birch shrub when she came to.

But there was one remaining chore FuFu hadn't taken care of. He turned to Good and asked if she could assemble a transport.

Her mug shriveled and sunk in instantly... the reason he saved that chore for last. But of course she could. She held a triple crown moving large groups in a hurry. She only looked so helpless because she HELD the crown EONS AGO.

"And so who do you suggest I leave behind," she snarled.

"Look Ante, we don't have much time," FuFu said, keeping a marble on the Soldier waiting by the Trap. "The city is sending over mobiles to help you all get loaded up."

"Loaded up," Good huffed, her patience wittled to brittle, indicated by how long it took her to finish her thought. "Fu, do you really believe that CROOK is gonna just NICELY pack us up," she finally got out. "...And whisk us off to EXACTLY WHERE!?!"

She missed hearing his reply because Ante PrayedUp got to praying. "WHY...WHY...WHY..." she wailed. "We've been through SO MUCH! OH CRISIS! PLEASE FIX IT!"

FuFu whispered in Good's lobe, repeating what she missed. "It's going to be alright. We must trust him..."

At this point, the marker constantly moving, she had no choice BUT to BELIEVE. They couldn't stay if what was true, was true. Seeing the stressed Antes... and the Chancellor and Captain FuFu on their way to who knew where, plus the innocent tikes, none who deserved ANY of this, she had to do what was in the best interest for all.

She was asking FuFu about where he and the Chancellor were headed, and when he expected they might return, when Pokey suddenly appeared, BREAKING the SOUND BARRIER.

"Hey! I know YOU," he said pointing at the city Soldier still waiting by the Trap. "You WORK for that BIG ORANGE CRUMB," he screeched in his mealy-clammy voice, breeching a small gathering of Antes.

The chitter-chatter STOPPED. All attention fell on the little tike headed for the city Soldier, jabbing bugs left and right demanding a path be cleared for him. "MOVE! GET OUTTA MY WAY," he shouted, sounding like a Licey Crabby lush.

"What are YOU doing in here listening at this Yik Yak YIKKITY YAK," yapped the kid. "Now where's THAT BIG FAT HOPPER!"

The Soldier watched amused. The Antes DID NOT, none more than Just. POKEY, from the dreg he hatched, had always been his own little mant, doing what he wanted when he wanted, often encouraging other kiddies to follow his lead, BUT ENOUGH WAS ENOUGH!

Good started to move. She hadn't seen Pokey in some time, but Jumpy jumped ahead of her. "I got this," she huffed, reaching the kid as he delivered one of his famous well proscribed kicks.

The Soldier wasn't amused any more. He went for his blaster... a nick before—WHACK—Jumpy hit the kid so hard his mullet whipped around twice, spinning TWO full circles.

"OUWEE!" he cried out, sounding like his weird regular self. "That hurt," he whined, before changing his tone yelling, "YOU SAW WHAT SHE DID! BLAST HER YOU SUMMAGONBLASSE!"

Antes Just, Jumpy, Bitter...and the angriest

Antes jumped into action. Bitter had him by his connector. Just got a ligger. And Jumpy was still swinging, wildly. "Not this time," Just was heard saying.

Good tried to get between the Antes but was unsuccessful. They were really worked up, stirring the Soldier to intervene. "How about he goes with us," he offered. "We can drop him off by an Infirmary to get his ligger reattached..."

"Umm...No thank you," Good replied. She wasn't that despondent. "We have our OWN Infirmary in here!"

This was the moment Pokey recognized her. He hadn't seen his favorite Ante since his infirmary, and wasted NO TIME leaping all over her, squealing and slobbering, "kisses... Kisses... gimme more Kisses!"

The Soldier's marbles got EXTRA wider. No matter what these bugs said, or were trying to pull off, THIS WAS NO KIND OF KID! This strange mock up, ironically resembling the ex-Chief County, was WAAAYYY OVER THE LINE...BEFORE he began shrieking, "BRING ME MY YUM-YUM! I WANT MY YUM-YUM!"

This time the obvious could not be scooped up and tucked away with a nooky. But Good tried. "Give him here," she said to Just, who she suspected of sneaking in unnecessary extra licks. Pokey squealing 'OUWEE' tipped her off.

"I will NOT," Just said. "Me and Jumpy got it. We're turning this one over to this nice Soldier. Let's let him take Pokeymon to get checked out and fixed."

"Nooo...what are you saying," Good cried. Yes, Pokey had gotten beside himself more than she'd ever seen, but HE WAS STILL A KID!

Just ignored Good though. The creepy peewee LUSH had worn out his welcome. Wasn't no sense hanging onto a pest. She passed him over Good and into the whiskers of the Soldier. And be joggonnit if the lurid bug didn't wrap ALL six of his wiry cylinders around the Soldier. IT WAS BIZARRE...and even so Good made one final attempt to rescue the BRAT.

"No! Wait a tick..." she protested, stopped by Ante Prayed Up.

"Wait...let's hang on a tick," intervened the ultimate Prayer Warrior. "I done prayed on this. Crisis said let him go. Last thing we need is MORE TROUBLE traveling with us!"

............The End..........

Other Books by the Author

Memoirs

Black Table
God Be the Glory
Babies Raising Babies

Novels (Series)

Leiatra's Rhapsody (I)
Something Xtra Wild (II)
This One I Got Right (III)
Rye n the Rump (IV)
My Love (V)

Other Fiction

Pretty Inside Out
A Piece of Peace
Tehuelche
Pleasure
Double Dare
Lock Box
Big Bully
Copy Cats
Mindless
Painted Cats
****NEW Front Page News*

Short Stories

My Blackberry
Storytella

Poetry

Atlóta
GEM
A Blast From the Past
Civil Talk

About the Author

RYCJ is a book reviewer, blogger, publisher, and storyteller. Since 2009 she has written dozens of books in a mosaic of genres, and has read and reviewed hundreds of books. She is the ultimate book lover, passionate about reading and writing stories that educates, entertains and inspires.